# EVERY NEW YEAR

## LOVE AT LAST

### KATRINA JACKSON

Editor: Aretha Kaitesi Tibandebage

Cover photographer: Adrienne Andersen @ItsAAndersen

❀ Created with Vellum

*For Eric.*
*Even though I know this wouldn't have been your thing. You still would have bought a copy and brought it to every get together just because. I'll miss your laugh. rip*

# CONTENT WARNINGS

Parental illness (cancer)
Mentions of parental illness (diabetes and hypertension)

## DECEMBER 31, 2001

*E*zra Posner really didn't want to be at this party. Actually, if he'd realized that his roommate, Miles Jefferson, would force him to leave the comfort of their dorm room and trek halfway across campus and then halfway up a hill, he would have pretended to be asleep until Miles left without him. He didn't like parties. And he certainly didn't like New Year's Eve parties in the woods with the kids who'd decided — or had no other choice but — to stay on campus over winter break. They'd hiked into the hills surrounding their semi-rural campus to have their own New Year's Eve celebration; all crushed together around a bonfire and listening to someone's cheap boombox on low so they could keep an ear out for campus police.

The smell of smoke and cheap vodka made Ezra's stomach turn. This wasn't how he'd wanted to spend his New Year's Eve and he was growing more annoyed that he'd let Miles drag him up here by the minute. He turned to his best friend and found him sloshing cheap swill into a red plastic cup and frowned. When Miles saw Ezra looking at him, he chuckled while pouring nearly half a bottle of orange juice into the cup – "for taste," or more accurately to hide the burn of bottom barrel liquor – and held the cup out to Ezra. He raised his own cup for a toast.

"Cheers," Miles said, smiling at Ezra with raised eyebrows. He'd given him that same smile when they'd met at summer orientation before immediately suggesting they become roommates. Ezra raised his eyebrows at his friend, took the smallest sip he could manage and cringed. But Miles didn't notice. He was too distracted by Mei Barnes, the actual reason they'd come out tonight. She'd been the singular object of his attention all fall semester. Every week — sometimes every day — Miles had subjected Ezra to very detailed lectures about how Mei was literally the best, most perfect, beautiful girl on campus; maybe even in the world. Miles was the king of hyperbole.

Ezra watched as Miles clutched his cup tight with nerves and started inching through the crowd toward his crush and once again marveled at seeing his normally confident and sociable friend turn into a ball of nerves, even though it was obvious to everyone who knew them that Mei was as obsessed with him. Ezra shook his head stepped back into the shadows trying to avoid the smoky heat of the bonfire. He hoped — for Miles's sake and the sake of his productivity — that those two would finally get together so he could get some peace.

But just because he was rooting for their relationship, didn't mean Ezra wanted to sacrifice his liver in celebration. He dumped his drink into a nearby bush, tossed his cup into the trash bag by the "bar" and went in search of a place to sit, hide, and wait for this all to end.

He settled onto a cold flat-topped rock and wished he'd worn a thicker sweater. He pressed the button on his digital watch to check the time. Eleven o'clock on the dot. He sighed. He didn't think he could last another hour out here, but he didn't want to leave Miles, especially not with how fast he and Mei were guzzling their drinks, smiling nervously at one another as if this was the first time they'd ever met. He wished again that he'd pretended to be asleep when Miles had burst into their dorm room, a towel around his waist, shower cap on his head and shower caddy in one hand yelling excitedly at him to "get ready nerd, we're going to a party." Ezra also wished he hadn't paid such close attention to the refrigerator magnet they all received at orientation about drinking responsibly and looking out for your friends, so he could have slipped down the hill without feeling guilty.

Either way, he wished he was back in his dorm room working, because these were peak productive hours, and work was the entire reason he'd come back to campus immediately after Hanukkah. If he was going to submit the 3D scale model of his efficient train engine on time and have even half a chance of winning the Gilder prize, he needed to be giving it his full attention during every free moment of every day. He couldn't afford to waste these few precious weeks before spring semester started, watching someone else's teenage romance and edgy underage drinking in the woods. He checked his watch again. One minute after eleven.

"Anybody sitting here?"

Ezra jumped at the voice. He looked up and couldn't quite see who was standing in front of him with the bonfire behind them casting shadows over his vision, but he didn't need light to recognize her. He would have known that voice and silhouette anywhere.

Candace Garret was tall, almost as tall as him, with big curly hair that framed her head and gave her a few inches more height, wide hips and the brightest smile he'd ever seen. She was also way out of his league. He knew that. She knew that. Everyone knew that. Because Candace Garret was way out of everyone's league.

"Hello," she said again, leaning close and waving a hand in front of his face.

His vision adjusted as her lips spread into a small smile. Ezra was mesmerized by the flash of her bright white teeth and her even, flawless, deep dark brown skin that seemed to drink in every bit of light around them.

"Anybody in there?" she laughed.

He jumped from the rock and their heads collided.

"Ow," she whined.

"Shit, I'm sorry," Ezra said, panicked, his own head beginning to throb. "Shit."

His face heated and his eyes widened. What if he'd given Candace Garret a concussion? He'd have to transfer schools, he couldn't live with that embarrassment. She was rubbing small circles on her forehead but still smiling at him, which only made him feel worse. But ringed around that shame was the same awe he always felt in her presence.

"Calm down, Ezra. I won't press charges. This time." Her voice was calm but playful.

"I— You know my name?"

She laughed and shook her head.

Ezra loved Candace's laugh. So much so that he'd catalogued and ranked his favorite moments of becoming absolutely mesmerized by it. In descending order, Ezra's top five Candace Garret laughs were:

5. Once in the middle of their Chem II lab. He'd become distracted and accidentally ruined three days of an experiment.

4. Once in the dining hall during the lunch rush. He'd heard her above the din and mistakenly dumped an entire ladle of ranch dressing on his grilled cheese sandwich rather than the salad he'd forgotten to make because he'd been too busy trying to get a glimpse of her across the room.

3. He'd been rushing from English to the engineering lab when he'd heard her distinctive twinkle wafting along the late fall breeze. His head whipped

around as he searched for her on the Oval. When he'd found her, Candace was surrounded by half the basketball team and they were fighting each other for her attention. She was ignoring them and reading a comic book, laughing as she turned the pages.

2. That one time Miles had begged him to tag along to Mei and Candace's dorm room. Ezra had spent the entire hour leaning awkwardly against her desk — too terrified to take her up on the offer to sit on her bed — while Miles had entertained them with jokes Ezra never heard because Candace's laughter took over all his senses.

1. Well actually, he'd forgotten his number one favorite laugh because it was immediately replaced by this one. Every other time he'd heard that throaty melody, he'd been a bystander; accidentally infringing on someone else's moment with her or her own moment with herself. But when she finally laughed with him — at him — it felt so much better, even if it shouldn't have. It sounded so much sweeter.

"Of course I know your name," she said, pulling him out of stasis. "My roommate and your roommate have been playing cat and mouse with each other since orientation." She laughed as she turned and pointed at the party.

Ezra assumed she was gesturing at Miles and Mei. The two had basically imprinted on each other from the moment they'd met, and he and Candace had been unwitting spectators to the inevitable. But he didn't look their way, so he couldn't be sure, because for the first time all semester Candace Garret was looking at him. Talking to him. Laughing at him. And it was heaven.

When she turned back, her smile slipped slightly but only for a second. "Why are you over here all by yourself, Ezra?"

Her voice was different than he'd ever heard it. Deeper, maybe? Intimate, he hoped for a fleeting second.

"I don't like parties," he admitted quietly.

Her smile narrowed to a grin and it made him feel like they shared a secret. "Yeah, neither do I," she said. "Especially not outdoor parties with cheap liquor and a severely high chance of starting a forest fire."

He smiled, or at least he thought he did. "This is really irresponsible."

"Totally. But we're supposed to be the brightest of the bright. The best of the best," she said sarcastically and rolled her eyes. He always liked that about her; that she could seem older and wiser and smarter than everyone else around them with a simple inflection of her voice, a wry smile and a graceful tip of her head.

"I-if you don't like parties, why are you here?"

She moved to the rock he'd jumped from and lowered herself onto it gracefully. She did everything with grace. Candace was the exact opposite of his awkward, gangly mess of an existence. She looked up at him and waited until he sat back down. Next to her. His hands started to sweat as he lowered to the rock, perching on the edge so he could leave room between them because he knew she hadn't meant for him to touch her; not even accidentally. She couldn't have meant that; life couldn't be so perfect as to give him his most cherished — albeit secret — fantasy.

"I'm here for the same reason you're here probably," she finally said. "To watch out for my roommate."

"Oh. Yeah," Ezra said. This time he did look at the party and his eyes zeroed in on their roommates. They were standing in the middle of the clearing making out, swaying slowly together even though the loud rap music blaring from the stereo was up tempo. Ezra might have thought their first kiss after months of pining would be gentle and slow like their swaying. It was not. They were attacking one another's mouths. Aggressively. And they didn't seem to care who saw them.

"So gross," Candace muttered under her breath.

"Exactly how much have they had to drink?" He could feel Candace shift on the rock, closing the distance between them. Clearly accidentally.

"Too much. Not enough. Who knows? I think tonight was just a reason to make it official. That gross kiss is what young love looks like, my friend," she snorted.

He turned to her and gulped before speaking, he was so nervous. She'd called him 'friend.' "What would you be doing if you weren't here?"

She really seemed to think about her answer before she made eye contact with him and shrugged, "Don't know, actually. Maybe reading or washing clothes since the laundry rooms are empty for once. Something boring for sure."

He frowned slightly. "That's not what I would have imagined," he breathed.

She slid across the rock; her left thigh pressed against his right. Ezra swallowed a gasp. "I'm not nearly as deep and interesting as everyone thinks," she said, almost shyly. And then she straightened, her elbow grazing his ribs. "What about you? What would you be doing?"

He had to force himself to breathe normally before he could answer. And even when he was able to speak, his voice sounded strained, tense. "Easy," he croaked. "I'd be working on my submission to the Gilder engineering competition," he said. He could still feel the sharp, sweet pain of her accidental touch.

"And what's that?"

"Engineering innovations prize. The winner gets half a million-dollar investment to build a real model of their submission and career mentoring."

"That's amazing. When is it due?"

"Senior year."

She blinked rapidly. "What?" She turned fully toward him, her left leg bent, and the dull point of her knee dug into his thigh. "It's not due for three more years and you're already working on it?"

He gulped. So much of her body was touching his. He tried to regulate his breathing and slow his heartbeat by sheer force of will. "It's a huge deal," he said. "They only give one prize every four years. There are people who've been working on their submissions since high school. And alums always coming back to enter. Technically, I'm behind. I really should be in my room working on my project." He said the last sentence — the same thing he'd been thinking for the past hour — but for the first time he didn't mean it. For this beautiful, unexpected moment, Candace's leg touching his was so much more important than the prize that had been his singular obsession since high school.

And then what would surely be the best night of his life got even better. He tried not to tense when her hands landed on his shoulders, but he did. Because Candace Garret was touching him on purpose. She turned his torso toward her.

She was beautiful. Her lips were parted in shock. Her eyes were wide. And then her mouth shifted from that wry grin to a full-on, prize-worthy, brighter than the sun smile that took his actual breath away. "You're an interesting guy, Ezra Posner," she whispered. "Real interesting."

And then she kissed him.

"*C*an I put my flats in your purse?" Mei asked.

Candace wanted to tell her no. She wanted to tell her best friend that her purse wasn't community property. That she did this constantly, asking them all to hold her wallet and keys and lipstick so she didn't have to bring a bag when they went out. She wanted to tell Mei that was inconsiderate and entitled, but she didn't. She never did. Because above everything else, Candace hated conflict. And on a scale of one to worst friend ever, this hardly rated. So she just sighed, opened her crossbody bag and let Mei shove her ballet slippers into the front pocket of her purse.

"Thanks, Can," Mei trilled.

Candace rolled her eyes.

"We ready?" Miles asked impatiently from behind them.

"Ready," Mei called and ran toward him.

Ezra appeared where Mei had been standing and checked his car's back door. It opened. Mei had forgotten to lock it.

Candace rolled her eyes again. "Sorry."

"It's okay," he said quickly. Not that he would have said anything else, because Ezra didn't get mad or annoyed or frustrated with Mei or anyone else. He was shy, sweet and accommodating. As far as Candace was concerned, Ezra Posner was too nice for his own good.

"It's not," she mumbled as she locked the front door and closed it.

"Do you need help?" Ezra asked as they started to walk to the BART station behind Mei and Miles.

She turned to him and frowned in confusion.

"With your bag? Do you want me to carry it for you?"

She smiled and felt her body relax a bit. "No, I'm okay. It's not heavy. I'm just being bitchy."

They stepped onto the escalator and he turned to her. "You're never bitchy. You're the exact opposite of bitchy, actually."

She smiled at him. "Funny. I was just thinking the same thing about you."

He smiled, like a real genuine smile, which was a very rare thing for Ezra. As far as Candace could tell, Ezra had three kinds of smiles; a pained, thin line that wasn't so much a smile as a grimace; a brief lift of the right side of his mouth, always the right side; and a shocked — always shocked — spread of his lips that showed that one slightly wonky tooth on the left side of his mouth. They were all endearing in their own way. Especially to her.

"You were thinking about me?" he asked in that quiet voice he always used with her, as if he was genuinely shocked that she knew his name, sat next to him in Western Civ II, or had ever wasted entire afternoons cataloguing his limited repertoire of smirks. As if he still couldn't understand why they were friends and never could imagine that sometimes — all the time — she wondered if they could be more.

She wondered what would happen if she told him that of course she thought about him. That he was the most interesting guy in their year, and she hadn't encountered one guy that held her attention like him. She thought about telling him that sometimes she felt as if she couldn't think about anything else *but* him.

"The train's coming," Mei yelled down at them. "Hurry up."

Their eyes widened and they took off up the escalator. Candace made it to the platform first, but Ezra overtook her and reached the turnstile before her, because he was wearing tennis shoes and she was tottering around on a pair of heels that made her close to six feet tall and every step a precarious adventure. She made a mental note to write about this for her Women's Studies final essay and pushed herself to the limit trying to keep up with him.

He pushed his card through just as the train arrived.

"Candace, come on," Mei yelled at her from the edge of the platform.

"I'm not spraining my ankle to catch a BART train, Mei," she yelled back. She shoved her ticket into the machine just as the doors opened and Mei and Miles jumped aboard. Ezra was caught somewhere between waiting for her and making it into the car before the doors closed. If she weren't running for her life — metaphorically speaking — she would have doubled over in laughter at the way confusion contorted his face adorably. But she was running, so she pushed her affection for him to the side. Making this train was an imperative.

BART service to San Francisco on New Year's Eve was great, but a hassle. On a normal night, the trains might be crowded with drunk people, there might be a fight in one of the cars or on the platforms and there would absolutely be a homeless person walking the length of the train telling stories about his glory days during the Summer of Love while asking for spare change and telling everyone to never drop acid; just regular shenanigans. Tonight, the trains would be full of people at their most inebriated and annoying. There would absolutely be a fight or five, someone was going to vomit and more on a seat, and the nice homeless men would be replaced by a gang of rich, angry frat boys from the Midwest, who would probably end the night passed out and riding the train to the end of the line, their wallets and jewelry having mysteriously disappeared.

This would be a long night, and Candace knew the longer they waited to get to the City, the worse it would be. Most crucially, the longer it took to get to the City, the more likely she'd have to stand in these heels until midnight. And that was absolutely out of the question. They had to make this train if they wanted to get a decent seat on one of the good benches at the Embarcadero Center. But still, Candace was not going to sprain an ankle to make this specific train by running. She didn't believe in running for buses, trains or men, so this was a magnanimous move on her part as far as she was concerned and she planned to make sure they understood that.

Ezra hopped onto the train but he was angled out of the car, his body blocking the doors just in case they started to close. He extended his arm toward her and the smile on his face was glorious, different; a new category all together.

Candace extended her arm and their hands touched just as a chime indicated that the train would soon be departing. Ezra's hand closed around hers and he pulled her from the platform onto the car just as the doors began to slide shut, wrapping his arm around her waist to keep her steady. Their bodies crushed together. She couldn't stop herself from laughing with delight, not because they'd made the train but because Ezra was holding her. They were looking at one another in a way they certainly never had before. Candace wondered if Ezra's eyes were a different shade of blue under this light, darker maybe, more penetrating? She was thinking about telling him that she liked this new stormy blue she'd never seen before when their train car erupted in applause.

Ezra frowned and Candace turned her head to glare at the rest of the car in confusion. Everyone was very not sober or on their way to being, and clapping at them as if they'd just won a gold medal at the Winter Olympics.

"You made it," Mei said. Miles kissed her in celebration or because those two could hardly keep their hands off each other.

Candace furrowed her brow and turned to Ezra. He shrugged and grinned — that brief lift of the right side of his mouth. The train began to move and then quickly plunged into the Caldecott Tunnel, turning on the track, shifting her body against his. She could have stepped away, put some distance between them and caught her breath. The train wasn't technically packed enough for them to be so close. Not yet. But she didn't move. Instead, Candace leaned into Ezra. And he let her.

❧

*I*t was almost midnight.

They'd staked out a good spot at the Embarcadero. They'd have a perfect view of the fireworks and there were low concrete benches for the girls to sit on and "extend the shelf life of these heels," Mei had said.

"Or," Miles said, "you two could put on your flats and we can push through the crowd by the water." Ezra appreciated that Miles wasn't giving up on his plan. No matter how many times Candace and Mei shut it down. But they didn't even bother to respond to him this time.

"Come on, Ezra. What do you think?" he asked.

Ezra lifted his eyebrows and shook his head quickly, meaning that he wanted to stay entirely out of this disagreement. He didn't care where they were as long as they were together. But he could tell that Miles took his silence to mean something else.

"Of course," Miles rolled his eyes and looked briefly at Candace.

Ezra frowned at him and they had a silent standoff.

"Oh, it's almost time," Mei shrieked.

The crowd around them began to buzz with excitement.

Mei shoved her disposable camera against Miles's chest. "Take a picture of us."

Miles sighed as he wound the film and brought the camera to his face. Candace and Mei posed on the bench they'd half occupied, their sides touching, their faces close together and their smiles posed and unnatural to show off their glittery makeup.

"Make sure you get our matching shoes in the shot," Mei instructed. "And then a close-up of our makeup."

"This isn't a fashion ad for broke co-eds, Mei," Miles said as he snapped some more pictures.

"Come on, Ezra," Candace said to him.

He shook his head again. "I hate pictures," he mumbled.

"I know. But we need to document the moment anyway," she said, extending her arm toward him.

He stood, stunned at the thought that Candace knew he hated pictures. Almost as stunned at the idea that Candace had been thinking about him and her hand in his as he pulled her onto the train and her body pressed into his side as the car had jerkily traveled along its tracks. She took advantage of his shock and pulled him down onto the bench next to her. She and Mei posed while Ezra tried to hide his sheer panic at being close enough to Candace to smell her perfume. Again. Twice in one night.

It was entirely possible that nothing would ever beat this moment. This might even be the best New Year's Eve of his life. Well, second. Nothing could beat Candace kissing him last year. Even though they'd never talked about it and he'd never had the courage to ask her out; that was still the best New Year's Eve ever and in the top five nights of his life.

But then the countdown started. Mei shot up from the bench into Miles's arms. He picked her up and she wrapped her legs around his waist. She grabbed her camera from him and began to take pictures of everything; the early fireworks, the crowd, close-ups of Miles's face, everything.

Candace stood and Ezra followed, mostly just because he didn't know what else to do with himself.

"It's so loud," Candace said, leaning toward him.

"Do you want to be my New Year's kiss?" he blurted out and then swallowed the panic he felt at being so bold.

She smiled. "Again?"

He nodded as the crowd began to count down. The ruckus and the time limit of this question — let alone the fact that he had even asked it — made Ezra's heart beat faster and his hands sweat. It was as if the entire city was counting down, not to 2003, but to his fate. Or maybe his heart was beating erratically at the way Candace was smirking at him. As if she'd been waiting a year for him to ask just this question. But of course, she hadn't. It was dark out and that look was probably just a trick of his imagination and pathetic heart.

"Why me?" she asked.

"Because you're perfect," he yelled, loud enough to be heard over the erupting crowd as the countdown seemed to speed up.

Candace shook her head and rolled her eyes. "I'm so far from perfect, Ezra. How many times do I have to tell you that?"

"Three!" Mei yelled at the top of her lungs.

He wanted to tell her that she *was* perfect to him and nothing she could say would ever change that. He wondered if he could tell her that he knew — apparently better than she did — how great she was. He wondered if that would make him sound like a stalker. And maybe it would, because sometimes he felt like one, studying her like he did. But either way, he knew how amazing Candace Garret was, because he considered himself an expert on everything about her. The words were a jumble in his chest and he tried to figure out the right order to loosen them.

Apparently, he waited too long.

Candace sighed and rolled her eyes again. And then she slapped her hand onto the back of his neck and pulled him forward. "Oh, Ezra," she breathed, just before their lips touched.

"One!" the crowd screamed, and the fireworks erupted, hundreds of flashing cameras illuminating the Embarcadero. Ezra barely registered it all. Every firework and flash and scream faded to nothing when compared to Candace's scent and her taste and her tongue sliding against his.

He smiled against her lips and moaned into her mouth and couldn't believe that her answering moan — which he felt, rather than heard — was real and not some figment of his imagination like all the other moans had been.

This night and this kiss might have tied last year as the best New Year's Eve of his life, but it blew last year out of the water when Candace moved his right hand around her waist and placed it onto her ass. His other hand followed, and they ground into one another in the middle of the city-wide celebration.

Best New Year's Eve of his life. Best night ever.

"*E*verything alright, kiddo?"

Ezra nodded at his dad without turning toward him, wanting to avoid the weary look in his eyes and the gray tinge to his skin. He couldn't have looked much better, which was why he'd also been avoiding looking at himself in the mirror. The few times he'd left his mother's bedside to use the bathroom or go for a walk down to the hospital cafeteria at his father's suggestion, he'd avoided every reflective surface he passed. He was basically a carbon copy of his father under normal circumstances, so he knew what exhaustion and grief looked like and he didn't have any desire to inspect it more closely. He turned his head just a fraction of an inch more, trying to unhear his dad's pained voice.

The sounds of his mother's labored breathing and the rhythmic beeping of the monitors attached to her were comforting and terrifying at the same time. He didn't know where to look or what to do with his hands or his sadness or his anger.

"Hey bud, you should go eat," his father said, following his words with a comforting hand on Ezra's forearm.

"Not hungry," he muttered. His eyes filled with tears and he wiped them away with his fist. He didn't know why he was crying right now, but ever since his mom had been admitted to the hospital, he'd been tearing up near constantly.

"You need to eat. Your mother would never forgive me if I let you waste away too."

That last word fell from his father's lips as a strangled cry and in the end that was what drove Ezra from his mother's room; not his own non-existent hunger. He needed to get far away from that sound. He wanted to scrub his brain with bleach and wipe it from his memory. But he couldn't. So he practically ran down the hall. He pressed the button to call the elevator, but he was too restless to wait and pushed open the doors to the stairwell. He ran down three flights in a heartbeat, and it still wasn't fast enough or far enough away from that memory of his dad's voice. On the first floor, he considered running out into the night, but he couldn't. He couldn't stray too far. Just in case. He'd never forgive himself.

So he turned to his right and headed to the cafeteria like his father suggested. He wasn't hungry, but he didn't have anywhere else to go. There was only one place he wanted to be, and he felt selfish for even thinking it.

He walked down the hallway in a daze, not really seeing anyone he passed. He grabbed a small fruit salad from the ice well by the cashier just because. He paid for it by simply pushing all the money in his pocket toward the cashier. He was thankful when she sifted through the bills and coins, extracting what she needed and pushed the rest back to him.

He mumbled something that maybe sounded like thank you and walked away. He found a table near the back of the cafeteria, far away from everyone else, and sat heavily in an old, scratched plastic chair. He didn't touch his fruit. He still wasn't hungry.

"Anybody sitting here?"

Ezra startled and looked up. He blinked rapidly to clear his vision, but he still didn't believe what he saw. Candace was smiling down at him, Miles and Mei at her side.

"What..." he couldn't finish the question. He couldn't think.

"Your dad thought you could use some company," she said.

"And we're your best friends," Mei added.

"Actually, I'm your best friend," Miles corrected. "They're just your regular friends."

Ezra noticed Mei roll her eyes in his peripheral vision, but he never took his eyes off Candace. "You're here?" he croaked.

She smiled as she slid into the seat next to him. "Of course I'm here, Ezra. Where else would I be?"

"*S*o how does it feel?" Mei asked, leaning across the table and snagging a couple of Candace's fries.

"Do you want me to order a basket for you?"

"No thanks. Yours always taste better when we share." Her best friend winked. "Now come on. Answer my question. Candace Garret, how does it feel to be out of college an entire semester earlier than the rest of us regular achievers?"

Candace rolled her eyes. "Technically, I'm not done for real. I just finished all my coursework."

"Finished all your coursework for a double major in Art History and Spanish with a minor in Sociology," Mei said. "And now you're off to spend an entire semester in Ecuador. How does it *feel*?"

Candace ducked her head to hide her smile. "Weird. Hella weird."

"Yeah, that's what I thought," Mei chuckled. "You gonna miss me?"

Candace snatched her basket of French fries away from Mei's grasp. "Absolutely. I won't know what to do with myself when I can finally eat an entire basket of French fries for the first time in three and a half years all by myself."

Mei frowned, "It won't be as fun as you think. It's gonna go right to our hips."

Candace put her basket of fries in the middle of the table. "I'll be back for graduation."

Mei snatched two fries and shoved them into her mouth with a smile. "You better," she mumbled around the food.

"Well, hello there, ladies," Miles yelled from across the bar.

"Shut up," Candace and Mei yelled back.

He pretended to be affronted, but slid into the booth next to Mei, their bodies crushing together after so long — three hours — apart.

"Hey, Candace," Ezra said shyly, as he slid into the booth next to her, his eyes trained on the table.

"Hey," she said back, always enjoying the way his neck and cheeks turned bright red whenever she spoke to him, even though they'd all been a very tight quad for three years now. It was cute. Frustrating, but cute.

"Are you— Are you all packed?" he asked, still avoiding her eyes.

"Mostly. My mom and dad are coming up next

week to grab my furniture and all the clothes I don't need. But my bags are overstuffed for Quito."

"When do you leave?"

She didn't answer him right away. She waited. The sound of Mei and Miles kissing and laughing with each other — lost in their own world — met her silence. Finally, he looked up at her and made eye contact, like he always did when she waited long enough.

"Tomorrow morning," she finally answered.

The color drained from his face.

"So we gotta live it up tonight," Miles said unexpectedly, jolting them out of the moment.

"Yeah, we do. We're gonna send my girl off right," Mei echoed.

Candace and Ezra groaned.

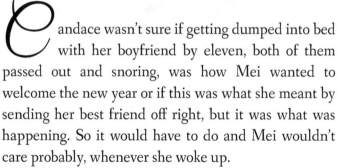

*C*andace wasn't sure if getting dumped into bed with her boyfriend by eleven, both of them passed out and snoring, was how Mei wanted to welcome the new year or if this was what she meant by sending her best friend off right, but it was what was happening. So it would have to do and Mei wouldn't care probably, whenever she woke up.

"They're kind of sweet when they're passed out," she said to Ezra as she stepped back to look down at their friends.

"Quieter at least," he mumbled irritably.

She snorted a laugh as they watched their friends

naturally gravitate to one other in their drunken slumber. Candace chuckled as she turned to walk out of the room, Ezra on her heels. He closed the door gently, even though she was certain nothing was going to wake those two up.

"So, what should we do for the next hour?" she asked.

Ezra looked around the living room. It was piled high with boxes of Candace's clothes, too many clothes for her parents to pick up after she'd left. "Do you need any help packing?"

"Sure," she said, even though she'd already told him she was finished.

She walked into her bedroom. The room was mostly empty. She'd taken all her posters and art prints down from the walls, packed away all her jewelry and trinkets. Her closet only had a few hangers left inside with the outfit she was traveling in tomorrow. And her suitcases were jam packed on the closet floor. But her bed was still made and topped with her favorite jumbo brown teddy bear that up until now had gone with her to every place she'd ever lived.

"Are you taking Teddy with you?" Ezra asked.

She turned to him and smiled. He stood just outside the threshold of her room, too nervous to enter. She reached for his hand and pulled him inside, walking him across the room and pushing him onto her bed. He landed stiffly. She pretended to ignore his flushed cheeks.

"I wish, but I can't. My parents are taking him home."

"I'm sorry," he whispered. Because of course he would.

"It's okay," she said, even though it wasn't. "How's your mom?"

He ducked his head and smiled. "Better. Her hair's long enough to almost put in a ponytail so she's teaching my dad how to do French braids."

She loved the way he looked in that moment; so happy he could burst. She loved him. But he... Well, she didn't really know what he thought about her. He was too hard to read. He was so nervous around her even after three years that he still dissolved into a red-faced stuttering mess when she tried to talk to him. She couldn't even imagine what he would do if she tried to flirt with him for real.

Three years of not really knowing where she stood with Ezra made her second-guess herself. She wanted to walk across the room and kiss him, or put his warm hand on her breast and stare at him until he squeezed. But what if he didn't respond? She didn't know how Ezra felt about her; not really. It wasn't indifference, but she couldn't rightly say that it was interest either. Sometimes she caught him looking at her as if she was the only person in the world. He'd kissed her two out of the three New Year's Eves they'd spent together, but he'd never asked her out. He never called her just to say hi or to go to the mall, just the two of them. So Candace looked away and swallowed all that unrequited love she felt for him like she had been for years. Because if she was wrong — if she'd been reading Ezra wrong all this time — she knew she wouldn't be able to handle his too kind rejection. Not right now.

"So give me an update on your Gilder submission. When is everything due?" she asked.

He swallowed loudly. "February first."

She sat on the bed next to him and bounced a couple of times before she felt strong enough to turn to him with a smile that looked as normal as she could manage. She bent her left leg; her knee grazed his thigh. "Nervous?"

He nodded.

"Nervous about the prize or nervous about sitting on my bed?" she blurted out before she could stop herself. Maybe that one glass of champagne she'd drank earlier had gone to her head.

"Both," he squeaked.

"Ezra," she whispered his name. She'd always loved the way it tasted on her tongue.

He swallowed slowly.

"Ezra, are you going to miss me?"

His entire neck had turned the brightest shade of red Candace had ever seen. When he turned to her, his pupils were fully dilated and he looked as if he might be on the verge of passing out. But he managed to nod.

"Do you remember our kiss freshman year, Ezra?"

He nodded again.

"And sophomore year?"

He'd never stopped nodding, so she took that as a yes.

"Do you want to kiss me goodbye, Ezra?" The question was an innocent tease, but she couldn't be sure exactly who she was teasing, him or herself. She was terrified of his answer.

His eyes widened in shock, but his nodding sped up comically.

She exhaled the breath she hadn't realized she was holding and reached out tentatively, placing her hands flat on his chest. She felt his muscles jump and heard his breath hitch even as he leaned into her touch. She smiled at him and moved her hands slowly up his pectorals to circle his neck. Her fingers slipped into his hair as their heads dipped forward. Their mouths moved closer and closer until their lips were almost touching. Their eyes locked and just as their lips met, he whispered her name into her mouth. It was divine. It was everything she'd ever fantasized about at night in this room, her hands in her underwear.

This kiss was nothing like that first kiss three years ago. That kiss had been tame, soft lips moving together and over in a heartbeat, even if Candace had spent the past three years thinking about it. This started off, in some ways, like that second kiss: tentative but hotter by the second. But it quickly morphed into something new; something Candace had only ever dreamed of experiencing.

This kiss was soft lips that spread on a shared gasp, wet tongues moving tentatively forward. After that first spark of connection, Candace smiled in surprise as Ezra's tongue pushed confidently into her mouth, gliding against her tongue, his lips pressing and prying her mouth open. She wouldn't have thought Ezra capable. She was happy to be wrong.

They fumbled a bit, his hand on her hip when she wanted it higher. But that was okay. With his tongue stroking hers she suddenly felt brave enough to grab his hand and place it on her breast like she'd been considering. And maybe he was braver too, because he used his mouth to push her head just slightly back so he could deepen their kiss. She smiled against his mouth.

She moaned and he pulled back sharply. "Is that okay? Am I doing it right?"

She could have screamed, but she laughed and nodded impatiently. "It's more than okay, Ezra. Don't worry."

He smiled shyly and she pushed him back onto her bed. She crawled on top of him and dipped her head. Their mouths crashed together again.

His hands moved to the hem of her t-shirt and tentatively slipped underneath. She smiled against his lips. She'd been waiting three years for this.

"Is this okay?" he asked again as his hands covered her bra-covered breasts and he trailed soft kisses along her cheek.

She nodded and then shook her head.

He pulled back immediately.

She sat up to straddle his waist and locked eyes with him as she lifted her shirt over her head and then reached back to unhook her bra. Candace wished she'd had the forethought to turn the light off, but she also loved watching the shock and arousal play on Ezra's face as she bared her breasts to him.

His arms were locked stiffly at his sides as if he was terrified to touch her bare skin. She grabbed his hands and gently placed them on her waist. And then she waited.

"I'm a virgin," he whispered.

"I know," she said. "We can stop whenever you want."

His eyes had been locked on her breasts but flew to her face. "Why would I want to stop?"

Her shocked laughter filled the room. "You're still so very interesting, Ezra Posner. Whenever I think I get you; I don't."

He smiled shyly as his hands moved across her skin slowly, dry and warm, leaving a path of electricity in their wake. His fingertips blazed a trail up the soft flesh that spilled over the waist of her jeans, up the rounded planes of her hips, and across her rib cage. He cupped her breasts gently.

"Play with my nipples," she whispered, part instruction, part plea.

He moved his thumbs over them, circling each bud softly. "Like this?"

She nodded. "You don't have to be so gentle."

He nodded back and began to pluck at them as he bit his bottom lip in concentration. She smiled. She'd seen this look on his face before. In the library computer lab, during their Biology III midterm, while they studied with Mei and Miles at the campus coffee shop, whenever he inspected the salad bar in the dining hall. She'd always dreamt that he would look at her that way and imagined what it would do to her body if he did.

"Ow," she hissed.

"Shit, sorry." He moved his hands away, holding them up in apology.

She smiled down at him and grabbed his hands, moving them back to her breasts. "It's okay, Ezra. Just don't twist that hard, okay?"

He nodded and began tentatively massaging her breasts again.

Once they'd reestablished their rhythm, her eyes closed, and her hips began to circle at the waist as she ground into his lap. She moaned when she felt his mouth cover her right nipple. "God, yes." Her head fell back in ecstasy.

Ezra had always been quick at picking up new skills. He was also a hard worker and very focused on doing things right. And just as Candace had always secretly hoped, when he turned his attention toward pleasuring her body, it was amazing. His head moved from one breast to the other, kissing and licking at her while she rode his lap, trying desperately to get herself off on the growing bulge in his pants. She cupped the back of his head, scratching at his scalp, gently pulling his strands through her fingers. She whimpered when he stopped, already missing his touch. She looked down at him, confused, and the sight of him looking up at her, her breasts in his hands, made her shiver.

"Can we reposition?" he asked, oh so politely as usual.

She couldn't help but smile down at him. "Of course, Ezra."

She crawled off his lap and he jumped from the bed excitedly, pulling his shirt over his head.

Candace had never seen Ezra without his shirt on and since he seemed to swing between scorching and glacial with her, she wasn't sure if she ever would again. She greedily drank in every new part of him just in case this was the only time she got to see it. She was surprised at how sexy she found the veil of dark hair on his chest and down his stomach. Her gaze followed that hair to the waist of his jeans and then her attention settled on the bulge she'd been riding. She sucked her bottom lip into her mouth.

"Can we...?"

She looked at his face. "Can we what, Ezra?" She smiled.

He swallowed again and took a deep breath. "Can I taste you?"

Her mouth fell open in shock and her eyes widened. "Ezra, have you ever eaten a girl out before?"

He shook his head quickly, but he didn't blush, Candace noticed. "But I've had dreams."

"Have you?" She couldn't help but laugh.

"Dreams about you," he said.

The laughter died on her tongue. "Have you?" she whispered.

He looked her directly in the eyes and nodded. "Always. Can you teach me?"

Candace could have screamed again. Why hadn't he ever said anything? Three years. They'd been friends for three years and he'd never said anything. Not once. And she had no idea why.

The only thing that kept the frustrated yell from her throat was that she'd known almost from the moment she'd met Ezra at freshman orientation that she'd have to wait for him. And so far, he'd been worth it. She let out a frustrated breath and nodded up at him. His smile was so big Candace could hardly think as she tried to memorize it.

She leaned back against Teddy and unbuttoned her jeans. She shimmied out of them with Ezra's help and lifted her hips as he grabbed her underwear. She would have worn something sexier if she'd ever imagined that Ezra Posner would be kneeling between her thighs, red-faced with lust rather than embarrassment, shirtless, with a more than impressive bulge in his pants. But now that he was, who cared that she didn't have sexier panties? Certainly not Ezra, who placed them on the floor gently without looking, his eyes laser-focused on her sex.

She pressed her knees together and she could have sworn she heard him whimper. She liked it. "Are you ready, Ezra?"

He nodded, his hands fisting the bedsheets on

either side of her hips in anticipation. She spread her legs again slowly and then lifted them to rest her feet on his shoulders. He licked his lips.

Candace had to bite back a moan. Did he even know what he was doing to her?

She reached between her legs. "Give me your hand."

He nodded, his eyes still trained on her. She grabbed his index and middle fingers and ran the pads of his digits down her lips.

"How does it feel?" she whispered in a shaky breath.

"Wet," he croaked and then cleared his throat. "Soft. So soft."

They moved his fingers up and down and then she spread them, spreading herself open for him. She heard the sharp intake of his breath as he saw her for the first time.

She moved his middle finger to the base of her sex and pulled a moan from his lips as his finger slowly moved inside. She watched him as he pumped his digit in and out slowly — so damn slowly — his eyebrows bunched in concentration.

"Is this okay?" he asked again.

"You could add another," she whispered, her own breath ragged.

His hand stopped and he looked up at her. "Are you sure?"

She bit her bottom lip to try and stifle the smile, but she failed. "Very."

His free hand gripped her hip and they both moaned as he slipped one more finger inside her, massaging her gently. This time he watched her face as he worked her over. Her chest rose and fell faster and her eyes drifted closed.

"Can I taste you now?"

She whimpered. He sounded needy. It was so wonderful to finally be on the same page, she thought to herself. "Yes," she moaned. "Just lick me. Or kiss me like you kissed my mouth." She wasn't even sure if her voice had risen high enough for him to hear until his tongue swiped up her lips.

Her legs fell open and she cried out as he did it again and again with increasing pressure.

She was going to tell him where her clit was and ask him to suck it, but his fingers were still working her over and his wet tongue was so nice that words were becoming harder to conjure. So when his tongue accidentally grazed her clit, she reached down and cupped the back of his head to keep his tongue just there, knowing that he would catch on. Ezra was the smartest boy she knew.

His fingers dug into the soft flesh of her hip with the perfect amount of pressure. Then his tongue scraped over her hard clit again and she groaned. He lifted his head. She loosened her grip and did the same. She watched and moaned as he ran two of his soaked fingers up her lips and pulled back the hood to expose her sensitive nub. "Is this...?"

"Yes. Please," she groaned, her hips lifting from the bed, trying to close the distance to his mouth.

"What should I...?"

"Suck it, Ezra. Please." Of all the ways she'd imagined tonight unfolding, she'd never expected that she would beg — actually beg — Ezra Posner to suck her clit. But as it happened, she'd once had a dream exactly like this, so she wasn't mad about this development at all.

His mouth covered her again and he sucked her clit into his mouth like she was the fountain of youth.

"Oh god," she moaned, and her head fell back.

He pushed his fingers back into her sex and turned his hand to stroke her inside at the same rhythm as his mouth. Candace's legs began to shake and her sex clenched around his fingers. She moved her hands back to his head, not that she was at all worried that he might stop. Her hips began to rotate. Her body had developed a mind of its own. The only thing that mattered was that her pussy stayed as close to Ezra's mouth as possible.

She gasped and moaned and then cried out as her orgasm unexpectedly rippled through her. Her entire body shook and her breathing was nothing more than vulgar pants. It was the best orgasm of her life. And Ezra seemed hell bent on pushing her over again because his fingers and mouth didn't stop moving as she clenched and shuddered and gushed onto his hand. Her entire body felt like an exposed nerve that Ezra somehow knew exactly how to touch.

When she couldn't take it anymore, Candace finally pushed him away, albeit reluctantly. The room was full of the sound of their labored breathing. She felt the warm puff of his breath as he placed soft kisses on her inner thighs and could only groan weakly at the perfection of this handful of moments.

When his mouth finally disappeared from her skin, she opened one eye to peek at him and moaned.

He was licking her off his hand.

She sat up on her elbows, ready to ask Ezra if he was sure he'd never done that before, and where the fuck he learned to rub her that way. She was planning to ask him those and a million more questions while also switching places so she could return the favor, when the sound of fireworks outside caught their attention. There were sporadic bursts at first and then the sound became a popping crescendo. And then they heard shuffled footsteps down the hall.

"Oh god, I'm gonna puke," Mei groaned before the bathroom door slammed shut.

Candace turned back to Ezra and smiled. "Happy New Year," she breathed.

They dissolved into quiet, intimate giggles.

DECEMBER 29, 2019

*E*zra checked his watch and sighed. He'd been trying to miss this flight all day. He'd pressed the snooze button on his alarm twice — something he never did — and taken an extra-long shower. He'd puttered around his kitchen making a breakfast he wasn't interested in eating, then eaten it as slowly as possible. He'd even washed the dishes, wiped down the counters and taken out the trash. He'd even sat down to watch a movie. His mind kept wandering and when he saw the credits rolling he had no idea what he'd just seen, but that was two hours gone; still not enough. When he'd finally trudged back to his bedroom, he wasted as much time as he could reorganizing his collection of — mostly unworn — ties before finally packing his suitcase. When his driver, Carl, arrived on time, he'd sighed at his own inability to deviate from his schedule. Not even when he wanted to.

On the way to the airport he'd silently rejoiced

when they'd gotten stuck in traffic on the I-80 and been just as silently pissed when Carl had taken the streets to make sure he made it to SFO with time to spare. He couldn't be mad at the man for doing his job. Ezra paid him good money to get him where he needed to be on time and usually in a hurry. But just this once, he wished Carl had been less than stellar. At the departing curb, Ezra shoved down his disappointment and thanked the man nonetheless.

He checked into his flight, handed over his suitcases and began to walk leisurely to his gate, stopping in every store in the terminal, window shopping for things he didn't want or need; anything to waste a few more minutes. But no matter how much he dawdled, Ezra finally had to accept that he was going to make his flight when he spotted his gate a few feet ahead.

Missing this flight would mean he'd have to cancel his upcoming meeting and email his team to postpone finalizing their contracts. His COO and Board of Directors would probably kill him, and with good reason. Ezra wasn't the kind of man who ran away from responsibility, but there wasn't anything he wanted less in this moment than to board this plane. He considered going to the closest airline desk and buying a ticket to Hawai'i or Montana or any flight leaving immediately. He felt desperate and he hated it.

Across from his gate, he spotted a newsagent and turned inside just as his phone rang. He frowned when he saw Miles's name on his screen.

"What do you want?" he asked in greeting.

"Is that how you say hello to your best friend?"

"Yes."

Miles laughed. It sounded genuine, but not as light as it used to. The only way Ezra could have described Miles's laughter nowadays was burdened. "I was just checking to make sure you were at the airport."

"Yes, mom," Ezra sighed.

"Don't 'yes mom' me. I'm going to tell your father about this, young man." Miles laughed at his own joke.

"I'm going to hang up on you," Ezra warned.

"You better not." Ezra heard Miles sigh. "When are you coming back?"

He navigated the tightly packed aisles of the newsagent to get to the refrigerated cases. He grabbed a bottle of water and began to peruse the books, avoiding Miles's question. "Not sure yet," he eventually mumbled.

"Any chance you'll charter a flight and rush home for my annual New Year's Eve party?"

Ezra was in a tricky place in his life at the moment; absolutely not where he'd planned to be in his mid-thirties when he and Miles had met during freshman orientation. He'd imagined that by this age he'd be married with kids and running his own tech start-up. He hadn't ever expected that having the latter would feel so hollow without the former. And no one could have convinced him that he'd be standing in the airport giving serious consideration to buying a family-sized bag of M&M's, terrified at the thought of boarding a flight to attend the most important meeting of his career and equally as terrified of what would happen if he didn't.

"Let's play it by ear," he said half-heartedly.

Normally Miles would have pressed the issue, but he didn't this time and Ezra was both grateful and sad about it. There was probably a sense of relief on Miles's part. The New Year's Eve party had once been the social highlight of their year but maybe with Ezra out of town, Miles would give himself permission to cancel it. He was just about to suggest that when a big curly Afro caught his attention in his peripheral vision. He turned quickly but not quick enough, and it was gone in a flash. His mouth fell open and he shook his head. Couldn't be, he thought and tried to collect himself.

It wasn't her. What were the odds?

And even if it had been her, it wouldn't matter. It shouldn't matter, he reminded himself.

But in that almost glimpse of what certainly was not Candace, Ezra's heart had sped up and he could feel the familiar blush building on his neck. He felt eighteen again and he hated himself for it. It shouldn't have mattered that that could have been Candace, but it did. And it always would. That was why he was leaving; why he'd scheduled this meeting for the end of the year and in another country.

"Actually, Miles, I'm definitely not going to make it," he said.

He couldn't go back. Not again.

~

*C*andace couldn't miss this flight. If she did, Sarah would never forgive her, she'd be written up and worst of all, she'd probably have to be home over New Year's Eve. And she couldn't have that. Never mind that the reason she was running across the terminal like a mad woman was because she'd spent most of the day trying to miss this flight. She'd woken up, looked at her packed suitcase and considered calling in sick. The airline could probably find someone else to cover Sarah's itinerary.

She'd gone through her regular pre-flight routing — shower, breakfast, coffee, then lounging around the house — wondering about so many things. What if she spent New Year's Eve at home? What if she put on that slinky champagne-colored dress that made her skin look like the truest, deepest ebony and went to a party? What if that party was Miles's annual New Year's Eve get together? What if Ezra was there? So many possibilities, she'd thought while running her fingers over the sequins on her dress, daydreaming about his hands doing the same. She'd lost track of herself for so long that when the notification on her phone chimed, letting her know that her ride share driver was close, she hadn't had any time to think. She snatched the dress from its hanger, threw it into her suitcase and was out the door in a heartbeat.

On the way to the airport, she watched the city disappear behind her, conflicted, but not enough to ask the driver to turn around and decided to take that indecision as a sign. If she really wanted to stay, she would be, but for what? She was going to make her flight and follow through with her plan to make this New Year's Eve different; to finally get over him.

She carried all her self-doubt and fears and wishes with her as she checked her bag, wound her way through security, chatted with the TSA agents she recognized and made her way to her gate. By the time she paid for the large bottle of water at the newsagent closest to her gate, she'd managed to stuff all her sadness into a tight ball that she could ignore for a few hours at least. She smiled at the gate agent and showed her badge and then waited for them to unlock the jet bridge. She waved and walked through the door and then immediately let her smile slip. When she stepped onto the plane, she exhaled briefly, finding some solace in the familiarity of her job, at least.

"Ooooh girl, what are you doing here?" Jorge yelled, walking up the aisle toward her.

"What's that supposed to mean?"

"Exactly what it sounds like, shock and judgment. I can't believe you let Sarah scam you into taking over this flight. Her grandmother has died twice in the last six months!"

Candace laughed and shook her head. "She didn't scam me. I wanted to go to Quito."

It was true. She hadn't been back to Ecuador since she'd spent six months there during her last year of college. She'd worked a quick turnaround between

Oakland and Chicago with Sarah and let the other girl spin a yarn about a family reunion and surprise funeral. Sarah was legendary for hitting up everyone she worked with to either swap or cover shifts, with various repetitive sob stories that were as effective as they were probably fake. But when Sarah had mentioned Quito while they were standing on the people mover heading to baggage claim, something inside of her clicked. She'd said yes before she knew what she was doing. That too had felt like a sign.

The last time she remembered being really happy and free had been on the way to Ecuador, before she'd been a real adult with real adult responsibilities, making real adult mistakes. It seemed farfetched when she said it out loud, but Candace hoped returning to Quito might help her find herself again. The fact that it gave her an excuse to run away was a bonus.

"Well, scam or not, I'm happy you're here instead of her," Jorge said, lifting Candace's bag into the overhead compartment. "Working with her is like working alone. And working with her *and* Mark," he said and lowered his voice to a whisper, his eyes shifting to the rear of the plane, "I don't deserve that kind of torture."

She nodded, "Well, you're welcome. I guess you'll only have to deal with half the torture."

"So you wanted to go to Quito, huh? Why? You got a man down there I don't know about?"

Candace laughed again, the irony and absurdity of that statement making her wheeze. "I don't have a man. And I'm sure not keeping one in a foreign country."

Jorge frowned, "Shame."

They burst into laughter and started the pre-flight check just as the pilots stepped onto the plane.

Candace sank into the routine of safety checks and deliveries and manifests and plane preparation to take her mind from all the questions in her head. She wondered if this was the right decision. She wondered at all the wrong decisions she'd made and how she might have made different choices. But she had to stop that and accept the truth of the unknown. She didn't know if running away was the right decision or a colossal mistake, but she couldn't bear to spend another year wishing she was with Ezra, or being with him and feeling alone.

~

*E*zra still wanted to miss this flight. He stared at the screen listing all the departing flights and gave Hawai'i serious consideration for a few minutes. But he once again dismissed the idea, because he didn't want to skip Quito and go somewhere else. If he didn't get on this plane, there was only one course of action for him. If he stayed in California, he'd leave the airport, call a cab, go straight to Miles's house and camp out in his home office/guest bedroom and wait for her. He knew it. And Miles would know it, even if he wouldn't say it aloud.

There was only one thing stopping him from taking that course of action: he didn't trust that she'd show. She'd skipped last year without a word — no email, no text message, no voice mail, nothing. She'd been off doing... whatever she was doing, while he'd waited for her in vain. He didn't have the heart to live through that again.

He'd spent the last almost two decades in exactly the same place with Candace and he couldn't do it anymore. Not because he wouldn't; he absolutely would. Left to his own devices, Ezra knew he'd wait for Candace forever, on the slim hope that she would come around. That's why leaving was his only option. He needed to break his old pattern and try to start a new one.

But still, he kept his mind and his heart focused on Candace right up until the very last moment. Ezra had a First Class ticket, but he stood across from the gate, leaning against a hollow column, breathing deeply and mentally fighting with himself through the pre-boarding for families with small children, those who needed more time to make it down the runway, and veterans. He clenched his boarding pass in his hand as First Class and Mileage Elite members disappeared through the gate. He stayed rooted in place as zones one to infinity followed. He only moved when the gate agent called for final boarding, while staring directly at him.

He walked slowly forward and smiled as he handed over the crumpled, slightly damp piece of paper in his hand.

She smiled back, "Welcome aboard, Mr. Posner."

He walked down the bridge slowly, much more slowly than he should have considering he was probably the last person to board. All the while, he wanted to turn back. He tried to tell himself that there was a lesson to learn in this moment, but his brain and heart didn't care. Instead, his mind kept replaying the crystal-clear image of eighteen-year-old Candace leaning toward him. *"You're an interesting guy, Ezra Posner,"* her beautiful, soft lips had said. It was the first lie she'd ever told him.

His eyes were downcast as he walked toward the plane, but as he neared the open cabin door, he pulled the strap of his messenger bag over his head. His entire body froze when he saw her. He knew this image wasn't a mirage or some other figment of his imagination. If his brain had conjured Candace, she wouldn't be looking at someone else, smiling, covered nearly from head-to-toe in a terrible flight attendant's uniform. He never had before, and he never would. No, when Ezra dreamt of Candace, she stared at him with bright eyes, that haughty smirk, naked, gasping, biting, sucking, clenching, moaning, shuddering over him. Beautiful. Perfect. His.

This was no mirage, because he'd finally accepted last New Year's Eve that even if she was beautiful and perfect still, she would never be his.

And then she turned toward him.

# CHAPTER 1

*C*andace used a specific smile while she was working. Wide, but not too wide; teeth, but not a lot of teeth; never deep enough to show her dimples. It was the kind of smile that worked on every passenger, no matter their race or sex, young or old, angry or sad, happy or indifferent. It was multipurpose — able to defuse every sticky situation, no matter how big or small — and also pointed, making each passenger feel seen and heard. This smile was her best defense. It was part of her uniform. This smile was a skill. It was just as important as being able to maneuver those damn carts down the skinniest airplane aisle or shove a suitcase just barely within TSA regulations into an overhead bin. Learning how to smile in just the right way to make passengers feel comfortable, while reminding them that she was absolutely not the one to fuck with, was crucial to her ability to perform her job. Which was why it was necessary that she never let it slip. And it was only because of her training that when she turned to the jet bridge and saw Ezra Posner standing there, staring at her, she managed to smile at him — not too wide, not too much teeth and betraying none of the shock and anxiety she felt. Candace was many things — restless, indecisive, disorganized and a failure — but she was also a professional.

"Welcome aboard, sir," she said. She wondered if her voice sounded strained. She extended her arm toward him; maybe reaching for his boarding pass, maybe just hungry to touch him again after so long.

Ezra didn't move. He just stood there, his boarding pass clutched in his hand and a carry-on bag in the other, staring at her.

He wasn't eighteen or twenty-one anymore. He didn't flush at the sight of her. Or when he was nervous. Or embarrassed. Or happy. Or awake. Near her.

"Welcome aboard, sir," she said again. Her voice was definitely tense this time.

A baby's cry from the jet bridge mercifully disrupted the awkwardness of the moment. A mother with an infant in her arms and a toddler walking beside her came into view. Candace exhaled in relief at this temporary reprieve.

Ezra seemed to come almost to his senses and stepped aside. The mother didn't question it and nudged her daughter forward.

Candace pulled her mouth into that familiar smile

and bent down to the toddler. "Hello there, sweetheart," she said to the little girl as she stepped forward.

"Plane," she trilled happily up at Candace.

Her mother sighed, "This is her first flight." Candace noted the bags under her eyes and the weariness in her voice.

"Papa," the toddler yelled.

"We're going to visit my husband," she added.

Candace smiled and nodded, stepping back for them to board the plane.

"Welcome aboard," she said to the children as they passed. "Let me know if you need anything," she said to the woman and made a mental note to check in on her before takeoff.

She watched them move slowly down the aisle, the mother balancing the baby on her hip and encouraging her other child forward with her free hand. She watched to make sure they were okay and also to put off turning toward Ezra again. But it couldn't be avoided forever. *He* couldn't be avoided forever.

Candace had tried.

She took a deep breath before she swiveled her head back to the jet bridge. Ezra was still standing there, seemingly rooted to the spot. Staring at her.

She smiled wide, wider than she normally would in this situation; assuming she'd ever trained for a situation like this. Her cheeks hurt. "Welcome aboard, sir," she repeated, because she couldn't think of anything else to say. What was left to say between them?

And maybe he realized that, Candace thought sadly to herself, as he took one tentative step forward.

When they were in college, Ezra was great at shrinking into the background. Candace used to call him The Magician, because one second he was there and the next he'd receded so far from the center of the crowd that she sometimes had to search high and low to find him. But it was a nickname she couldn't share with anyone else for fear someone might ask the very valid question, "Why are you always looking for Ezra Posner?" And she didn't have an answer for that. At least not one that wouldn't bare her soul completely. Just like she didn't have an answer for the butterflies in her stomach even after all these years.

He took a few more jerky steps forward.

She wanted to tell him to hurry up because she wasn't sure how long she could keep this smile on her face without crying, and they needed to finish boarding and check the manifests. But she also wanted to tell him to slow down a little so she could watch him walk. In the end, she ground her teeth to keep from saying anything at all and his steps became slightly less awkward the closer he came.

When Ezra reached out to hand over his ticket, Candace let her face relax into her work smile because it was open, if not as aggressively friendly, and wouldn't betray the emotional storm in her chest. She focused on making sure her hand wasn't shaking when she grabbed his boarding pass. She also made sure not to overreach; she wasn't sure she could handle it if their fingers touched.

Candace had to smooth the softened paper some to read it. "5C. Follow me, sir." She led him the short walk to the front of the plane. She wished it had been longer. Or that Jorge had been standing at the door when Ezra turned that corner. Or that she hadn't let Sarah scam her into picking up this route.

She turned around and avoided making eye contact with him, extending her arm toward his seat. "Would you like something to drink, sir?"

He shook his head. "Stop calling me 'sir,'" he hissed. He sounded angry, or maybe confused.

Candace's eyes shifted to his.

"Please. Don't call me sir," he whispered softly.

Candace used to be able to discern all of Ezra's tones of voice and facial expressions, but she was rusty. She couldn't tell if that whisper was sad or furious or something more painful for him, and maybe for her. Left to her own devices, she would spend the entire flight trying to parse all the many notes in his voice and the variable meanings of his words. She'd spent years hoping for something more from Ezra; hoping she could decipher something in his voice or his silence that might let her know exactly what he was thinking and how he felt about her. She couldn't do that anymore. She'd wasted so many years of her life doing just that.

"I... can't. Not here," she said, looking quickly away, aiming her words at his right ear. "Not now."

She saw him nod from her peripheral vision and then he mercifully slipped into his seat. She took in a deep breath and then put on that fake smile again; as if she were slipping on a suit of armor, preparing herself for war. Because maybe she was.

~

*E*zra clutched his cell phone in his right hand, turning and turning and turning it around on his bouncing knee. He considered calling Miles, but Mei was who he actually needed to speak to, and he couldn't call her. Or maybe he could. Even after three years he wasn't sure about the etiquette of divorce in a friendship group. Ezra's parents were still married and had only seemed to grow stronger each year they were together — every cancer-free year they shared — so he was completely unprepared to watch Miles and Mei's marriage fall apart. Untangling almost two decades of friendship was too much for any of them to handle, especially when his and Candace's relationship had been privately ruptured at the same time. He needed to call Mei, but he wasn't certain that he should. So he bounced his knee and turned his phone over in his hand and he watched her.

He didn't want to watch her, but he did. Old habits die hard or never at all; especially when that old habit was being in awe of Candace Garret. She and the other flight attendants were flitting back and forth down the length of the plane. Ezra tried to catalogue the changes in her since he'd last seen her in person — as opposed to pictures on social media. Four years. That was the longest they'd ever been apart since they'd met. And as he watched her, he could feel every day of that time in his soul.

Her curly afro — the exact one he'd seen in the newsagent but convinced himself couldn't be her — seemed softer, but maybe that was just because he wanted to touch it. Her skin seemed to glow even under the terrible lighting, but maybe that was just because he'd always loved the way her rich tone seemed to shine as if she was lit from within. As if nothing could shine brighter than her, especially not to Ezra's eyes. Her uniform was a bland mix of blues and grays that did nothing to accentuate her figure, and yet the curves of her hips and breasts still looked as lush as ever.

But just as he did, her voice startled him.

"Hello, ladies and gentlemen. Welcome to Aero-Plan flight number 2365 with direct service from San Francisco to Quito, Ecuador. I'm your purser Candace and I want to welcome you aboard."

Ezra didn't hear anything else she said. He flew enough to probably be able to recite this welcome message and safety demonstration from heart. Rather than listen, he watched her. She stood by the closed cabin door, holding the receiver to the messaging system close to her mouth. She was leaning against the wall, her ankles crossed and one hand on her hip. Her eyes were cast down as she spoke. It was a relaxed stance, but something about it struck him as sad, which wasn't a word he would have ever used to describe Candace before. He couldn't help but wonder if she looked that way because of him.

He forced himself to look away, his heart thudding in his chest. He had to remind himself not to fall into old patterns. He couldn't keep creating an alternative version of Candace in his heart just so he could imbue her with feelings for him she clearly didn't have. He couldn't keep giving himself permission to wait for her, holding out hope that theirs was some kind of fairytale. Not again. Not anymore.

He looked across the empty seat next to him, out the window. There was nothing to see, just concrete and planes rolling slowly around the tarmac. In his peripheral vision, he saw her begin to walk down the aisle. She was smiling as her head swiveled from row to row, checking seatbelts and directing passengers to put their chairs in the upright position, stow their bags under the seats in front of them and "Please turn your phone off or put it in airplane mode, sir."

He started at the sound of her voice so close. It took him a few seconds to realize that she'd been speaking to him. By the time he looked up, she was already moving from First Class into the main cabin.

Ezra looked down at his phone. He didn't know why, but he checked his text messages and email. Scrolling back and back until he realized what he was looking for.

She returned to First Class. "Sir, please turn your

phone off or switch to airplane mode for takeoff," Candace said. Ezra thought she sounded angry, or maybe annoyed.

He looked up at her. "You really weren't going to show up again?" He lobbed the question at her quickly. It caught her off guard and her mouth fell open. But before she could answer, he asked her the question that had formed in his mind as he'd scrolled through his messages, confirming that none were from her. "And you weren't going to tell me? Again?"

*E*zra clutched his bottle of beer in one hand and pushed the sliding glass door to the patio closed behind him as he returned inside. Miles's living room was filled with people he knew but didn't know well enough to want to talk to. And even worse, they all wanted to talk to him now that his company had gone public.

He hadn't thought so many people at their annual New Year's Eve party would care, let alone be interested in pitching their half-cocked business ideas to him as if he was going to fund all their dreams. He'd been Miles's geeky, awkward best friend for so long, he hadn't thought anything could shift his social position. But he'd apparently severely underestimated the power of money. He bet Candace would cry with laughter when he told her about his naïveté.

Although, as it happened, Candace was the issue. It wasn't that he hadn't thought of this possibility, it was simply that whenever he thought of her, he let himself hope in the face of all sound evidence that that was a terrible idea. He'd been looking forward to this night for years, desperate to recover some semblance of the easy familiarity of their last New Year's Eve together.

New Year's Eve 2015 had been nearly perfect. It had felt like college again. Candace and Mei had commandeered the kitchen to bake and sing off-key to all their favorite R&B songs, while he and Miles caught up by the grill over beer.

By the time the rest of the guests showed up, the house smelled like chocolate cake and grilled meat, the four of them were tipsy and it had only taken a look. Candace excused herself upstairs and Ezra, adept at making himself invisible, followed her soon after. Ezra had no idea what had happened at the party downstairs. He didn't care. He hadn't shown up to Miles and Mei's for that. He'd shown up to catch up with the other three before the party and then spend the rest of the night in the spare bedroom, reacquainting himself with every inch of Candace's body. And he had.

It was perfect — a literal dream — when Candace gasped his name into his ear just as the fireworks started and the downstairs crowd cheered to welcome the new year. He'd looked into her eyes, her warm, wet sex clenching around him, and hoped that this year would finally be their year.

After so many false starts and almost-shoulda-coulda-beens, Ezra had let himself believe they were finally starting the relationship he'd been waiting patiently for since college. He hadn't expected to wake up alone, or to find out two months later that Candace was in a new relationship with someone who wasn't him. He'd skipped the next two New Year's Eve parties, unable to imagine being in the same room as her and her boyfriend.

Ezra might have skipped this New Year's Eve if he hadn't caught the change in Candace's relationship status on Facebook. Single. That word had been emblazoned on the back of his eyelids for months. He'd wanted to call or text her. Or fly to wherever she was and... Do what? He didn't know, so he'd waited. He was more than used to that. He hadn't realized what he was waiting for until Miles emailed an invitation to his new annual New Year's Eve party and it seemed like a sign. All he had to do was show up and everything would be as it was, he'd thought.

What his hunger to see Candace had hidden was that nothing was the same as it had been three years previous. Miles and Mei were divorced. Their tight foursome had disintegrated as their friends had separated assets and sat through hours of mediation and finally signed divorce papers. But still... Ezra had hoped.

His and Candace's annual reunions were a tradition. Some things could stay the same, couldn't they? Or maybe they could change for the better. He'd finally moved back to California and Candace was single; there was no better time to reconnect than this.

So, Ezra had carefully dressed for Miles's party thinking of all the possibilities with Candace. He hadn't let himself even consider that she wouldn't show.

When Miles and Mei had been together, the invitations to their party had been printed on the best card stock they could afford. The two would spend weeks planning and prepping for a blowout that lasted well into the new year. The few hours before the rest of their guests showed up was a time for the four of them to catch up and bring back their college glory days. But the divorce ended all that, as Ezra finally realized the moment he'd arrived at Miles's condo. Instead of his and Mei's ultra-modern house in the Oakland Hills, Miles's new apartment in El Cerrito looked like a luxury version of their off-campus apartment in college, replete with a futon and just enough furniture for a handful of grown men to watch sports in comfort and not one coaster more. The party was a BYOB potluck. Instead of Mei's huge menu catering to all their friends' tastes, Miles had ordered pizza and wings. Instead of a meticulously curated playlist of the year's best music, the television was tuned to ESPN and the guys had hung out in the living room watching highlights of games Ezra had never seen and didn't care about.

He'd spent the night checking and rechecking his watch, pacing from the kitchen to the front door to look out at the street. He couldn't fully acknowledge to himself that she wasn't coming until midnight. The finality of the ball dropping had nearly brought Ezra to his knees. He'd always thought — hoped — that the rollercoaster of his relationship with Candace was just a matter of timing. A kiss at the campus bonfire when they were first years and Candace had a firm no dating rule; a kiss with literal fireworks and a crowd cheering around them; a chaste but fierce hug in the hospital that lasted much longer than it should have while Ezra cried in Candace's arms; cunnilingus in her near empty bedroom interrupted by their puking friends; sex each New Year's Eve while he was home for the holidays. He'd been certain that it was all leading to something, and he'd planned to finally tell her that.

But Candace was MIA and Ezra drove home that night sober, sad and alone. As he crossed the Golden Gate Bridge, a few errant sparkles lighting the sky, he'd decided that he was officially too old for this. He'd loved Candace for nearly half his life, but it was time to finally accept that she didn't feel the same.

He'd made a solemn vow to himself as he looked at his drawn face in his bathroom mirror that this had to end. It was finally time to get over Candace Garret.

# CHAPTER 2

*I*t hadn't happened immediately after graduation, but they had grown apart. One day, Candace, Ezra, Mei and Miles had spent nearly every day together and the next it was like they were living on four different planets. Well, three planets; Mei and Miles were certainly on a planet together. In reality, they'd drifted apart gradually, so slowly Ezra had barely noticed. He'd naively thought graduation wouldn't change them. But if things had to change, he'd hoped that he and Candace would drift closer together, not further apart. He'd been wrong.

She hadn't come home for graduation. She'd decided to stay in South America and travel with a guy she'd just met. Three months later, he heard from Miles that she was in Jamaica, and then she popped up in New York before spending six months in Toronto. Ezra had felt as if a small part of his soul died every time he heard that Candace was somewhere new with someone who wasn't him. But he'd also lived for every scrap of information about her; a geographic location, a story about a new under-the-table job. He was hungry for any news about her, even if it hurt. A mangled snippet of a funny story Mei couldn't quite remember in detail while the three of them were waiting for the gates to open before the Oakland A's and San Francisco Giants game; a random anecdote about how she'd changed her hair, but never a picture; a throwaway comment about a new book she was obsessed with and then a discreet interrogation for the title, so he could read it and feel close to her. But never a coherent picture of what her life was like and, crucially, if she missed him.

After a year, he had to accept that the answer to that question was obvious and should have been obvious by her terse email congratulating him for winning the Gilder prize and then radio silence. She didn't miss him. She never had. And he was a fool to have ever hoped she would. It was a lesson he'd had to learn and re-learn more times than he would ever be comfortable admitting. And apparently, he wasn't done learning it just yet.

He watched her officially welcome the passengers to the flight and announce the drinks service, waiting desperately for her to look his way. She didn't. She put her hand on her hip and stared down at her feet as she spoke, never once tripping over the announcement she must have made thousands of times. When she was done, he watched as she knocked on the cockpit door and spoke to one of the pilots briefly. Someone two rows above him and across the aisle pressed the overhead button to call her and Ezra hungrily — pathetically — drank in the curve of her elegant neck as she smoothly pressed the button to turn off the call and leaned over the passenger to ask what they needed. He reveled in the soft whiskey sound of her voice, the tinkle of her laughter and the curve of her hip as she placed her hand there and listened. He even took in the shape of her as she walked toward the front of the plane. But he ducked down in his seat and watched her over the chair in front of him when she returned, so she didn't see him. Not that she looked his way. When she walked past him down the aisle, it was as if he wasn't even there. He pushed himself up in his seat, feeling foolish.

How long was too long to pine after someone who clearly didn't want you? Ezra had been asking himself some version of this question for his entire adult life and in just a few minutes he'd fallen back into that old pattern of wanting Candace in vain. That's when he reminded himself that the entire reason for this trip was to break the bad habit of wanting the only woman he couldn't have. And he reasoned that it was only right that he got to see her one last time before he forced himself to forget about her for good.

"Pssst," the old man across the aisle said.

Ezra turned to him and frowned. "Yes?"

The man held up the latest issue of *Tech Times*. "Is this you?"

Ezra shook his head automatically, even as he stared at his own smiling face on the cover.

"Yes, it is," the man said and turned to the woman sitting next to him.

Ezra didn't need to hear what he was saying to get the gist, especially when the older woman, who was maybe the man's wife, leaned forward to squint at Ezra. Her small eyes darted from his face to the cover. When she reached for the eyeglasses perched on top of her head, Ezra exhaled.

"Okay, you're right. It's me," he leaned forward to whisper across the aisle.

"I knew it," the man said triumphantly, beaming at Ezra. And then he extended the magazine across the aisle face up. "Any chance of an autograph?"

Ezra nodded and reached for the magazine just as Candace pulled back the curtain separating First Class from the main cabin. He looked up at her, the back of his neck getting hot from embarrassment. She was looking down, but not at him — never at him. Her eyes were glued to the magazine.

He'd have thought there would be nothing to see in her gaze, but he was shocked to find that she looked... well actually, Ezra didn't know. There was a time when he'd known all of Candace's facial expressions, cataloguing them like the lovesick fool he was. But this one was new; he'd never seen it before. And that shouldn't have mattered. Not really. But Ezra was pathetic and that unknown facial expression on

Candace's face did matter, because at least it wasn't indifference.

~

"*I* need you to do me a favor," Candace hissed at Jorge in the back galley.

"You sound like Sarah. Are you about to ask me to cover your return because no can do, ma'am? Once we land in Quito, I'm hopping on the bus to the hotel, showering, putting on my shortest shorts and heading out to find me a man to ring in the new year with."

Candace rolled her eyes. "I'm going to ignore you comparing me to Sarah because we're friends and I need your help. Besides, I'm staying in Quito for a few days, so chill. I need you to take over First Class and Business for me."

"Huh?" Jorge frowned.

"I can't get into it, but I need to switch cabins with you. Please."

Jorge's eyes shifted from left to right. "Girl, let me get this straight. You want to take over the packed, plebian ass economy seats even though there is a married couple in row 30, seats A and C who are right now almost certainly hurtling toward divorce even though we're barely at cruising altitude? And in return you want to *give me* a cabin that might have a man rich and almost single enough to be my first mistake of the new year? Am I hearing you correctly?"

Candace put her fist on one hip. "Don't make me

take it back," she said. Jorge didn't need to know that she would absolutely never do that.

He put his hands out toward her and shook his head, "Haha, just kidding. I'll do it."

Candace exhaled. "Thank you. I really appreciate this."

"Um... you're welcome," he said skeptically. He turned back to the cart he was currently filling with refreshments. Technically that was her cart now, but Candace let him finish the task. She *was* giving him First and Business.

"So, 30A and B are breaking up?" she asked, looking down the aisle and trying not to focus on the dark blue curtain cordoning off the main cabin from the premium seats.

"A and C, girl," Jorge corrected.

She turned to him. "What about B? Who's in between them?"

"Some dude. I don't think he's related or even knows them."

"Why not?"

Jorge smiled. "He asked me if I could bring him a bag of popcorn."

They ducked back behind the bathrooms to laugh. When a passenger pushed out of the bathroom — even though the captain had yet to turn off the seatbelt light — she and Jorge tried to rein in their silliness and get back to work.

"Alright, you're good to go," he said.

"Thanks."

He turned and smiled at her. "No, thank you. And if you think I'm not going to make you explain what's going on, you're dead wrong. Be prepared to spill after refuse service, bye." Jorge crossed his feet at the ankles so he could turn slowly and smoothly while he waved with just his fingers.

Candace rolled her eyes again. She normally would never have let him get away with such annoying behavior, but he really was doing her a favor so she couldn't afford to rock the boat. Putting as much distance as the plane allowed between herself and Ezra mattered more than dunking on Jorge.

It was pathetic, but there was something about seeing Ezra on the cover of that issue of *Tech Times* that made her feel so small she could hardly breathe. The conflicting emotions she felt were almost too many to handle. She was so proud of him — she always had been — but that pride was tinged with shame. Ezra was a tech giant on the cover of a magazine, and she was the woman asking him if he wanted nuts or cookies. She didn't think it could get any more embarrassing than that. And she couldn't bear to see pity in his eyes. So she'd run away, and not for the first time.

She took a deep breath, checked over the cart, made sure the aisle was clear and then she backed out into the aisle to start the drinks service.

She tried to keep her mind Ezra-free as she served but handing out drinks would never be more engaging than thinking about Ezra and how soft his beard looked. The repetition of her job was as much a reason to love and hate it. She said the same things — "Would you like something to drink? How about you?" — and the passengers asked the same questions — "Do you have decaf? Coke? Tomato juice?" She hardly had to think at all, which gave her mind ample time to keep wandering back to row five, seat C. The only aisle that stole her attention for a bit was row 30. Jorge was right, seats A and C were absolutely sniping at one another across the lap of a complete stranger who was thoroughly enjoying watching their marriage dissolve up close and personal.

To keep her mind from Ezra, Candace worked overtime to remind herself why she'd said yes to this trip; why she'd let Sarah con her. This trip was supposed to be a new beginning. She wanted to find herself in the exact city where she'd been lost. It was dramatic and maybe wouldn't make sense to anyone else, but it made sense to her and that's all that mattered. As she passed out the last row of drinks and snacks, she decided that it even made a kind of sense that Ezra was on this flight, since she'd lost herself in Ecuador all those years ago partially because of him. It wasn't his fault per se, but she'd never have let Marcel convince her to live like a nomad for a year if she hadn't been trying to drown her sadness in adventure and just okay rebound sex. It wasn't healthy, but Candace decided to hold onto that ancient hurt, hoping that it would help her survive the next ten hours.

She'd just stashed her cart away and turned toward

the aisle when the curtain cordoning off the premium and main cabins fluttered. Candace sucked in a breath as Ezra appeared in the aisle. They locked eyes across nearly the entire length of the plane and Candace felt immediately trapped. She took two steps back as he began walking toward her. But there was nowhere else to go. So she did the only thing she could do; she pulled the door to the nearest bathroom open and jumped inside.

Desperate times and all that.

~

*E*zra should have stayed in his seat. What did it matter that Candace had walked through the curtain to the main cabin and hadn't returned? Why should he care if she stayed on the other side of the plane for the rest of the flight? He was supposed to be getting over her. He wondered all these things as he unbuckled his seatbelt, stood and pulled the curtain back.

He wondered other things when he saw the wide-eyed shock on her face and the way she scurried into the bathroom to hide from him. He wondered why he wasn't turning around. He wondered why she'd always mattered so much to him. Why he never meant nearly as much to her. But most of all he wondered why he couldn't let her go, not even when he was flying across the continent to do just that.

He knocked on the door to the bathroom.

"The other one's open, dude."

Ezra turned to see a tall, bald man looking quizzically at him. He hadn't heard him walking behind him in the aisle; he'd been so focused on Candace. Always so focused on Candace.

"Um," he said, stepping past the bathrooms and out of the man's way, "you can take it. I'll wait for this one."

The man squinted at him, "Why? What's wrong with this one?"

"Nothing's wrong with it, I just need to talk to the person in this one."

The man eyed him for a few seconds and then shrugged. "First 30A, now this," he mumbled. Ezra didn't know what that meant but he was happy when the man opened the bathroom door and disappeared. He took another breath and knocked on the other door again. "Candace," he whispered.

He wasn't sure if he'd meant to whisper her name that way — like a plea — but he'd done it, and he guessed there was no going back now. But she didn't respond.

He knocked again.

"Sir, there's no one in the First Class bathroom," one of the other flight attendants whispered to him, as if he was crazy for walking past the bathrooms behind Business and all the way to the back of the plane like a commoner.

"I don't have to use the bathroom," Ezra said. "I just need to talk to someone in this bathroom for a second."

The flight attendant wrinkled his nose.

Ezra sighed and knocked again. "Candace, I'm not leaving. Just open the door," he said, loud enough that people a few rows ahead turned to see what all the racket was about.

"Sir, I'm going to have to ask you to return to your seat."

"Why?"

"Because it's a federal offense to assault a flight attendant while in the air. Now please return to your seat before I contact the Air Marshall."

"What, I—?"

The bathroom door opened and the men turned to see Candace looking resignedly at them. "Don't do that, Jorge. I know him. He's... Ezra's harmless," she said, still refusing to even look his way.

"Are you sure?" Jorge asked. "Because I'll let the captain know and we can turn this whole damn plane around." He glared at Ezra as he spoke.

"I didn't do anything. I wasn't going to do anything," Ezra said and turned to Candace. "I just wanted to talk."

She wouldn't look at him.

The other bathroom door opened and the other man stared at them for a few seconds before he turned to Jorge. "So about that popcorn?"

Ezra squinted at them both, but Candace took charge, just like she used to in college when they were running late for one of the dances in the student union, which only got packed and sweatier the longer they went on. She stepped out of the bathroom and pushed past Ezra. She pulled open one of the metal drawers lining the back of the plane and snatched a small bag of chips from the compartment.

"This is the best we can do," she said as she handed the bag to the other passenger. "Now please, I'm going to have to ask you to return to your seat."

"Why does he get to stay back here?"

Candace was always the levelheaded one in the friend group. Mei was always much more likely to start a ruckus and Miles was a wild card — just as likely to stoke Mei's flame as talk her down — while Ezra was full of silent, anxious happiness just to be involved. That usually left it to Candace to keep them all in check; until she couldn't. Everyone had a limit and Ezra watched as Candace neared hers. Her mouth flattened in a line, and she squinted her eyes. He stepped back out of the line of fire on instinct.

But apparently Jorge knew what that look meant because he stepped in between them, his back to Candace, and smiled at the passenger. "Hey, I heard 30C say something about a prenup."

The man's eyes widened. "Oh shit, I knew it!"

Ezra's eyes squinted as he watched the man scurry up the aisle. "What just happened?"

"Apparently the couple in row 30 decided to get a divorce just after takeoff. That guy is sitting in between them and he's loving the drama," Candace said.

Ezra turned to her, a confused smile on his face. "How? I would have asked to move seats or crawled under the seat in front of me. That sounds hella awkward."

Candace opened her mouth as if to speak, but then she clamped her lips shut and looked away. A pit formed in Ezra's stomach at the movement. It was a reminder that he'd lost so much with Candace, not just the sex or the object of his infatuation, but his friend. He knew that whatever she'd been about to say would have been great, probably funny, maybe scathing; definitely something worth remembering. And instead of telling him, she'd bitten her tongue.

He couldn't for the life of him understand how they'd fallen so far.

"Candace," he said.

She shook her head and then the plane lurched just as the seatbelt sign illuminated. He watched as she exhaled in relief and then lifted her eyes to his. "Please return to your seat," she said to him, as if he was just some other passenger and not her best friend or the man who had rung in the new year with his face between her legs more than once.

She spoke as if he'd never meant anything to her at all. And as he walked back to his seat, he guessed that was because he hadn't. Ezra was surprised he still had pieces of his heart large enough to break, but he did. What a terrible realization to have at 30,000 feet in the air.

# CHAPTER 3

"Okay girl, spill," Jorge whispered as he rushed to the back of the plane.

"Shhh, we need to get ready for the dinner service." Candace hoped the gravity of the task would distract Jorge from gossiping, but she was grasping at straws and she knew it. Jorge had a nose and encyclopedic memory for messy in-flight dynamics. He lived for it and rated each flight by how entertaining he found the passenger drama. Candace usually didn't mind trading stories — being a flight attendant was more boring than people imagined — but it was decidedly less fun to be the object of his interest.

"No one's listening," he whispered, and then turned to preparing trays for the service carts. "Besides, we can multi-task."

"Mark hates gossiping," she said.

"I put Mark on the meals for the premium passengers. You know how he gets about that," Jorge said with a roll of his eyes. "And Mark hates spicy foods and fun, who cares what he thinks? Gimme the tea, girl."

Candace focused on moving the frozen meals in and out of the oven in a timely and safe manner, but much like the drinks service, the movements were programmed into her muscle memory and didn't require the kind of attention she needed to tune Jorge out. She turned to him and glared. "Don't pull a Sarah," she said, annoyed.

His face fell. "Ouch." He clutched his chest and took half a step back. He might have been hurt but Candace got her wish. He turned to the trays and gave his full attention to stocking her carts. Candace turned back to the oven and sighed in relief. She knew the reprieve couldn't last long but she would happily and enthusiastically take every second of it as she prayed for this flight to literally fly by. She needed to get off this plane.

She and Jorge worked in efficient silence for a blessed fifteen minutes.

"How are we doing back here?" Mark asked as he walked into the rear service area.

"Great. Almost done," Candace replied quickly. Her voice sounded strained, uncomfortably high-pitched.

"Perfect. I really appreciate how well you two work together."

"Yep," Jorge said, turning to her, "it helps when you're *friends*."

Candace slid another tray of cold vegetarian meals

into the oven and ignored the stress he put on that last word. "Do you need anything, Mark?" she asked instead.

"Oh no, I was just checking up on you two." There was a moment of silence and then she and Jorge turned to him for the first time. Candace noticed that his face was flushed. She'd never seen him look quite like this before so she couldn't be sure, but he looked excited. It was actually kind of unnerving.

"Is there something you want to tell us?" Jorge asked carefully.

"Did something...happen?" Candace added, thinking of the couple breaking up.

She only noticed that his hands were behind his back when he brought them forward and held out the issue of *Tech Times*. "Ezra Posner is in First Class. I'm freaking out," Mark whispered. "I'm a huge fan."

"Who?" Jorge asked, but then he gasped and snatched the magazine from Mark's hands.

"Hey—"

"Oh my god," Jorge said, his eyes darting from the magazine to Candace's face and then back again.

"I know," Mark said. "He's like a billionaire genius with a heart of gold."

"A what?" Jorge yelled, turning to her.

"Shhh," Mark and Candace said at the same time.

"A billionaire?" Jorge hissed at her.

The combination of Jorge's excited eyes and Ezra's smiling face on the cover was too much for Candace to handle. She turned away and began double-checking the carts in front of her even though she knew they were packed perfectly; she and Jorge really did work well together.

"I can't believe he's flying commercial," Mark said.

"Yeah, that's strange. Don't you think that's strange, Candace?"

"I wouldn't know. Let's announce the dinner service, guys." She straightened and smiled at Mark. "You don't want to get behind schedule, do you?"

Mark's back straightened predictably. "Yes, yes, let's get started," he said, but then his posture relaxed and he cringed. "I can't do it."

"Can't do what? Make the announcement? I'll do it," she said in a relaxed voice, even though she felt wound tight. She just wanted to get the rest of the crew on track. She needed to do her job and lose herself in it so she could forget about Ezra, even if only for a few minutes.

Mark shook his head and his eyes widened in fear. "No, I can't cover First and Business. My hands are shaking now," he said, "I'll probably drop his food in his lap."

"You can't be serious right now. He's just some tech guy," she started.

"Just some tech guy?" Mark exclaimed. "He's literally going to revolutionize the way Americans travel long and short distances around the country. His high-speed trains run on renewable fuel and have you seen his infrastructure plans?"

As it happened, Candace had. She'd seen almost

every early version of Ezra's plans to revitalize public transportation locally and nationally. He'd given her the first draft of his project proposal at the end of their freshman year of college and she'd taken it home with her. She hadn't understood one word of it, so she'd read it over and over again until she did. And when they met up a week before classes started sophomore year, she'd given him a response essay — mostly questions — of things he needed to clarify and expand upon and define that was nearly as long as his draft. She wasn't certain how Ezra would take critical feedback — especially not from her — but they'd had maybe the longest conversation of their entire relationship up to that moment and gone through each of her queries point-by-point. Candace had felt a kind of exhilaration at having the smartest person she'd ever met take her seriously and listen so intently to her suggestions. When he'd given her the next version of his report, she could hardly contain her glee when she'd seen how many of her suggestions he'd incorporated into his revisions. And her heart had practically burst at all the footnotes he'd added with questions for her.

Even after college, she'd read every article about him from interviews to fluffy PR pieces, as if keeping up with Ezra were her job. Over the years, she'd watched that germ of an idea grow and change in ways she couldn't have imagined, just as she'd watched Ezra become the kind of man she always knew he would. It was bittersweet. In college, she'd naively entertained the hope that she'd be right there by Ezra's side when he won the Gilder prize and began to build his company, because she believed in him and his work. So watching it all happen from the outside felt like a knife in the heart, even as her entire body was suffused with pride.

She took a deep breath and let it out shakily, fisting her hands behind her back. "If you love his ideas so much then go serve him his pasta with meat sauce and ask for his autograph," Candace said. "Talk to him about the company." Her face was hot, her head was starting to ache and all she wanted to do was hide in one of the bathrooms and cry.

"Do you think he'd...?" Mark started and then shook his head. "No, I can't. Oh my god, I couldn't. Sorry, can't do it."

Candace gave Mark a tight smile. "Fine, Jorge, can you—"

"Nope," he said way too fast, "I need to check back into the divorce court drama in the main cabin. Besides, First and Business are your territories."

"What is wrong with you two?" she screeched. She had to close her eyes, hold her face in her hands and take a few deep breaths to get herself together. She couldn't believe that she'd just yelled while on the job; a violation of the AeroPlan flight attendant code of conduct.

"Better question," Jorge said, "is what's wrong with you?"

"Yeah," Mark said, and Candace's eyes opened

quickly. "Normally you love First Class. Am I missing something?"

Maybe if Mark's hands had still been shaking or if his concerned eyes hadn't been darting between her face and Jorge's, Candace might have told him some version of the truth, especially if it would have gotten her out of switching back to the premium cabins. But she couldn't. She wasn't certain it was fear of being written up or pure cowardice, but she took a deep breath in through her nose, smiled and shook her head as she released it. "No, sorry. I just have a headache and I'm waiting for my medicine to kick in." She sounded much calmer than she had before.

Jorge sucked his teeth and probably rolled his eyes, but Candace ignored him. She focused on Mark and waited.

After a few seconds that felt like an hour, Mark visibly relaxed and smiled. "Sorry to hear that. But that's even more reason you should cover the premium seats. Fewer people and no crying babies," he said. And as if the universe was conspiring against her, the sound of a baby crying rent the air and Jorge and Mark both nodded at her as if to say, "See. Told ya so."

Candace exhaled loudly.

"Have fun," Jorge said.

She turned to him and glared.

He smirked at her as if to say that's what she got for not telling him about Ezra. And maybe he was right, she thought, as she turned to walk up the aisle. She wanted to curl up in the empty seat in 42E and cry.

She might have even considered parachuting from the plane. She felt completely wrung out and they were barely two hours into the flight. The only reason she was still upright was inertia.

And a pathetic desire to see Ezra smile wide enough to show that wonky tooth she'd always loved.

~

*E*zra had never directly admitted his feelings for Candace to anyone. Not his parents or Miles — even though he felt certain they knew — and definitely not Mei or his work friends. He'd always been too afraid that confirmation of his crush would get back to her and she'd push him away. Ezra had always known that Candace didn't love him the way he loved her. But they were friends. She was kind to him, she made him laugh, he'd never met anyone smarter, they had amazing sex, and sometimes when she moaned his name during her climax her voice sounded full of love. That was more than enough for him.

For years, all he could think about was everything he'd lose if she knew for sure that he wanted more than their casual hookups. He'd never imagined that not admitting how he felt would ultimately cost him everything anyway.

"Pssst," the old man across the aisle whispered. "Ezra. Can I call you Ezra?"

Ezra smiled wearily as he turned his head. "Sure. What should I call you?"

"My name's Martin, but everybody calls me Marty. And this is my wife, Alejandra," he said, motioning to the sleeping woman next to him.

"Nice to meet you, Marty."

"Nice to meet you too. I've never met a billionaire before."

Ezra's stomach lurched and he shook his head. "The company's worth a lot of money, not me. I'm comfortable, but not filthy rich," he said, in what had become a practiced response in the past few years as his company had gained a higher profile.

He'd been fully unprepared for all the strangers who read a profile of him in some newspaper and felt compelled to approach him on the train or at the grocery store to ask if he was actually a billionaire and then, why he was riding public transportation and picking his own tomatoes. He'd honed his response to two simple sentences that made him feel less exposed, something he'd always hated.

"Sure, sure," Marty said with a wink. "So, are you single?"

Ezra sighed. That was usually the third thing people asked after surreptitiously checking his left hand to confirm the absence of a ring there. Ezra hated lying. Lies took too much energy. But he could tell by Marty's forwardness that he wouldn't let him breathe if he was honest. They were barely two hours into a ten-hour flight and he couldn't bear to have this man shoving pictures of every ostensibly unattached woman he knew in his face, trying to force a promise of a date when he was back in town. As far as Ezra could tell, there was only one thing to do.

"I'm engaged, actually," he said, just as Candace pulled the curtain aside.

His face flushed when he looked up at her. He saw the pain flit across her eyes, even if he didn't understand it. And then he saw her entire face close to him.

"Candace," he said, just as the seatbelt sign illuminated.

She moved forward as if he hadn't spoken. Watching her walk away would never not break his heart, but this time there was something else mingling with that pain. It was fragile and probably completely ill-advised, and yet the pathetic hope that sprang up in his breast was an honest to God breath of fresh air.

He watched her walk away and then disappear into the small alcove across from the forward door. Marty was still trying to talk to him, but Ezra couldn't hear anything besides his beating heart. He unlocked his phone and opened his text messages. He began typing his message to Mei, finally ready to ask the thing he should have asked her the day after Candace kissed him freshman year.

Do you think I have a chance with Candace?

*H*e typed the message quickly and pressed send before he could second-guess himself. Because after eighteen years, it wouldn't be a second guess. He was probably on his millionth moment of hesitation. But he could feel time running out. Whatever was between him and Candace, he had to get it right now or never.

# CHAPTER 4

*A*ll flight attendants cry during a flight at least once. Definitely more than once. It was a hazard of the job. Being stuck in a metal cylinder with hundreds of cranky people crammed together and confined to their seats for hours at a time bred the worst kind of human behavior. But Candace had always found the most frustrating part, and the reason she usually broke down in tears, was pent-up anger. When passengers were at their worst, flight attendants had to be at their best; that was the AeroPlan party line. She always imagined that the responsibility and frustration of a regular flight — or many flights — built up in flight attendants' systems and had to be released one way or another. Sometimes, flight attendants lost their cool — and usually their jobs — by being... not at their best. Other people managed to work through the angst by having lots of casual sex with each other, passengers, whoever; stress relief was stress relief.

Some people walked right off the plane to the airport bar. But they all cried at some point.

Candace wouldn't have considered herself a crier before she got the job at AeroPlan, but she'd cried more non-Ezra related tears in her first year than ever before. The point was that crying was a hazard of her job. But this cry was the worst. She'd squeezed herself into the forward galley tears leaking down her face, swallowing years of frustrated sobs, but not because a passenger had been shitty to her or because the plane had been buffeted in the air in the middle of a storm and everyone had been strapped down for hours snapping at each other and afraid for their lives. She was desperately trying to staunch the flow of tears falling from her eyes because Ezra was engaged to someone who wasn't her. She pressed her body as close to the wall as she could get to make sure none of the First Class passengers saw her, and she cried as silently as she could, feeling shattered. This moment felt like rock bottom. It had to be. What could be worse than the fact that she'd been crying about Ezra Posner for almost two decades and he'd found someone else?

The sound of Mark's voice made her jump.

"Good evening, everyone. We'll be starting the dinner service soon. We have a selection of meal options..."

Candace couldn't add getting written up to this flight; she wouldn't be able to bear that, so she wiped her tears away and took a series of deep breaths, collecting herself as Mark ran through the announcement. She checked her supplies and tried to ground herself in the job. The familiar movements weren't as comforting as she'd hoped, but she eventually got herself together enough to dart into the bathroom, wipe her face with some water and put some eye drops in her eyes. She felt almost back to normal as she went to the first row and began the dinner service.

She could feel Ezra's eyes on her as she moved from each aisle to the front galley and back and she felt uncomfortable that even after four years and finding out that he was with someone else, his gaze still felt like electricity on her skin.

When they were younger, she liked to imagine that he'd never tire of staring at her. She used to fantasize that he was storing up every glimpse of her to tide him over while they were apart. She used to love flitting around Miles and Mei's New Year's parties, knowing that he was watching her, waiting for her, waiting for the party to reach full swing. Waiting for her to turn to him, pin him with a look and then disappear upstairs where he would slowly and surely strip her naked. He still stared then, but his gaze was followed by his touch, his tongue, his entire body. She'd always wanted more from those nights; declarations of love, a stammered invitation to dinner and a movie, some sign that this wasn't just sex. She never got it, but for years she convinced herself that he just wasn't ready; maybe next year. But the familiarity of his gaze now was the final clue she needed that she'd always been wrong about what his attention meant.

*"I'm engaged, actually."*

Ezra's eyes on her hadn't been the early seeds of love; it was just lust. She knew what he felt like inside her; how gravelly his voice sounded first thing in the morning. She knew what it felt like to let herself dream of a future with him in the hours between three and dawn wrapped in his arms, her fingers playing in the hair on his chest; decades of the two of them together just like that. But she didn't know what it felt like for Ezra to pick her up and take her to a fancy dinner, for them to hang out in her kitchen and cook dinner or fall asleep on his couch watching a movie.

It was one thing to feel eighteen or twenty or twenty-five again; pathetically in love with Ezra and afraid he couldn't love her back. But knowing that he'd only ever thought she was good enough to fuck ripped her to shreds. She had only ever been a fantasy to him. Not good enough to marry.

Candace had never felt so small.

She had to walk and stoop and serve while he watched her, her only place of respite the small galley that just barely hid her from view. Over and over again, closer to his seat each time. And then she was at his row. His gaze felt heavier here, her backside to him, as she asked the older couple what they wanted for dinner. She avoided looking his way as she walked back with the couple's meals, but then she couldn't.

Her training was clear; she had to look every passenger in the eye with a friendly smile when she served them. After she made sure the couple didn't want or need anything else, she took a deep breath and turned to Ezra, putting on her best work smile. He looked shocked, as if he hadn't been watching her. And then she second-guessed herself. Maybe he hadn't. Maybe she'd made up his attention today and their entire relationship. He smiled up at her, that grimace thing he used to do that was so accidentally charming and devastating all at once. It felt like a knife in the back.

"What would you like? Chicken or pasta?" she asked. She was on autopilot and her voice was flat, but at least it didn't break. At least she didn't cry in front of him. But then she frowned, her face warming with shame. "Sorry, kosher. There's a kosher meal for you. I'm sorry," she said, turning quickly away.

"Candace," he called after her, and her steps faltered the tiniest bit, but she didn't turn back.

*Fuckfuckfuckfuck,* she thought to herself as she pulled the kosher meal onto a tray with his salad, roll and dessert. *Shitshitshitshit,* she thought as she walked back down the aisle. She slid his food onto the tray in front of him. "What would you like to drink?"

"I— Water. Please."

She nodded and cursed herself in her head back and forth again. "Enjoy," she said and turned away.

He grabbed her arm, somehow gently circling her wrist and caressing her pulse all in a fraction of a second. "Candace," he whispered up to her.

It was wrong — terrible actually — what his touch and his voice could do to her sex. She was soft and wet in no time. Her mouth fell open, but a garbled sound was all that escaped. She should have pulled away and reminded him that assaulting a flight attendant was a federal offense or suggested that his *fiancée* probably wouldn't appreciate him touching another woman this way. But she didn't do that, because the part of her brain that didn't grind to a halt was currently remembering every time he'd ever touched her. That first New Year's Eve and every one after; that time they'd all gone to see a terrible vampire movie and she'd forgotten her coat so he'd draped his over her shoulders; or that last time they'd seen each other when he'd fallen asleep with his arms around her, his face buried in the crease of her neck. And by the heated look in his eyes, she guessed that his brain had taken a similar journey. It was terrible, and yet she couldn't look away.

"Well, well, well," Jorge said.

Candace pulled her arm from Ezra's grasp a little too hard and slammed her elbow into the headrest of the seat in front of the old man.

"Ow, shit," she said. "I mean shoot. I'm sorry, sir," she said to the man whose dinner she'd interrupted. "Can I get you another glass of wine?" It was what she always said when she made a mistake and thankfully, it worked.

Without turning back to Jorge or Ezra, she shot up the aisle to the galley. She heard Jorge's steps behind her. Her hands shook as she pulled the drinks tray from the shelves.

"Now you've gotta spill," Jorge said. "What's going

on with you and the billionaire?" he whispered. "Do you have a sugar daddy?"

"No," Candace said forcefully. "It's not like that at all."

"Well girl, what is it like? And when is it gonna get like that, 'cause that man is loaded. Don't deny it, Mark already told me."

Candace shook her head and circled her wrist, rubbing the skin Ezra had touched. Caressed. "He... Ezra and I were friends. We used to be friends."

Jorge shook his head and then motioned between them with two fingers. "You and I are friends. I have lots of friends that I've never looked at like that and that don't have more money than a small Midwestern state's fiscal budget."

Candace swallowed. "We *were* friends. And then we were s-something else. And now we're nothing," she said, even though it broke her heart to admit it. "I'm not anything to him anymore. I'm not even sure I ever was." She couldn't start sobbing. She wouldn't. But she also couldn't stop the tears from spilling from her eyes. "Are you happy now? Take this to 4B," she hissed and then pushed past Jorge to the toilet.

Once she'd locked the door behind her, she sat on the closed seat and cried as quietly as she could. Again. This would surely go down as the worst flight of her career. Hands down. And it wasn't even half over.

# CHAPTER 5

*E*zra ate his food but he didn't taste it. His entire body — every cell, every atom — was focused on Candace. He'd wanted to run after her when she pulled from his grasp and ask her if what he thought he'd seen in her eyes was real. He wanted to know what she'd been thinking during those few seconds. Was it the way he used to love kissing behind her knees just so she'd giggle, or all the times he'd coaxed her onto his face so he could watch her come on his tongue? Did she remember how much he used to love holding her as they fell asleep? Did she know that he dreamed about holding her like that every other day of the year? And those were just the first questions that came to mind. He had so many more; eighteen years' worth of questions he'd been swallowing, too unsure of the answer to muster the nerve to utter them.

But someone doesn't become a new person overnight or in the first few hours of a long-haul flight.

If that were possible, Ezra would have been out of his seat and down the aisle after her before she'd gotten more than a few rows away. He'd tell her how much he regretted all the times he hadn't chased after her or bit his tongue instead of telling her how much he loved her. But the other flight attendant had glared at Ezra before following after her, the seatbelt sign was illuminated, and Marty was still trying to figure out what was going on.

But the thing that really kept Ezra in his seat was that voice in his head that reminded him how pathetic he was to still be hoping he saw something in her eyes that looked like love; something that mirrored his own lovesick adoration.

Still, Ezra kept his eyes on the front of the plane, waiting for Candace to reappear. When she did, her face was a mask as she rushed down the aisle toward the main cabin. She didn't even look his way. He tried to catch the eye of the other flight attendant when he came to collect their trays, but he avoided Ezra's gaze as well. He didn't know what else to do with himself, so he sat and stared at the seatbelt sign, waiting for it to turn off or for Candace to come back.

Time passed slowly. His leg started bouncing again. He checked his messages. A few emails from his team in Quito. Nothing from Mei. The overhead lights dimmed and then finally the seatbelt sign turned off. Ezra was unbuckled and out of his seat in a heartbeat.

"Where ya going?" Marty asked.

Ezra didn't answer. He pulled the curtain open

and sped through Business Class into Economy. The aisle was almost entirely clear, and he saw her, in the back galley, talking to one of the other flight attendants. He stalked toward her determined to... do something. As he walked, other passengers jumped up from their seats and began to walk in front of him toward the rear bathrooms, blocking his view of her. Eventually, he found himself in a line for the toilets, four other people standing in between him and Candace.

He tapped the shoulder of the woman in front of him. "Excuse me, can I—?"

"No, wait in line," she said quickly.

"No, sorry, you don't understand," Ezra said.

She rolled her eyes over her shoulder, "That's what they all say."

He frowned and squinted at her in confusion. "Um, I'm not really sure what that means, but I don't need to go to the bathroom. I just need to get past you."

"Sure, buddy," she said, but didn't move.

Ezra sighed and resigned himself to waiting in line, shuffling forward slowly. He leaned around the woman in front of him every now and then to make sure Candace was still there, even though she'd have had to pass him to go anywhere else. Finally, the woman in front of him was at the head of the line and a toilet door opened. They all stepped aside for an older woman to pass and as soon as the toilet door closed, Ezra moved quickly into the back galley. His throat felt dry when he swallowed and his stomach was in painful knots.

"Candace, we need to talk," Ezra said in a soft voice.

She froze, but didn't turn to him.

The other flight attendant gasped. Ezra turned to him and smiled. "Sorry, I—"

"Oh my god, I'm a huge fan," he said.

Ezra could feel his cheeks warming. "Um, thanks. I really appreciate it." And he did, even if he didn't understand it. "I just need to talk to Candace."

"Is there something wrong? Do you need me to get you anything? A glass of wine? An extra dessert?"

"Um, no. Everything's fine," he said, his eyes darting to her back. "I just... Would you mind if I... I mean if we...?"

"I don't know..." he said, his eyebrows bunched in confusion.

"It's okay, Mark," Candace said. She finally turned around, but she didn't look at Ezra. "Can you take over the evening drink service in the main cabin? Tell Jorge to help you when he's finished in First."

Mark nodded. "If you're sure," he said, his eyes darting between them. "Oh my god," he whispered as he walked away.

Ezra shuffled out of Mark's way in the tight space. He turned to watch him go. The line to the bathroom was just a couple of people now. Ezra guessed this would be the most privacy they could hope for under the circumstances.

When he turned back to Candace, she was looking

at him, but she averted her eyes rather than make eye contact and it broke his heart.

"You shouldn't be back here, Ezra." She sounded sad and Ezra had never been able to handle when anything dimmed Candace's shine.

"Candace, I'm not engaged," he whispered, taking a couple of steps toward her. Not enough to crowd her, but closer, nonetheless.

She finally lifted her eyes to meet his and he felt the way he'd felt that first New Year's Eve when she'd leaned toward him: like the sun was shining down on him because Candace Garret knew his name. Candace Garret was looking at him. Candace Garret cared that he was single.

"You said—?"

"That old guy was about to tell me about his very single daughter or granddaughter or next-door neighbor. Everyone I've met in the past few years has tried to become my own personal matchmaker. I was just trying to head him off."

She squinted at him. "You hate lying."

He shrugged. "I do, but sometimes I have to."

She sucked her bottom lip into her mouth and shifted her eyes away.

"But not to you," he added. "I've *never* lied to you."

She looked at him skeptically, which hurt.

"So you're not engaged," she said, sounding just as unsure as she looked.

"I'm not seeing anyone either," he said. He had been. Over the years, there'd been a series of models he'd met at those strange fundraisers he went to but hated, and then a hasty three-month fling during the summer with an astrophysicist he'd met at a political event. But old habits die hard, and he'd broken up with her in the fall, unconsciously giving himself time to get over a woman who was just a placeholder for Candace. His entire life had been one long holding pattern as he waited for a future with Candace he'd been sure until recently would come. Even in the past year when he'd committed himself to getting over her, a part of him had still been waiting for her. Loving Candace came as naturally to Ezra as breathing, pathetic as it was.

"But you were... We're both..." she started but didn't finish.

He stepped forward again. Vaguely he heard the toilet doors open and close but none of it mattered. He was close enough now to touch her. He lifted his hand to her arm and stroked his thumb up to her elbow and back down to her wrist. The touch was fairy light. Her head lifted and their eyes met.

"I didn't show up last year," she said, even though he knew that.

"I did," he said, just in case she didn't. And by the way she worried her bottom lip between her teeth, he guessed that maybe she hadn't. "Why didn't you?"

She shook her head. "Mei needed me. We went to the City to go dancing." Her smile changed from wistful to pained. "We rang in the new year in the bathroom of some dance club. Mei was crying on my shoulder."

Ezra had a flash of a memory; Miles at midnight, a probably warm bottle of beer in his hand, his gaze blank as he stared at a painting on the wall. Mei had bought it to decorate their first apartment together after college. "I'm sorry," he whispered.

"So am I," she said. "You weren't going to go this year?"

He smoothed circles around her wrist. "I couldn't bear to show up at Miles's house and watch him pretend he didn't miss Mei, waiting for you not to show up again," he admitted. It felt like a two-ton weight had been lifted from his shoulders.

"You could have called me," she said.

He could have laughed and cried at the same time. "Could I? How would your boyfriend have felt about that?" His voice was harsh, full of all the bitterness he'd suppressed while watching that relationship play out over social media. She winced. He hated himself.

"Why did you do it?" he asked. He didn't elaborate. He wasn't even certain if he could have. There were so many things she'd done, so many times she'd turned away from him right when he thought they were on the precipice of something great. He'd always thought he knew Candace better than anyone, but he could never understand why she kept running from him, no matter how hard he tried.

"Why did I get a boyfriend?" she asked.

He nodded. This was one of the questions, so he went with it. He didn't expect the bitter laugh or the single tear that fell down her right cheek. He had to force himself not to move his free hand to cup her face and brush it away.

She tilted her head to look at him. "What was the name of the last model you dated, Ezra?"

He froze.

"How long did that last? What about the one before her? And before her? Did you take them out on dates? Buy them flowers for Valentine's Day? Did you go on vacations together?"

Candace's eyes were glassy with unshed tears and Ezra could feel the pressure of his own tears as his face warmed with the accusation in her words, even if he didn't understand it. And when she brought it all together, he wished he could have stayed ignorant.

"You took them out though, right?" Candace continued. "You went out in public with them. You took them to your business events. You didn't practically ignore them all year just to hook up with them in secret." Candace pulled her arm from his grasp and swiped at her teary eyes. She stepped back, putting more distance between them. When she looked at him again, her eyes weren't sad or angry. There was a depth of pain he'd never seen there before and it broke him anew to realize that she could ever feel that way about him.

"Don't ask me why I dated someone who had the nerve to tell me how he felt faster than twenty years too late," she ground out. "Besides, you're a billionaire now."

"Candace, I'm—"

"I'm sure you can find someone to hook up with you on all the major holidays. It just won't be me. Not anymore."

Ezra shook his head and reached for her again, a tear slipping from his eyes. "Is this a joke?" he said, which was the wrong thing to say.

Candace's laugh was so hurt and angry and bitter.

"That's not what I meant, Candace and you know it."

"Do I?"

"Why would you think I wouldn't want to date you? Why would you ever think I only wanted to be with you on New Year's Eve?"

She laughed again and he wanted to scream. Not at her, but at the universe. This wasn't at all the way he'd expected this conversation to go. Never, in all the years he'd been waiting for them to be honest with one another, could he have imagined this.

"Because you told me so," she said, swiping at her face again.

"When?" he practically screamed.

"The last night we were together. Just before you fell asleep. And you just told me that you'd never lie to me, right, Ezra? Never?"

"Candace—"

"What's going on back here?"

Ezra turned to see Jorge looking at them with wide eyes.

"I—" he started, but Candace cut him off.

"Nothing," she said in a flat tone. "5C is going back

to his seat now." She turned to him and her beautiful brown eyes were dead. "We're done here."

"Candace," he said, still shaking his head.

But Jorge once again stepped protectively in front of her. "Let me escort you back to your seat, sir," he said with the thinnest veneer of professionalism.

Ezra normally would have loved that, would have found a kinship with anyone who wanted to protect Candace. But the realization that *he* was the thing she needed to be protected from was too much for him to handle.

He let the man lead him away but he turned back to Candace just before he left the galley. She stared blankly at the wall with haunted eyes. Ezra felt numb and broken as he walked up the length of the plane back to his seat, completely and utterly alone for the first time in a long time.

*C*andace had had a shit year. She'd been passed up for a promotion she wasn't sure she wanted but damn sure knew she deserved; her landlord had raised the rent on an apartment she could just barely afford — with two roommates — and rarely saw because she was always in the air. Her mom had also had a scare with her diabetes that had been traumatic. Candace couldn't remember having done anything in the spring and summer besides fly, ferry her mom to doctor's appointments to give her dad a break, and hope his hypertension didn't also become an issue.

For months, the only thing keeping her going was knowing she'd see Ezra tonight. She'd been stalking Miles's Facebook for days, waiting for the obligatory "My boy's back in town" post. When the picture finally popped up on her feed, she'd gasped at finally seeing his grimacing face after so long. In the picture, Miles had thrown his arm around Ezra's shoulders and they were smiling and squinting into the camera. Ezra had grown out his facial hair a bit, the five o'clock shadow almost giving his angular face a menacing glare. Almost. He seemed bulkier, like he was weightlifting again. She'd lost herself staring at it for far too long, a year of delayed excitement flooding her veins.

She'd spent the past few days winding herself up into a ball of anxiety, but now that the day had finally arrived, she felt weightless with anticipation. It was a feeling she'd come to associate with Ezra because she only ever felt so free once a year. And this year, she needed the release of sinking into his touch more than ever. Candace had spent the entire day soaking and scrubbing and moisturizing her body, daydreaming about what his hands on her smooth skin would feel like after so long, wondering the entire time about what Ezra's blush would look like when he saw her.

She slipped on the pair of nude dark brown lacey underwear that she'd ordered months ago, specifically for tonight. She sat at the vanity in her bedroom, poured a small bit of coconut oil into her palm and then carefully undid her twists and arranged the crown of her curls in a way she loved. A way she knew Ezra loved.

She shimmied into the gold sequined dress she'd bought on deep discount in a sale the day after her mother told her that her new medication was working. The dress was more than she'd normally spend on a single item of clothing, but she'd considered the expense worth it, because it was Ezra. She sprayed herself with her favorite perfume — the same perfume she'd been wearing since senior year of college — and then looked at herself in the mirror. The rich gold of the dress accentuated the depth of her dark skin, the fabric flowed over her body, dipping deep into the cleft of her breasts, hugging her hips and flaring at the knee, highlighting the beauty of her curves. The curves she loved. The curves Ezra worshipped once a year.

She wished it was more.

The dress made her feel beautiful, but she hadn't bought it for that alone. Pathetically, she'd also bought it hoping it would make Ezra want more than this one night. Sometimes she fantasized about having the guts to broach the topic herself, but she was terrified of being rejected by someone she loved so much. Too much.

She ran her hands over her rounded stomach and hips and imagined Ezra doing the same. And then she swallowed all her fear and insecurities so she could focus on enjoying tonight. After the year she'd had, it was the least she deserved.

Decided, she stepped into her four-inch heels, grabbed her purse and headed out to have the best night of the worst year.

"*E*zra, can you help Miles move the couches out of the way before he hurts his back?" Mei yelled from the kitchen.

"I'm not an old man," Miles yelled over his shoulder as he walked into the living room where Ezra was trying not to watch the clock, waiting for Candace. "But actually, my back has been acting up," Miles whispered to him.

"What's that you said, old man?" Ezra yelled. "Arthritis?"

Mei's loud cackle floated in from the kitchen.

"I hate you," Miles said. "Help me with this damn *settee*," he ground out.

Ezra laughed and moved to help him.

For a few minutes, Ezra didn't think about Candace. He and Miles rearranged the living room furniture to make more room for people to gather. By the time they were done, both men were feeling old, huffing and puffing, faces flushed. Of course that was when Candace arrived.

"I'm here," she called from the foyer.

Ezra stood up too fast and his lower back tweaked. He groaned.

"Who's the old man now?" Miles mumbled just as Mei ran into the living room.

She breezed past them toward the front door. They both cringed as the sound of Candace and Mei's squeals filled the room.

Ezra snatched up his beer bottle and went to take a

sip. It was empty. Miles laughed and snatched the bottle from Ezra's hand, shaking his head as he headed toward the kitchen. Ezra glared at his back and fidgeted — smoothing his shirt down his torso, running his hands over his hair — his stomach fluttering and his neck warming. When Candace finally walked into the living room, Ezra's mouth went dry.

She was wearing gold, his favorite color on her, even though every color looked beautiful against her skin. Her hair was a soft, curly crown around her head. She was like one of his wet dreams come to life; as if she'd put herself together specifically to tempt and torture him. He wondered if that was a possibility, but immediately dismissed the thought.

"Hey, Ezra," Candace said, in the deep whiskey voice he missed 364 days of every year.

Ezra tried to smile. He wasn't sure if he succeeded. "Hi, Candace."

She smiled at him and he was certain his heart stopped.

"We're all together again. Finally," Mei said.

"Yes, we are," Miles said. "Let's toast to that."

He handed each of the women a glass of wine and passed Ezra another bottle of beer. Ezra took a quick sip before the toast; his mouth was so dry.

"To friendship," Mei said, lifting her glass.

"To family," Miles added.

"To something less corny and sentimental," Candace said.

Ezra spluttered a laugh. "To next year," he said.

"She said, '*less* corny,'" Miles muttered.

They made deliberate eye contact with one another as they clinked glasses. Candace and Ezra held each other's gazes as they sipped their drinks. Ezra thought he would fall apart at the intensity in her eyes and the way her soft lips rested on the edge of her glass.

"You know what we should be toasting?" Miles said. Ezra tore his eyes away from Candace reluctantly. "These drinks are better than that first New Year's Eve."

They all groaned.

"We didn't all drink that swill. Some of us," Candace said, gesturing to herself and Ezra, "had discernment, even then."

"We were nervous," Mei said, coming to Miles's defense as she walked to him.

Ezra watched as they molded themselves to one another and smiled at each other. There was something comforting about seeing them so close, even after all this time. And as Ezra took another sip of his beer, he snuck a quick glance at Candace and wondered if they would ever have that with one another.

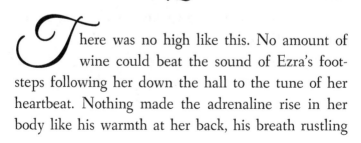

here was no high like this. No amount of wine could beat the sound of Ezra's footsteps following her down the hall to the tune of her heartbeat. Nothing made the adrenaline rise in her body like his warmth at her back, his breath rustling her hair, and the brush of his skin as he reached around her to open the door to Miles and Mei's spare bedroom.

The sounds of the party didn't travel all the way up here when the door was closed. She heard him gulp in the dark silence and smiled to herself at the familiarity of that nervous reaction. She turned around and found him staring at her.

Her nipples hardened. She loved when he looked at her this way. As if he couldn't wait to taste her. As if she was the most beautiful woman in the world.

"Did you miss me?" she found the courage to ask.

He laughed, just a huff of air, and she wanted to crawl out of her skin and disappear.

"Of course I missed you," he said. His voice stroked her skin and made her nerves tingle. Her nipples were so hard they hurt. She'd been wet all night but that grumble of his voice made her sex clench.

She laughed herself, a nervous exhalation of breath. "Prove it," she said. Begged.

Whatever complaints Candace had about their relationship, they'd always been completely in sync in the bedroom. It was instinctual. Their connection was so natural and easy and explosive. She'd never experienced anything like this with anyone else.

Ezra stalked toward her with a small smile on his face, his blue eyes dark and intense. But when he finally touched her, his hands were gentle as ever as he slipped his fingers under the straps of her dress and pushed them slowly over her shoulders, his knuckles dragging along her skin.

She was practically naked under the dress but for the lace underwear she'd bought for him. But the way Ezra touched her made her almost wish she'd worn more clothes so she could enjoy the pleasure of having his pupils dilate with lust as he undressed her for even longer. He ran the pads of his fingers around the waist of her underwear, caressing the soft skin there. Candace thought she would melt. She moaned and he captured her mouth, groaning as their tongues met and she wrapped her arms around his shoulders.

Ezra dug his fingers into her waist and she whimpered as he deepened their kiss and pulled her nearly naked body against his.

For a second, Candace thought there was no way this perfect kiss could get better, but then Ezra pushed his hand into the back of her underwear, prying her legs apart with his own as his fingers moved between her ass cheeks and grazed her wet sex.

Her head fell back on a screaming moan.

He kissed her chin. "Did you miss me?" he whispered against her neck.

She couldn't answer. Her knees were weak. Her heartbeat was pounding. "Missed" didn't seem like a strong enough word. "Ezra," she moaned, her only answer.

He laughed against the column of her neck and then licked his way down her clavicle, slipping two fingers into her aching core. "Feels like you missed me," he whispered against her right nipple before he licked it as his fingers began to move in and out of her in strong, slow strokes.

Candace shivered against him. "Too many clothes," she spluttered.

She could feel his smile against her breast. "I agree," he said, using his free hand to push her underwear over her hips. She happily helped him, shimmying until that expensive scrap of lace pooled at her feet, his fingers still buried inside her.

"I meant you," she said, pressing her body against his again. "You're wearing too many clothes."

He kissed her briefly. "I agree," he whispered against her lips, unfortunately pulling his fingers from between her legs.

Candace thought to help him undress but her body had a mind of its own. She stepped back to watch him, her hands caressing her breasts, tweaking her nipples, enjoying watching him as he watched her. His boxer briefs were tented by his erection, a wet spot spreading at the front, and she bit her bottom lip as her stomach fluttered with need.

"I missed you," she whispered, because she had. She'd missed him clothed and naked, touching her and across the room. His voice whispering in her ear and laughing loudly at one of Miles's jokes. Making her sex quiver around his shaft, the soft steel of him in her pumping hand. But more than anything, she'd missed what it felt like to see herself in his eyes. However inaccurate and shadowed by desire, there was nothing like realizing that he still saw her the way he had when they were teenagers.

She wasn't that girl anymore, but for a few hours a year, she could pretend.

He smiled at her as he bent to push his underwear over his hips. When he straightened and they were both naked, they burst into laughter at the awkwardness of being naked together, even after all this time.

Candace was wiping happy tears from her eyes when Ezra stepped forward, somehow always at his boldest when they were naked. He grabbed her hips and pulled her toward him. She wrapped her arms around his torso, suddenly nervous.

Not for the first time during one of their New Year's Eves together — not even the first time tonight — she had the urge to tell him how much she'd always loved him. But then he kissed her, smiling against her lips as he walked her back toward the bed. It was for the best, she thought, as she sucked his tongue into her mouth. It felt too good to be with him like this and she didn't want to spoil it.

He gently pushed her onto her back and then began to kiss his way down her body, touching and licking and sucking her into a frenzy.

"Oh god," she hissed when Ezra's mouth covered her sex. Her hips arched closer to his mouth and his tongue, and his strong, heavy hands settled on her hips, holding her in place. "Oh god," she moaned again.

Ezra licked her, slowly parting her lips and circling

her clit, smiling against her wet sex as if this felt as good to him as it did to her. Candace considered covering her mouth just in case someone heard her, but she didn't. She only moaned louder as Ezra sucked her clit into his mouth and licked at her opening and then groaned against her pussy, the deep vibrations pulling a high-pitched whine from Candace's throat. She came with a sharp cry, her thighs locking around his head and still he lapped at her, extending the life of her orgasm into beautiful echoes that made her scalp tingle.

When she looked down her body, she found his eyes on her and she came again. He smiled.

She was still shaking when he finally released her. He lifted onto his hands and knees. He kissed her mound and then used his mouth and tongue to travel back up her body. She groaned when he bit at her nipples and sighed as he licked up her throat. And then he was hovering over her, smiling down at her, his wet face shining in the light from the streetlamp outside. Candace smiled as she pulled him down, enjoying the hard weight of him on top of her and her taste on his lips.

They had to separate longer than either of them liked to find the stash of condoms at the bottom of Ezra's suitcase. The endeavor took longer than it should have because they kept stopping to make out around their laughter.

"Found it," Ezra finally said, holding the box of condoms up triumphantly. His back bent with a groan when Candace palmed his erection and squeezed.

"Finally," she whispered, leading him back to the bed, still holding his dick.

She pushed him onto his back as he'd done to her. She stood over him and tore open a condom. He caressed her leg just behind her knee and smiled up at her as if she were the sun. She wanted to taste him, but she was impatient and needed him inside of her now. She'd been waiting all year. But they'd have all night, she reminded her momentarily terrified heart. And then she crawled over him and sank down onto his hard dick, feeling once again as if she were floating.

But then Ezra grounded her.

"Candace," he whispered up to her, his hands on her hips.

She could feel his eyes on her as she began to ride him, her hips moving in slow circles.

"Candace," he groaned again. And again. And again, as she rode him faster and harder.

The room filled with their moans and cries and his name on her lips, her name on his.

They'd spent every New Year's Eve this way for nearly a decade, Miles and Mei's parties raging while they snuck off to be together. Eventually the familiar sound of fireworks exploding outside marked their dwindling time together. Their bodies were covered in sweat and they kept chasing just one more orgasm — and then one more after that — desperately needing to fill every moment they had together with enough memories for the coming year.

They heard the countdown in the house, the

combined voices loud enough to carry to their room. Ezra pulled Candace's face to his, close enough that they could look into one another's eyes as their hips moved together. Neither of them believed in New Year's resolutions, but when he held her like that, staring into her soul, she sometimes let herself imagine that he was making her a promise. He didn't ask her out on a date or surprise her on her birthday or do anything that might indicate that he wanted more than just this night, but every year, for that brief moment when their eyes and bodies were connected, Candace always found herself hoping for more and hoping he could see that in her eyes.

The fireworks were still exploding outside when Ezra moved his right hand between their bodies to massage her clit. She came in a clenching, wet rush and he came soon after. She collapsed on top of him and there were a few blissful breaths of calm. But as she rested her head on his chest, scraping her nails gently through his chest hair, she felt the exhilarated rush of knowing they had all night mingle with the dread that their night was almost over.

~

The sun wasn't out yet, but the sky had begun to brighten. They were exhausted. Candace burrowed her face into the pillow under her head as Ezra pulled her close to his chest. Her eyelids were drooping and his breaths had begun to deepen and slow. In a few minutes they'd both be asleep. And in a few hours one or both of them would have to rush out of here to get back to their real lives.

Candace wanted to let herself fall asleep. She more than needed the rest. But she wasn't ready for the night to be over. She wasn't ready to wake up and have to leave Ezra or to find that he was already gone. She wanted this to last forever.

She took in a deep breath of air, summoning up the courage to tell him how she felt, even if not the depth of her emotions. "I wish we could stay like this," she whispered.

Ezra tightened his arm around her middle and buried his face in the crook of her neck. She smiled.

"I can't wait for next year," he whispered, and placed soft kisses along her jawline.

He was asleep in minutes, his arms still around her, the heavy feeling of his mouth still lingering on her skin.

Candace cried silently until the sun was fully in the sky and then carefully crawled out of bed, dressed, and slipped out of Miles and Mei's house before anyone woke up.

She wished she hadn't said anything at all.

# CHAPTER 6

*E*zra didn't have the best history of good plane rides. When he'd moved to New York after college, his plane had an electronics malfunction and had to divert to a cornfield for an emergency landing. His parents had been so terrified when he'd told them about it two days later that they'd offered to pay for a train ticket so he could move home immediately. Another time, he'd been on a red-eye flight to New Orleans for Miles's bachelor party. He'd barely slept in the three days before — working night and day on the prototype of his efficient engine — so he'd been ecstatic to just sleep from gate to gate. But as soon as he'd collapsed into his seat, he'd been waylaid by an old man who spent the entire flight telling him — a complete stranger — his entire life story. But as far as he was concerned, nothing would ever be worse than ten hours on a plane with the woman he loved who refused to even look in his direction.

He slept in short intervals. His ears were so attuned to the sound of footsteps in the aisle that he woke up every time someone passed him, hoping it was Candace. It never was. She didn't come back to First Class until after the breakfast service, to collect refuse. When she made it to his seat, she angled the bag in his direction and averted her eyes. He didn't get another glimpse of her for another three hours as she'd rushed to the front galley and then back again.

He desperately wanted this flight to be over, but also, he didn't. For whatever reason, he was reminded of college graduation. He'd been standing on the Oval with Miles and Mei and their parents. Everyone was taking pictures before the ceremony started. He was smiling, but his focus was every-where else but at the camera lens. He was looking for Candace. He hoped she was just late, unwilling to accept the possibility that she really hadn't come back. He didn't want this plane to land for the same reason he'd been dreading the sound of the chapel bells to start the ceremony. If Candace hadn't shown up by those bells — and if the plane landed and she still wouldn't look at him — then there was a very real chance they would never see each other again. That fear was even stronger now that Miles and Mei were divorced and the connective tissue of their best friends couldn't hold them together. And even though he'd convinced himself that he was heading to Quito to get over her, sitting on this plane desperate for her eyes to swivel in his direction forced him to finally accept that there was no getting over Candace Garret.

He unbuckled his seatbelt and stood.

"What's going on?" Marty mumbled, his eyes fluttering open, still half-asleep.

"Nothing," his wife Alejandra said, patting his hand and smiling up at Ezra.

Ezra smiled back and then pushed the curtain aside to head into the main cabin.

He sped through Business Class and spotted Candace easily in the main cabin. She was holding a small baby on her hip and rocking side-to-side as she talked to a toddler standing up in her seat. The sight of her was like a violent punch to Ezra's gut.

When they were in college, Miles and Mei had always talked about kids with the kind of easy assurance of a couple on firm ground. "When we have kids..." was a common refrain when the four of them talked about the future. But he and Candace were much more circumspect. They weren't sure if they wanted kids, so they pledged to be the best aunt and uncle for any kids their best friends brought into the world. And every time his parents carefully mentioned the possibility of grandchildren, Ezra shook his head and shrugged noncommittally. But seeing Candace holding a baby clarified all of his indecision. He didn't have to have children, but if he were to have them, it would be with Candace. Like everything else in his life, it was Candace or bust. This moment was Candace or bust.

"Candace," he whispered softly when he was within earshot.

Her back stiffened, but she kept bouncing the baby in her arms as she turned slowly toward him. As she moved, Ezra saw a woman in the aisle seat next to the standing toddler, with an in-flight meal in front of her. It didn't take a genius to realize that Candace was holding the baby to give the mother a long enough break to eat.

"Is there something you need, sir?" she asked in the friendly voice she'd used for all the other passengers; polite, not warm, vaguely distant. Not the way she would ever have spoken to Mei or Miles.

His eyes darted to the mother and toddler and then the baby in Candace's arms. He swallowed and leaned slightly toward her. "I need to talk to you," he whispered.

"I'm busy," she said in a tight voice.

"I know," he said. "I just..."

"All done," the little girl announced.

Ezra and Candace turned to see the mother smiling indulgently at her daughter. She turned to them and reached for the baby in Candace's arms.

"Thank you," she said to Candace. "It was nice to eat with two hands." She pressed her son's nose as if it was a button and both of her children dissolved into peals of laughter. It was an adorable family scene and Ezra couldn't help but turn to look at Candace's profile. She turned to him with wide eyes and sucked in a breath before turning quickly away. She grabbed the woman's tray, waved at the toddler, and then turned on her heel toward the back of the plane. Ezra followed her.

In the back galley, she refused to look at him as she threw away the refuse and bussed the tray. He wanted to grab her shoulder and turn her to him, but touching Candace had always been a reverent act for Ezra. He lived for those invitations, when she opened herself up to him and welcomed his tentative touch. He didn't want to ruin all those beautiful memories between them in a moment of frustration, so he shoved his hands into his pockets as he spoke to her back.

"Candace, I don't know what I said — what you think I said — but I have never been ashamed of being with you. I can't even remember a time before wanting to be with you."

She slammed the tray into one of the carts and turned to him, her arms crossed over her chest and a scowl on her face. He met her eyes. He felt his heart — and hope — shrivel at her glare.

"I'm not calling you a liar," he said, just in case that wasn't clear. "I'm just saying that I know how I feel about you, how I've always felt about you. And no part of me has ever been ashamed to be seen with you. If I'd thought that you wanted more, there was nothing anyone could have done to keep me from you."

"If *I'd* wanted more?" she asked, her eyebrows furrowing.

He felt the plane dip down ever so slightly toward the ground, which underscored the urgency of this moment. He couldn't imagine what he'd said in some half-asleep post-orgasmic admission to make her think he wouldn't have reveled in finally being hers. But if she was right, if there was some hidden part of his consciousness that had given her this impression, he knew where it would have blossomed; the first crack in their bond.

"You didn't come back," he whispered.

The wrinkles between her eyebrows deepened and her scowl turned into a frown. "What?"

"Graduation. You said you'd come back," he smiled weakly. "I spent that entire spring semester psyching myself up to ask you out. I had it all planned out. I'd bought you flowers." He shrugged. "I borrowed money from my dad to buy you flowers. I gave them to Dr. Freedman instead. And I had a copy of my Gilder Prize speech to give you. I laminated it."

"Why?" she asked.

He was blinking faster than normal, the pressure of possible tears in his eyes. "I thanked you in it. Two paragraphs about how none of it would have happened without you. How lucky I was to have you as my best friend." Ezra smiled a bit wider this time as a few tears fell from his eyes. "Miles was pissed about that, actually. But the version of the speech I was going to give you ended with me asking you out on a date. A real date." He swiped at his face and took a few breaths, trying to get himself together. "But you never came to graduation. You didn't come home for three years."

Candace's mouth had fallen open in shock. Ezra's

cheeks and neck were hot with embarrassment. He'd decided long ago to never tell her this. It made him sound pathetic. But maybe he'd been wrong to say that he'd never lie to her, because hadn't he been lying about the intensity of his feelings for years? Hadn't he been pretending he *wasn't* head over heels for her? That he was perfectly fine just being her friend? That he didn't need more than one night a year?

He'd never thought of it this way and just next to the airplane toilets was an inconvenient place to have such earth-shaking self-realizations, but better late than never, he guessed.

The captain's voice over the intercom system cut into the tense, quiet moment between them. They stared at one another with wet eyes and mouths open, as the captain announced that they'd started their descent into the Quito International Airport. The sound of the seatbelt sign illuminating felt like a bomb in Ezra's ears and he jumped.

"I know you have to get back to work but I... I couldn't get off this plane without clearing that up. Even if I never see you again, I don't want you to go another day thinking I haven't been completely in awe of you for the past eighteen years. Every day. I'm sorry I didn't make that clear before now."

Candace hissed a breath and opened her mouth to speak. Just then, Jorge burst into the back galley.

"Sorry to interrupt, but we've got motion sickness."

"Oh God," Candace groaned.

"Yep. Just barely got him to the toilet. I'll clean it

up, but you and Mark are going to have to handle the landing procedures until I'm done."

She nodded and then her eyes shifted to Ezra.

He smiled sadly at her. "I'll get out of your way." He hesitated, clenching his fists in his pants pockets. "If I don't see you, Happy New Year, Candace. I hope next year is good to you. You deserve the best."

And then he turned away. If he'd thought moving on would make him feel lighter, he was wrong. Every step back to his seat and away from Candace felt heavier than the last; like he was leaving his heart and entire soul at the other end of the plane.

～

*C*andace felt shell-shocked. Somehow, what should have been a routine trip from San Francisco to Quito had turned into the worst of her career. It seemed impossible that a flight with no technical malfunctions or service issues or even many children had wiped her out, but it had. She found it hard to follow what Jorge and Mark were saying as they wheeled their bags to baggage claim.

At the carousel, Mark waved goodbye to them and ran to catch a cab to his hotel. He only had less than a day in Ecuador before working a short flight to Panama and then on to Chile, so he needed to get to sleep asap. She and Jorge were staying in Quito for a while and weren't in the same rush. Jorge hadn't checked a bag, but he waited around for Candace to collect hers, so they could travel to the hotel together.

But she was distracted. Her head swiveled around, her neck straining as she looked at the passengers from the flight; searching for Ezra.

"Looks like we missed him," Jorge said carefully.

Candace couldn't look at him. She was too afraid she'd cry. Again. But she deflated at his words.

"Is that your suitcase?" Jorge asked, pointing at the carousel.

Candace nodded and wiped at her eyes, pressing the pads of her fingers against her closed eyelids as he darted off to grab her luggage.

"Thanks," she whispered when he returned.

"Anytime. Now come on. First round at the hotel bar is on me."

She laughed. It sounded weak and reedy. They walked out onto the curb and the air was wet with humidity. They both looked up at the sky.

"It's gonna rain soon," Candace said.

"Yep."

She turned to look at the traffic around them and her entire body froze. "Watch my bags," she said, already walking away.

"What? Candace, where are you—? Oh."

She didn't look back. She kept her eyes on Ezra's profile. He was looking at his phone as a black town car pulled up in front of him. She sped up as he reached for the door handle.

"Ezra," she called out to him.

He turned to her with red-rimmed eyes. His full beard needed a trim. He looked beautiful. He always did. But that wasn't what this was about.

He turned to her as the driver stepped out of the car and walked to the opened trunk. He lifted Ezra's bag and put it in the trunk just as Candace reached them. And then the driver looked between them in confusion.

"Necesitamos un momento, por favor," Candace said in rusty Spanish.

The driver turned to Ezra who nodded, his eyes still focused on her.

"Así," the driver said and walked back to the driver's side.

Ezra's entire question was in the furrowing of his brow.

Candace swallowed. She was uncomfortable. She wanted a shower, a long nap, a good cry and a shot of whiskey, and not necessarily in that order. But before all of that, she needed to say this to him.

"I was going to come back. My return flight would have landed at SFO three days before graduation. I spent the first few days here homesick, thinking about how happy I would be to get back to The Bay. To spend all my free time with Mei and Miles and..." she swallowed and rubbed her wet palms on her skirt, "you. I thought about you every day for the first few weeks and that New Year's Eve together when we kinda defiled Teddy."

His face and ears turned a soft red. "If you were

going to come back, why didn't you?" he asked carefully.

There was an old pit of sadness in Candace's heart about that question. She'd harbored it deep inside herself for so long — too long — afraid to tell anyone of how deeply Ezra had once hurt her. How could he not know? Why did she have to tell him this? But she shook her head because none of those questions mattered now, she supposed, since this was the end anyway.

"You were supposed to email me. You ate me out on my childhood teddy bear and then nothing. You didn't even try and contact me while I was gone. Not until the end of the semester when you told me you won the Gilder Prize."

She could feel the sting of tears in her eyes, but she knew they wouldn't fall. She'd cried so many tears about this subject, she had no more water left to give. "I waited days and weeks and months for you to contact me. I was always waiting for you to get it. I was always waiting for you to make a move and then taking it when you didn't.

For once, I thought, you would act. That you'd finally take the first step to me because after that night, how could you not know how I felt about you? How could you not even email me to ask? And when you didn't, I realized it was because you didn't feel the same way about me as I felt about you."

Ezra shook his head. "Mei said you were busy. That you barely emailed her."

"I would have emailed you," she yelled at Ezra. "You were the only person I asked to contact me."

"I— What?"

She furrowed her brow.

"You didn't? The last thing you said was that you'd be back for graduation. If I'd known—"

"What do you mean, if you'd known? I left you a message."

"Where?" he yelled back.

"With Miles," she exclaimed. "I *told* him to tell you to email me. And you never did."

"Candace," Jorge yelled behind her.

She turned quickly to see their shuttle at the curb in front of him. She nodded and turned back to Ezra. "Look, I have to go. I'm tired."

"Where are you staying? I can drop you off," Ezra said quickly. Desperately.

She shook her head. "That's not what this was about. I just wanted you to know that I had planned to come back. Maybe I should have." She reached out to cup his face, enjoying the soft, downy feel of his beard under her palm. "I wish we hadn't waited this long or held all these things in. I wish we'd been more mature. Less afraid. But we can't go back and fix this. Maybe this is exactly how this was all supposed to play out."

"Candace—"

"Happy New Year, Ezra," she whispered sadly.

She practically ran to the shuttle, which was a mistake in the heat. She was drenched as she climbed onto the bus. Ezra was still standing by his car. He turned to follow the bus as it passed, his mouth open, his brow furrowed in confusion. Candace had to look away.

And then Candace's cell phone chirped with a new text message. She had to fish her purse from her bag. The message was from Mei.

What's going on with you and Ezra?
Where are you?
When are you two going to finally get it together?
Don't tell Miles I'm still single.

# JANUARY 1, 2003

*T*he sun was coming up by the time they boarded a BART train home. The train was packed but they managed to find four seats together. Mei and Miles sat next to each other, unusually quiet. Mei gripped one of Miles's hands with both of hers and he was twirling a long lock of her hair between his fingers. Ezra only noticed these things vaguely. He was exhausted and mostly just wanted to get back to his dorm room, shower and crawl into bed until the cafeteria opened for dinner. But the thing that was really occupying his mind — more than even his own exhaustion — was the weight of Candace's head on his shoulder. She'd plopped into the seat closest to the window and fallen immediately asleep on top of him. He'd been sitting stock still ever since.

His left arm had fallen asleep and the numbness was starting to hurt. He also really needed to yawn, but he stifled it, too afraid to move even a fraction of an inch for fear he'd startle her and she'd lean away from him. It was pathetic, but it wasn't a choice. Having the delicious weight of Candace's head on his shoulder was far more important that his own physical comfort.

When the train made a brief emergence from the tunnel, Ezra turned toward the window. He pretended to look out at his hometown and then inhaled deeply. Candace's hair smelled like coconut and vanilla. He fell asleep somewhere underneath the bay, surrounded by that scent.

He wondered if this was how Mei and Miles felt.

"*T*hanks for coming, kids. He really needed friends today," Mr. Posner said.

They all dropped their heads and nodded, unsure what to say to a man whose wife was dying of cancer. They all felt too young and immature for the gravity of this moment.

"No problem, Mr. P," Miles finally said for all of them.

Candace leaned back just a bit to see inside Mrs. Posner's room. Ezra was asleep at his mother's bedside, one of her hands clutched in his. He looked so peaceful. He hadn't looked so calm in months. She missed seeing him like that, as if the weight of the world weren't sitting on his shoulders. She missed the illusion that they were still kids in some ways. She missed him.

They hadn't seen each other all summer. Miles had been in San Diego working a summer internship at an architecture firm, Mei had been in Tucson at an artist's retreat and Ezra had been clear across the country on a summer developing course at MIT. Candace's friends had been off doing cool stuff and preparing for their futures while she'd been at home, working her regular job at the clothing store her mom managed, picking up random serving shifts at the diner her dad managed and saving every penny as usual. She'd felt lonely and abandoned, waiting for the school year to start.

This wasn't how they'd planned to spend their junior year. The day before classes had started, she and Mei had dropped off their suitcases in their new apartment and headed immediately out. They walked the four blocks to Miles and Ezra's apartment, feeling giddy about finally being back together. On the way, Mei had talked incessantly about how cool her residency was and Candace had done her best to skirt her best friend's questions about their time apart. There was nothing to tell and it made her feel an odd mix of jealousy and embarrassment — emotions she'd been avoiding acknowledging all summer. All that mattered was that she'd missed Mei, Miles and Ezra more than she could say.

When they'd arrived at the boys' apartment, Mei had banged on the door loudly as they'd giggled. Their laughter had died on their tongues when Miles opened the door.

"Ezra's mom has cancer," was the first thing out of his mouth.

Whatever normal Candace had been waiting all summer to get back to never appeared.

All semester, Ezra had split his weeks between school and home, wanting to be with his mom as much as possible. He and Candace barely saw each other. He was an engineering major; she was in Art History and their classes weren't even in the same buildings anymore.

She hardly saw Mei and Miles either. Sometimes the three studied together on Tuesday afternoons and they went to basketball games at least once a month, but more days than not she only saw Mei just before their first class on Monday and Wednesday mornings. And the apartment she'd imagined sharing with her best friend came to feel like her own as Mei spent more nights than not over at Miles's, especially since Ezra was so rarely there.

Shockingly, nothing was the same in their friendship circle without Ezra.

It was her idea to visit the Posners in the hospital, but now that they were there, she didn't know what to say. It had been okay downstairs in the cafeteria when Ezra had just wanted to sit with them and pretend as if everything was normal. They listened to Miles tell them about Christmas at his dad's new "condo for sad, divorced men." It had been more hilarious than depressing and by the end Ezra's eyes were wet with happy tears and he was leaning over the table, his body shaking with laughter.

But standing outside Mrs. Posner's hospital room, everything felt different. And not just because Mrs. Posner was weak and unconscious surrounded by beeping and whirring machines. She was small and frail and Candace couldn't help but remember how full of energy she used to be. She didn't look like the same Mrs. Posner who'd invited them to every Purim since they'd met Ezra and gave her son extra money so they could all have one great meal out before final exams, and none of them knew what to do with that.

But selfishly, the thing Candace couldn't get over was Ezra's warm hand squeezing hers desperately under the table, so tight it almost hurt. She squeezed his back just as hard. For a couple of hours, it was almost like things were back to normal. He didn't speak, he only cried a little bit and he laughed at Miles and Mei's jokes as he held onto Candace's hand for dear life. She wanted to ask him why; what it all meant. But of all the bad timing in their relationship, this was the worst.

"We're gonna go, Mr. P," Miles said. "But we can come back tomorrow or the day after if you... I mean, if that's okay."

Candace's eyes shifted back to Mr. Posner. His eyes were rimmed with red behind his glasses and he pulled them off to wipe at the tears running down his cheeks. He nodded. "That'd be great. I think he'd like that."

"Do you need anything?" Candace asked.

Mr. Posner shook his head, sniffled and put his glasses back on his face. When he turned to her, he looked like a sad version of his normal self; still kind and open but shattered. He looked like Ezra; like how Ezra would look in twenty years.

"We'll be fine, kiddo. Thank you. Just come back. I know he'll be happy to see you."

They said their goodbyes and walked to the elevator. When the doors opened, they turned and saw Mr. Posner still standing outside his wife's hospital room, seeing them off. They waved at him. He waved back.

They rode to the lobby in silence, Miles and Mei holding hands while Candace tried to understand the way Mr. Posner had said "you," as if Ezra would be happy to see her especially. Not just the three of them, but her alone.

And then she stamped down on her heart and ego and prayed that Mrs. Posner would be okay.

"Do you have everything?" Candace's mom asked for the fifth time just that morning.

"Yes, ma," she whined, even though she once again checked to make sure that her passport, travel checks and emergency credit card were all in her purse. They were.

"It's just that if you need anything, I can have your dad speed over there."

Candace smiled. "My plane starts boarding in twenty minutes. We'll be in the air before dad even got out of traffic on the bridge. I'm fine. I'm not a little girl anymore."

"You're my little girl," her mother said.

"You're adorable, you know that? A great egg. I raised you right," Candace laughed.

"Shush. Do you have your calling card?" her mom asked.

Candace frowned. "I don't know actually," she said.

"Candace," her mother groaned.

Candace could practically see her mother wringing her hands right now, surely aggravating her arthritis. She bent down and opened her backpack. She felt certain she did have the international calling card her aunt Sophie had gifted her for this trip, because she'd packed, repacked and double and triple-checked her bags with a detailed eye days ago. But with the panic in her mother's voice, she decided to lie, not wanting to give her parents one more thing to worry about.

She exhaled in relief when she found the card at the back of her travel pouch. "I've got it. It was in my travel pouch with all my other important information," she said happily.

Her mother exhaled as well. "Good. Good. I'm going to miss you, peanut."

Candace smiled. "I'll miss you too, mama."

"Promise me you'll take care of yourself. I don't know what I'd do if anything happened to you while you were so far away."

Candace could feel the pressure of tears in her eyes, but she blinked them back. "I promise, mama." She tried to lighten her voice to put her mother at ease. "Watch, you're crying on the phone, but I bet the next four months are just gonna fly by."

"I hope so," her mother whispered.

And that was the problem. Candace wanted to live

a little, to live on her own without feeling the weight of her parents' anxieties. They loved her so deeply that they never quite let her fly the coop. It had taken three years of saved wages, applying to every scholarship she could find and a year of dropping hints that she wanted to study abroad for her parents to "let" her travel farther than southern California. And as happy as she was to go, Candace still felt guilty about leaving them.

A single tear slipped down her cheek and she wiped it quickly away. "Mom, I've gotta go. Dr. Montero is getting the class together before we board."

"Okay, baby," she said, even though she sounded everything but okay. "You'll call as soon as you get there?"

"I'll try, mama. As soon as I find a phone, okay?"

"O-okay. Have fun, peanut."

"Thanks, mama. I love you. And tell daddy I love him too."

"I will, baby. I will."

Candace hung up the public pay phone and stared at it for a few seconds, giving herself a few moments to feel her guilt and sadness. Her parents deserved that at least.

On an impulse, she fished another quarter from her purse and dialed her and Mei's landline.

After Mei and Miles had interrupted her encounter with Ezra, they'd spent a couple of hours taking care of them before Ezra sent her to bed so she could rest before her flight. When she'd woken up,

Miles and Mei were once again passed out in Mei's bed, Ezra was snoring on the couch and the bathroom smelled strongly of bleach. She'd briefly considered waking Ezra up, but he looked so peaceful that she changed her mind. But her eyes kept darting to his prone body as she frantically threw the last of her clothes into her suitcase.

She had to make two trips to bring her bags down to the curb. Each time she opened and closed the front door, she silently hoped he would wake up. He didn't. She spent the entire cab ride to the airport regretting that they didn't get to say a proper goodbye or talk about what last night had meant. So, she called home, hoping that he was finally awake.

Her heart throbbed with every ring until finally someone picked up.

"'Lo."

"Miles?" Candace asked.

"Hey, Can. You on the plane?"

She squinted. "Obviously not. You hungover?"

"Very. I think I'm gonna die. Never drinking again."

"Good idea. Hey, is Ezra there?"

"Mmmm, nah. He went to get breakfast. He promised me bagels if I didn't throw up again. Might not be able to keep my end of the bargain though," he said and then burped. "Wanna talk to Mei?"

"No," Candace breathed. "I left her a card. Hey, can you tell Ezra that I called when he gets back?"

"Yeah."

"And like, can you..." Candace hesitated and frowned. She turned to look at her gate and saw that Dr. Montero really was rounding the class up before boarding now.

She wanted to tell Miles to tell Ezra that last night was amazing and totally worth the three-year wait. She wanted Ezra to know that there had been a moment last night, when his face was buried between her legs, that she'd seriously considered not going on this trip. She wanted him to know that she wished they could spend their final semester together. But that would be too much information to tell Miles even if he hadn't been severely hungover.

"Can you just tell Ezra to email me as soon as he gets back? I won't be able to email him until I land in Quito but... please, just tell him to email me, okay?"

"Yep. Will do. Have a good flight, Can," Miles said, yawning.

"Thanks," she said, and put the receiver back on the cradle.

"Candace," Dr. Montero called. "Vámanos."

She sighed and then turned. "Ya voy," she called back, and grabbed her backpack from the ground. It was corny, but just before Candace walked onto the jet bridge, she stole one more glance across the boarding area to the bank of payphones.

She boarded that plane certain that there would be an email from Ezra when she arrived in Quito. That when she came back for graduation, he would take her out on a date to a jazz club in San Francisco. That he would come to her parents' house for the Fourth of July and she would be his date to his cousin's wedding in August. But of all the emails in her inbox when she landed, none were from Ezra.

And it cracked Candace's heart in two.

*U*sually a good shower was enough to help Candace feel like herself again after a flight. She'd go straight to the hotel room, shuck off her uniform, shower, put on a dress that made her feel human and then head to dinner. But once she got to her hotel room, the idea of leaving again made her feel sick.

She still stripped out of her uniform and stepped into a shower so hot she should have been worried she might scald her skin, but she hardly felt the heat. She didn't feel the slightly scratchy wash cloth on her body, because her mind wasn't in that shower stall. Her mind was back at the airport, Ezra's soft beard under her palm, poring over every word they'd said to one another. She needed to memorize every detail because she was convinced that that final "happy new year" would be the last one between them. When she stepped out of the shower, washed her face, moisturized her body and dressed, she felt clean, but not like herself. She wasn't sure if she ever would again.

She'd just finished dressing when the hotel phone rang.

Candace rushed to the desk by her bed, her heart pounding with the irrational hope that it was Ezra. It was Jorge.

"Meet you in the lounge in five?" he asked instead of saying hello.

"Yep," she responded in a high-pitched voice that made her wince.

"Okay girl, see ya," he said and hung up.

Candace put the phone back on the cradle and looked around her hotel room. It was kind of a train wreck. Her suitcase was open on the luggage rack and her uniform was in a crumpled pile on the floor. Normally she would have sent the uniform straight to housekeeping and fully unpacked, but she was only staying in this hotel for one night and she'd be in Quito for a week, so she decided not to bother. She also wasn't working her flight home, so what did it matter if her uniform wasn't clean and pressed to AeroPlan regulations?

She took in a deep breath and decided to leave. She knew that if she dawdled, she'd crawl into bed and cry herself to sleep, and even though the idea of being around people made her chest constrict, thinking about crying more tears about Ezra made her feel worse. So she slipped into a pair of sandals, grabbed her purse and room key and hurried out the door.

The bar wasn't hard to find. While the check-in desk was near deserted and quiet, she could hear laughter and a mix of Spanish and English chatter from the other end of the lobby as soon as she stepped off the elevator. She followed the sounds to tall wooden doors flung open to the hotel lobby. She made a beeline to the bar and had the most intense feeling of déjà vu as she looked left and right to see men and women in business suits and waiters moving between tables in crisp white shirts and crimson vests. But it was the bar itself that made her mind struggle to grasp onto a memory that lay just beyond her mental fingertips.

She didn't remember this hotel and it wasn't particularly close to the Universidad San Francisco where she'd studied, but she couldn't shake the idea that she'd been here before. And if she had, her only motivation would have been to indulge one of the three great obsessions of her life at that point — jazz, Ezra, and chicha. And since Ezra had been back in California, she sat on one of the bar stools and assumed it must have been one of the other two.

The bartender stopped in front of her and smiled widely. "What would you like?" he asked in heavily accented English.

She forced herself to smile back at him. "Una copa de chicha, por favor," she ordered, cringing at how bad her accent sounded to her own ears.

He nodded and moved quickly away.

By the time he'd returned, Jorge was slipping onto

the stool next to her and a band was taking the stage at the head of the room.

"Chicha?" Jorge asked.

Candace nodded and he turned to the bartender to order the same. When his own glass arrived, they toasted one another and took a sip.

"Yeesh," Jorge hissed as he swallowed.

Candace's right eye twitched and she shook her head as she put her glass back on the bar. "No way I came here for this," she said.

"I hope that's not the only reason you took this flight," Jorge said.

She shook her head. "No, I meant before. I came to Quito senior year of college and I'm pretty sure I've been to this hotel before."

"Yeah?"

She nodded, "But I don't know why. I thought it could be the chicha, but this tastes like bad grain alcohol."

"Why waste the good shit on the tourists?" Jorge said.

She nodded again as the bass player plucked out a few exploratory notes, pulling her attention to the stage. "If it wasn't the chicha, I thought it could be jazz. I was a huge jazz snob then."

"Oh yeah?" Jorge laughed.

Candace watched as the drummer began to softly rasp his sticks against his set and she felt her body ease. "It was one of the things we had in common. I loved Billie and Ezra had this thing for Benny Goodman, 'cause they're both Jewish." She smiled despite herself. "He was always too nervous to talk music with me directly, but we were friends on Myspace and I used to love going to his page to listen to his playlist. It was all Benny Goodman until I told him I liked Billie Holiday. When I went to his page a few days later he'd added a couple of Billie songs. For me, I always thought."

As she spoke, the band's exploratory notes turned into a soft murmur and she felt certain that it must have been the house jazz band that had pulled her here all those years ago. She doubted this was the same band, but that sense of familiarity only grew as they played a soft rhythm that coaxed the tears she'd been fighting for hours to spill down her cheeks.

Jorge pushed a cocktail napkin into her hand and she dabbed at her eyes with a sad, painful laugh.

"So, the billionaire?" he asked when she'd gotten herself together.

She nodded and took another harsh sip of her drink. "He wasn't a billionaire then, of course. He was just my really shy, awkward, brilliant friend. And I was totally in love with him."

"But he wasn't in love with you?"

The tears fell faster. Jorge pushed the stack of napkins toward her. "Nope," she said, and wondered if Jorge could hear the bitter notes in her voice. "Apparently he was in love with me too. And I never fucking knew it."

"So that's it? You two were in love with each other in college?"

Candace took another sip of her drink and laughed again. She wished it was that simple. Maybe then the two of them could have run into one another on that flight and started where they left off. But there was so much history between them, and so much hurt. "After we graduated, I thought I needed to move on. I traveled for a couple of years. Avoided him. He stayed at home for a while, started his company. Dated a girl from high school. I dated a string of really fine but really broke men," she said with a laugh.

"That is the best way to waste your twenties, if you ask me," he said and squeezed her forearm.

She didn't disagree. Besides all the wasted time with Ezra, she cherished more in those three years than she regretted.

"Then what happened?"

"Our best friends got married," she said with a smile that faltered as she thought about that day, and then the day Mei called to tell her that she'd left Miles. "I went home for the wedding. He'd always been attractive, but when I saw him in that tuxedo..." she said, biting her bottom lip.

"Did he have the beard? Lord, I hope he had a beard."

Her smile widened; her eyes glazed over as she remembered. "They got married on New Year's Eve so he had that good cold weather beard. It was nice and lush and he had one gray hair on the point of his chin."

Jorge groaned.

"We left the reception early and had sex all night. It was perfect."

Jorge straightened excitedly in his seat and playfully swatted her arm. "Girl, then what the fuck? Why are you here drinking this lighter fluid and crying with me instead of sitting in some luxury ass penthouse with him?"

Candace blinked. Her eyes were too glassy to blink away her tears and her wet eyelashes felt as if they were weighing down her lids. "He'd just moved to New York. And then I moved home and neither of us were interested in a long-distance relationship, I thought. I don't know. We never got the communication thing quite right. But the sex..." She bit her bottom lip again. "That was always fire."

"So not the best foundation to be living on either side of the country," Jorge acknowledged.

"But he came home like clockwork for Hanukkah with his parents and he stayed for New Year's Eve with our friends and we hooked up every year."

"Okay, wait," Jorge blurted. She took the opportunity to wipe her eyes again. "Was this a straight-up friends with benefits type situation? Or were you two still in love?"

Candace didn't know why she was bothering to wipe her eyes because Jorge's questions only seemed to make fresh tears fall. "I really wish I had known you then," she said. "I don't know if I was willing to admit it at first, but I was still in love with him. I'd never loved any of my trifling boyfriends because loving Ezra didn't leave room for anyone else.

And by the time I realized that I'd never stopped loving him, I was too terrified to ask him how he felt. I had no idea what he'd say. So I kept hooking up with him once a year, waiting for him to make a move."

"But he never did," Jorge said sadly.

"No, that's not quite true. The last New Year's Eve we were together I told him how I felt, kinda, and he did the same."

"Ummm," Jorge said, his voice full of skepticism. "I'd like to hear that verbatim."

Up until this point, Candace had been avoiding Jorge's eyes, too afraid to see judgment or pity there. But she took a peek at him now and saw sadness. It wasn't quite pity or judgment but it still poked at the exposed nerve in Candace's life that was all the things she wished she could go back and do differently with Ezra.

She took another fortifying sip of her drink and cringed. "We'd spent the night together," she hedged.

"Knocking boots. Got it," Jorge corrected.

"And we were exhausted. I told him I wanted to stay together with him like that. In bed." The tears were really flowing now. She dabbed at them but wasn't sure if that helped at all. "And he told me he couldn't 'wait until the next New Year's Eve.' Because I was in love with him and he just wanted to hook up with me once a year."

Jorge squeezed her forearm and rubbed her back as

she broke down at the bar. She could only imagine what the other patrons thought of her. If Jorge was embarrassed by her tears, he didn't show it and she was beyond thankful for that. He simply moved more cocktail napkins within her reach and let her get it out.

When her quiet sobs finally waned, Jorge slid her drink in front of her and lifted his own. They both took deep gulps and then shuddered at the taste.

"So that was it? You haven't seen each other since?"

Candace sighed and put her elbow on the bar so she could rest her cheek on the heel of her left hand. "Our best friends separated a month later. I started dating that shitty art critic and it was just easier to keep not talking to each other like we always had."

Jorge pinned her with a fierce stare and frowned. "You're gonna hate what I'm about to say. You know that, right?"

Candace blinked and smiled weakly. Her body felt heavy with exhaustion and bad alcohol. "Definitely."

"I think you misunderstood what he meant the last time you saw each other. And I love you, but it was kind of a cowardly move to almost sorta tell him that you wanted to be with him while he was probably half asleep."

Maybe under different circumstances Candace's back might have stiffened in censure, but she was so tired and her drink was so strong. She could only nod, because deep down she knew Jorge was right. Maybe she'd always known, but she was too terrified to consider that possibility or accept that she'd over-reacted.

"He told me on the plane that he's always wanted to be with me."

Jorge started. "Then why are you here?" he yelled.

Candace didn't have to think about the answer to this question; she'd spent the entire final leg of the flight reminding herself of why it was too late. Why it had been too late long before Ezra had ostensibly rejected her four years ago.

She wiped at her face one more time. "Because when I came here for my study abroad, I left him a message. I told him to email me and he didn't." She clenched her fist around her glass. "I spent three and a half months waiting for him to email me."

"Girl, why didn't you email him?"

"Because I'd waited three years before that for Ezra to tell me how he felt. I batted my eyes at him, I sought him out at every party, and I never dated anyone else seriously because I just knew that sooner or later, Ezra would ask me out and I didn't want to have to dump anyone else for him. I didn't want to use anyone else as a space filler for him, because I just knew we were meant to be together. But it never happened. So when I came here, I was certain that once we were so far apart, he'd finally get it together. It was his turn to seek me out, but he didn't, not until he wanted to tell me that he'd won a prestigious award." The tears started again. "And it wasn't even an email just to me. I was so heartsick for him; I would have been overjoyed about that. But it was a group email.

That's when I realized that I didn't mean that much to him. Certainly not as much as he meant to me."

Jorge's face was full of sympathetic pain. "So, you didn't go home for three years?"

She nodded her head.

"And when you finally did go home, you started having sex but it never turned into more?"

She nodded again.

"Fuck," Jorge breathed. He turned to the bar abruptly, raising his hand to get the bartender's attention. "We're gonna need tequila for this," he said.

The bartender put two shot glasses in front of them and they downed them quickly.

It tasted worlds away from the cheap chicha. They sat in silence for a few minutes. The jazz band had moved from a slow standard that Candace recognized as a Cole Porter joint to something she didn't recognize but liked nonetheless. She tapped her fingers on the bar as Jorge seemed to be deep in thought.

"Okay. Once again, you're not gonna like this, but sometimes friendship sucks," he said. "In a few minutes we're gonna walk across the street to a restaurant the cute concierge told me is great. We're gonna get you hydrated and fed and then in bed, hopefully with little to no vomit."

Candace grimaced.

"And then tomorrow we're gonna meet for breakfast and strategize about how you can get your billionaire back."

"Jorge," Candace said, shaking her head.

"Don't give me a hard time. I'm making a sacrifice here. My bucket list has a line item for fucking a billionaire on it, but I love you so I'm going to forego that to secure your happiness."

Candace rolled her eyes.

"Besides," Jorge said, "I might not believe in God — to my mother's everlasting shame — but I do believe in love and fate and romance. And there is no way the universe put that man on *your* plane and you two in the same city over *New Year's Eve* for any other reason than you two being together."

"It could be closure," Candace offered, her eyelids drooping.

"Oh no, you don't," Jorge said. He pulled too much money from his pocket and put it on the bar and then helped her stand. Candace leaned into his side as they walked out the bar's side door onto the narrow sidewalk and across the cobblestoned street.

"It *could* be closure," Jorge conceded as they stepped into a queue outside of a tiny restaurant down the block. "But it sounds to me like the two of you suffer from a chronic inability to be absolutely crystal clear with each other. I saw the way he looked at you. And there's no way that was about closure."

"How did he look at me?"

Jorge smiled; the adorable upturn of his lips was hopeful. "Like there are billions of people in the world and the only one who matters is you."

Candace had to look away and swipe her cheek against her shoulder to catch the tears.

"And that's saying something because that uniform does no one any favors," he added with attitude.

They both burst into laughter.

*E*zra's eyes fluttered open when the sun streamed through the two walls of floor-to-ceiling windows in the penthouse. He should have closed the shades before he went to sleep but he hadn't. He'd only had enough energy to shower and fall into bed. He hadn't even eaten or turned on his computer to go over the paperwork for today's meeting, because he couldn't get Candace's words out of his head.

> *I waited for you.*
> *We can't go back.*
> *Happy New Year, Ezra.*

He'd slept terribly. He'd spent most of the night trying his hardest to figure out how he'd gotten the past almost two decades so wrong; how he'd misunderstood someone he thought he knew so well. None of it made sense and his jetlagged brain and broken heart couldn't figure it out. He turned away from the window and threw the covers over his head. He just wanted to go back to sleep and dream about Candace, conjuring that scene at the airport. An alternate version where she'd gotten into his car and talked to him, listened to him, a version where she said, "happy new year," not as a final goodbye but with laughter.

His phone chimed and he grabbed it out of habit. He sat up quickly when he saw Mei's name in his messages.

What's going on?

*C*andace used to poke fun at Mei for always answering a question with a question. The problem was that Ezra didn't have an answer for her. He sighed and checked the rest of his messages. There were a few texts from his team, letting Ezra know they'd all arrived, inviting him out to dinner and double-checking the time for their morning meeting, and then finally asking if everything was alright.

Ezra ran a hand through his hair and scratched at his scalp. He wanted to ignore the barrage of messages, but he couldn't. Miles had always joked that Ezra was the dad of their group; his deep sense of responsibility so strong he'd probably go prematurely gray. So instead of wallowing, he tapped out a quick group message to his team, assuring them that he'd arrived in Ecuador safe and sound and that he'd see them all in a few hours.

And then he opened the message that had actually pulled him fully awake. It was from Miles.

Call me.

*E*zra's stomach clenched. Miles was the most talkative person he'd ever known, even in text messages. He couldn't remember a time when his friend had ever messaged him just two words. He pressed the green call icon at the top of the screen and cleared his dry throat as he crawled out of bed.

"Hey," Miles said when he picked up.

"Hey," Ezra croaked.

"You sound terrible."

Ezra walked out of his bedroom toward the bar and grabbed a bottle of water. "Do you want me to hang up on you?" he asked and then cracked open the bottle and swallowed nearly half of it.

"Normally I'd joke about how you'd never, but I'm not feeling in a joking kind of mood right now," Miles said in a subdued voice.

Ezra lowered the bottle of water from his lips and frowned. "Hey man, what's going on? You don't sound like yourself."

Miles sighed, which made the alarm bells sound in Ezra's brain.

"Do you think we made a mistake?" Miles asked in a quiet voice.

Ezra's eyebrows bunched. That question could mean anything and it was one that he'd been rolling over and over in his head for hours, maybe longer. The answer he always arrived at was yes, but he couldn't pinpoint the moment he'd ruined one of the most precious relationships of his life.

But Miles couldn't have been calling him to ask about Candace. "Did who make a mistake, Miles?"

"Me and Mei," Miles said, his voice nearly giving out on his ex-wife's name. "With the divorce, I mean. Do you think it was a mistake?"

Ezra collapsed onto the couch in the living area. This conversation had been years in the making. During the divorce, Ezra had flown back to California to help Miles move out of his and Mei's old house. He'd gone to view nearly two dozen condos all over the Bay Area so Miles didn't have to make the decision alone. Every day he'd told Miles he could talk to him whenever he wanted, but Miles had always put on a thin smile and refused. He'd stuck to the story that he and Mei had made a mutual and mature decision; no friend therapy necessary. But three years later, he seemed to feel differently.

"I can't answer that for you, Miles," Ezra said, quietly. "But if you're rethinking the decision, maybe it's time you talked to her."

"Yeah, maybe," he said unconvincingly.

Ezra felt the hypocrisy of his statement as he was saying it. Why had he never given himself this advice with Candace? Maybe not in college when even the thought of her made his entire body flush. But why not after Miles and Mei's wedding, or when they started hooking up each year? Why hadn't he tried then? Those questions made him think about what Candace had said on the airport curb.

*I told him to tell you to email me.*

"Hey, Miles, can I ask you a question?" Ezra said tentatively.

"Yeah, of course." He sounded excited to change topics.

"Do you remember—"

"I remember everything," Miles said, sounding like his regular, cocky self.

Ezra hoped that was a lie as much as the truth. "Do you remember our last semester of college?"

"Barely," Miles interjected, contradicting himself. Ezra rolled his eyes. "We were in the library every day. Everything just kind of blurred together."

Ezra nodded, because that was true. Ezra had been finishing his submission to the Gilder prize, Miles had two internships and Mei was writing her undergraduate thesis.

"Not all of us," Ezra corrected. "Candace was in Ecuador."

"True."

Ezra swallowed. "Did Candace ever...? Before she left, did Candace tell you that I should email her?"

"Why would she tell me? Why not Mei?"

Ezra shook his head and ran his free hand through his hair again. "Right? I know. But... did she? Did she like, pull you aside or send an email after she arrived or something?"

"Nah. Can didn't email anyone while she was gone. She was on her 'eat, pray, love' tip."

Ezra didn't want to call Candace a liar because she never had been. But maybe she was mistaken, he thought to himself. Maybe she thought she'd said something to Miles but hadn't. There had to be an explanation.

And then Miles started. "Oh shit," he said. Ezra's stomach dropped and he felt queasy. "Yeah, she called the house phone from the airport. She was looking for you."

Ezra jumped up from the couch, his heart pounding in his chest.

"You went to get breakfast bagels from the diner and Mei was still passed out. But I told you about that, right?"

Ezra was blinking so fast he could barely see. "No," he ground out. "You never told me that."

"You sure?" Miles asked, incredulous.

"Yes. I'm sure. If you'd told me I'd have emailed her."

"Wait." Miles said, "You didn't email her while she was gone? Like at all?"

"She said she wanted to disconnect."

"Yeah, I know. She was all dramatic back then. But, like, she was our friend, Ezra. Even I emailed her a few times. I mean... they were mostly just funny chain emails, but I still kept in touch. I didn't want her to think I'd forgotten about her."

"I..." Ezra couldn't finish the sentence; he was so overcome with conflicting emotions.

Miles sighed. "Look, I'm sorry I didn't tell you about her phone call. I was hungover, but that's not an excuse. I knew how in love with her you were. Not that you ever admitted it to me. But..." There was a pregnant pause and Ezra wanted to crawl out of his skin. "The thing I've never gotten about you two is how fucking obvious you were."

"What do you mean?"

"I mean," Miles said carefully, "you used to turn the same shade as a cooked lobster every time she came around. And whenever you dipped from a party, if anyone needed to find you, I always just sent them straight to Candace, because she was basically a homing pigeon for you."

"What?" Ezra breathed.

"Everyone knew you two loved each other *except* y'all and I never could understand how that was possible."

"I didn't... I didn't know."

"Did you not know? Or was it that you couldn't

accept that someone like her might be interested in someone like you?"

Ezra didn't answer and he didn't have to. They both knew the answer to that question. "But why didn't she...?" he asked in another half-formed question.

Miles laughed sadly. "Maybe we both need to talk to Mei. We might be divorced but it's not my place to divulge stuff she told me in confidence that Candace told her knowing she'd only tell me. But with that said, you might want to consider why you always put Candace on a pedestal."

Ezra frowned again. "Of course I put her on a pedestal. She was smart and funny and the sexiest person in our class."

"Well that's rude, because I was hella sexy in college," Miles said, trying to lighten the mood. It might have worked under other circumstances, but Ezra's entire world felt as if it had been turned upside down. "Look, Candace was great. Candace still is great. But she's human and you never let her just be regular and flawed. Not in college and not after."

"What does that mean?"

"It means that maybe if you'd let Candace step on solid ground, you'd have realized that she could have had damn near any guy in college, but she kept choosing you. She kept holding out hope for you. But did you ever choose her? Like, really choose her?"

"I—"

"Nah, don't answer me now. Think about it. Just really think about it. And whenever you have an answer, how about you call Candace and tell her instead of me?" Miles said sagely.

Ezra swallowed and nodded. "Okay," he said finally. But remembering why Miles had told him to call him, he said, "And maybe you should think about calling Mei."

Miles huffed out another one of those sad laughs and they said goodbye.

Ezra looked at the clock on his phone. Now that he was fully awake, he needed to get dressed and spend some time preparing for his meeting. But instead of rushing off to the bathroom, he stood at the floor-to-ceiling windows and looked across the city and thought about all the things Miles had told him.

He thought about all the missed opportunities. All the ways he might have done things differently. All the time they'd wasted. And he wondered if Candace was right, that this was really the way things were meant to be.

# CHAPTER 7

"There he is," Tommy said, as soon as Ezra stepped off the elevator into the hotel lobby.

Ezra's steps faltered as he came face-to-face with his COO and Board of Directors and the relief in their eyes. They'd probably been terrified he wouldn't show up today since he hadn't returned their calls or emails until this morning. There was so much riding on this meeting and he never would have put them through that kind of uncertainty under normal circumstances. But seeing Candace on his flight was as far from normal circumstances as he could imagine.

He'd never put his emotional turmoil on their shoulders, however, so he smiled at them and pushed aside the bone-deep weariness he hadn't been able to wash away or sleep off.

"Good morning, everyone. I'm sorry I was MIA yesterday."

"Is everything okay?" Martina asked tentatively.

"Everything's fine. I just had a... difficult flight and I was exhausted when I landed. But I'm here. You're here," he said, gesturing toward the assembled group, "and we're gonna get this deal hammered out and signed. Alright?"

Martina and some of the rest of the Board smiled back at him, visibly relaxing, while others tensed a fraction more. He could understand both reactions.

"Did breakfast arrive?" Ezra asked, gesturing toward the boardroom. "Come on, let's eat and get started." He ushered them into the boardroom. He took a deep breath and closed the double doors behind them.

Just as the boardroom doors closed, Candace wheeled her suitcase into the hotel lobby. She'd barely slept the night before. She'd showered and re-packed her suitcase while the sky was dark and then sat on her bed, waiting for the sun to rise so she could leave. She left a message for Jorge with the address of her new hotel and then headed out into the city.

She could have taken a cab, but Candace needed the walk to clear her head. She'd always loved walking in the city early in the morning. She'd done it more times than she could count while a student here, meandering through the streets as she pored over her anxieties and fears and sometimes cried, passing off her tears as sweat in the perpetually warm climate.

As she headed toward the city center, she thought about all those walks before, trying to quantify how many of them had been about Ezra, losing herself in the past as the once familiar city came to life around her. There were hardly any tourists out besides herself, and that too felt familiar. She felt buffeted by the cars speeding past her on the sometimes narrow streets, the smells of cooking food, a baby crying somewhere in the distance and the melodic Spanish she could only understand in snatches. Mostly, she felt anonymous. Some people turned to her with a smile or a confused stare, but just as many went on with their morning routines, navigating around her and her suitcase deftly and with hopefully only minor annoyance.

The closer she got to her hotel, the more important it seemed for her to remind herself why she'd accepted this flight from Sarah. When she was twenty-one, Quito had seemed like a refuge. She'd originally applied for the study abroad to strengthen her Spanish and she'd thought it would look good on job applications. She'd imagined it as a semester-long break from reality as she prepared for the future. But Quito became like a warm blanket that she threw over herself as all of her plans back home fell apart.

Candace had decided against going home the day after Ezra's one and only email and a month after being rejected from every job and internship she'd applied to. She met an itinerant bartender and hooked up with him, hoping to bury her heartbreak in a whirlwind romance that was more whirlwind than romantic, because all she'd really wanted was to run away from all her failures.

It was heartbreaking to be back and immediately

confronted with all the ways very little had changed in her life. She was employed but still unsure what she wanted to do with her life. She still felt as if she hadn't realized all the potential her parents had fought to cultivate in her and protect. And while she was still in love with Ezra Posner, she felt certain that whatever window of opportunity for them to get their relationship on the right track had long since closed. Candace felt like a failure in too many ways to count.

She arrived at her hotel with little to show for her walk besides a sore shoulder from steering her heavy suitcase down the street, a sweaty back and a vague triumph that while her Spanish comprehension wasn't as strong as it used to be, it wasn't so bad that Dr. Montero would think he'd failed her. And at the very least, that made her smile as she stepped up to the hotel's front desk.

"Checking in?" the concierge asked in English.

"Yes," she said, "but I'm early. I understand if my room isn't available."

"We can check. Name?"

Candace waited as he checked his computer. She looked around and her eyes latched onto someone in a uniform carrying a carafe of coffee into a room across the lobby.

"You're in luck," he said, pulling her attention back to the front desk. "Your room is ready and you're welcome to check in early."

Candace smiled. "Perfect. Thank you. Oh, do you have dry cleaning services?"

"We do. We can come pick it up for you or you can take it to housekeeping yourself."

"I can bring it down after I get into my room. Where is it?"

He gestured. "It's just across the lobby there. On the other side of the elevators."

"Okay, thanks," she said with a smile. And on its own volition, the smile stayed on her face as she handed over her passport and credit card and took the elevator up to the third floor — the highest floor she could afford — and pulled her dirty uniform from her bag.

As she headed back down to the lobby, Candace rode the wave of a few minutes of good news and accepted that if she really wanted to know what was next for her, she had make decisions she'd been avoiding for too long in the vain hope that the uniform would show her the way. She'd come to Quito the first time and waited; waited for Ezra to email her, waited for one of the jobs she'd applied for to pan out; waited for all of her hard work to pay off. It hadn't. And while it had rocked her, it hadn't killed her. And that was what mattered.

She didn't know where Ezra was and she couldn't worry about that. She'd spent almost twenty years putting her life on hold or veering wildly off-track because of him. Not anymore. That relationship had broken her heart so many times before that there was nothing left to break. She might always love Ezra, but that wasn't enough. Love hadn't been enough for Mei and Miles; she'd been a fool to imagine that it could be different for her and Ezra.

As she pulled the door open to housekeeping, Candace made her first New Year's Eve resolution ever. In the future she just wanted to be *less* of a fool for love. Baby steps, she thought to herself with a smile.

~

"Alright, now your pensions," Ezra said. "This is the biggest issue for me."

"I agree," Martina said.

"If this goes wrong, I don't want anyone to lose their retirement."

"No one wants that," Tommy interjected. "But the pensions are our collateral. We can't afford the company without it."

"You can if you buy five per cent less of the company," Ezra said as he made deliberate eye contact with every member of the Board.

This had been the sticking point in their negotiations for months. They might have been able to close the deal a full four months ago but for the issue of how to protect his employees' retirement funds. Ezra had built his company from the ground up. He'd personally hired every person in this room. He believed in them and they'd believed in his vision. This company meant so much to him because of these people and he only wanted to do what was right. The buyout they were negotiating would make him richer certainly, but would also give his employees a share of the profits their collective labor had created. This move was the only reason he'd taken the company public; maximizing their worth so he could transfer a controlling stake to his employees.

It wasn't a benevolent decision, even though he knew that's how tech magazines would spin it as soon as the sale went public. But as far as Ezra was concerned, this was fair. This was right. And his old hippy parents would appreciate it.

But however important this sale was, and however unsure the future, he wasn't comfortable risking his employees' retirements in the process. Unfortunately, the only way to underwrite the offer without asking them to raise more money was to use their pensions as collateral. But if they bought fifty two percent, they wouldn't be gambling their entire futures on the company not collapsing in the foreseeable future.

Ezra would never be able to live with himself if their company failed and his employees were left destitute because he hadn't been vigilant on this point.

"You'll still have controlling interest," he said carefully and not for the first time.

"But there are more of us than you," Tommy said.

"True. And I understand you want to give each other the short-term benefit of more profits, but I want to make sure you're set long after this deal and long after one of our rivals improves on our ideas.

You know how this industry works. Once we unveil the new engine, it's out there. Soon enough, someone is going to think of something we didn't and find a way to make it work better." Everyone at the table squirmed in their seats. "Look, I'm not saying we can't weather that storm. I'm just saying that right now we have the opportunity to make this deal happen *and* prepare for the worst-case scenario. That's all I want."

The room was silent and he wanted to keep explaining himself, but he'd been harping on this point for so long that they all knew his stance. Everyone around the table, representing every area of the company from R&D to maintenance, knew his position. Some agreed with him, some didn't, and he couldn't browbeat the latter into becoming the former. He knew that and he hated it. He reached for the cup of coffee on the table in front of him and brought it to his lips to give them time to think.

He wasn't sure if it was the jetlag, the tension in the room or the lingering emotional turmoil of the past day, but he missed his mouth and poured black coffee onto his button-down shirt instead of into his mouth.

"Shit," he said, jumping from his seat.

Nearly everyone at the table either pushed their napkins toward him frantically.

"It's okay," Ezra said with a laugh. He lifted a calming hand and dabbed at the stain on his chest. "Remember this is why I shouldn't be your boss. Who knows what I'll spill on our next prototype?"

The joke seemed to release some of the tension between them.

"Look, I'm going to go change. I'll be back in a few

minutes. Eat some more breakfast and talk. And make a decision." He smiled. "But whatever you decide, I'll go along with it. You don't have to agree with me just because I'm the boss. And soon enough I won't even be that." They all smiled at him as he walked from the room.

Ezra rushed up to the penthouse to change his shirt. But he didn't hurry back, wanting to give the Board as much time as possible to come to a decision. He took his time checking his email and his phone, hoping for a text from Miles or Mei, or even — the saddest, most pathetic part of his heart hoped — Candace. He was disappointed three times. Just before he walked out of his room, he grabbed his shirt, deciding to take it to housekeeping while he was stalling.

Back in the lobby, he marched to the front desk and was immediately directed to housekeeping.

His eyes darted to the boardroom doors as he passed, his shirt clutched in his hand. He ran his other hand through his hair and took a deep breath as he walked around the elevators, pushed the door open and froze.

"How long will it take?" Candace asked the woman behind the counter.

"We can have it ready later today," the woman responded in accented English.

"Oh, there's no rush, I'm here for a few days," Candace said, shaking her head.

"Okay. We can bring it to your room when we clean tomorrow, if you like."

"Oh, that's perfect," Candace said. "Gracias."

"Si," the woman responded.

Candace turned from the desk and froze. Ezra heard the sharp intake of breath when she saw him.

"What are you doing here?" she asked in a whisper.

"This is my hotel," Ezra said in shock. "What are you doing here?"

"You own hotels now?" she asked, as if that was the most pressing issue. As if any of his material possessions mattered more than the fact that for the second time in two days, he and Candace were in the same place at the same time by accident.

That couldn't be a coincidence and Ezra refused to let this moment pass without fighting for Candace; something he should have done long ago.

# CHAPTER 8

*C*andace didn't believe in fate. She couldn't. There were too many things that could go wrong in life, so many decisions she could make or not make, so many paths she could take and then regret. There were so many things that seemed certain, but in the end weren't. She'd lived that. She'd lived that with Ezra. If Candace had ever believed in fate, the past decade of having Ezra right at her fingertips but never being able to fully keep him had cemented in her mind that nothing was promised. And Miles and Mei's divorce had shown that nothing written in the stars was permanent. So her brain just couldn't understand why Ezra was standing in front of her right now.

When she'd decided on this trip, a few nights at a relatively affordable luxury hotel had been a splurge. It wasn't the most expensive hotel in the city, but it was the best she could afford and she'd thought that if she was going to spend New Year's Eve crying, she wanted to do it on the best cotton sheets the hotel had to offer. All she'd wanted was a soft place to land while she got over Ezra. But here he was, standing in front of her, looking somehow even sexier than the last time she'd seen him, which was supposed to be the last time she'd see him.

"When did you move into hotels? Mei never told me that," Candace said, shaking her head.

"I don't tell Mei all my business moves," Ezra replied.

"But you tell Miles everything. And he tells Mei." She hesitated. "Told," she corrected, with a cringe.

Ezra flinched at the word as well. "I bought this place last year," he said, gently. "After the divorce."

"Got it," she nodded, looking everywhere but at his face.

He stepped toward her and she was too shocked to move away. Or maybe shock was just the excuse she used not to have to step away.

"What are you doing here, Candace?" he whispered.

She wished he hadn't. She wished he'd asked her that question in his regular voice instead of dropping to that deep whisper that she associated with the middle of the night, his mouth on her bare skin and his sweat-slicked body moving against hers, inside hers. She couldn't handle being reminded of that in this too-bright room.

She swallowed and focused her gaze on his shoulder. "I wanted to treat myself for New Year's."

"So you'll be here for New Year's too?"

Her eyes lifted sharply to his, which was a mistake, because for some reason in this moment, Ezra looked like he had in college. His blue eyes sparkled in the fluorescent light, the tops of his cheeks were a soft red, and the corners of his mouth had lifted into that almost grin that wasn't a grimace but also wasn't a real smile. For a disorienting moment she felt eighteen again, and the full force of the crush that had never really gone away washed over her.

"You're here for the new year?" she whispered back.

He nodded, absentmindedly, his eyes focused on her mouth. She watched him watch her and knew that she should put some distance between them; that this was a mistake. But she couldn't move, not until the door behind them burst open and they had to jump out of the way of a luggage rack.

The moment was enough to clear Candace's head. She couldn't go back. Not even if she wanted to. She stepped out of the incoming porter's way, surreptitiously putting distance between herself and Ezra. The man pulled a stack of laundry bags into the room and Candace watched him primarily to avoid having to look at Ezra.

And then she felt his hand brush her wrist, his touch so light she could have imagined it. Candace shivered.

When she turned to Ezra, he was smiling at her like she used to wish he would. Like when he opened his mouth it would be to tell her that he loved her and couldn't live without her. But he never did. And she'd lived in this puddle of disappointment before.

She took another step back, shaking her head.

"What's your room number?" he asked.

"No. I meant what I said yesterday, Ezra. We should just let this end."

He swallowed and gripped his right hand in his left, like he used to when he was nervous or uncomfortable. His eyes weren't sparkling anymore; they were dark and sad. "I don't know why we just keep missing each other," he said mournfully.

She sucked in a sharp breath. She felt as if her entire body was breaking, now that her heart was nothing but dust.

"But we're in the same city on New Year's. In the same hotel," he said, his tone brightening.

"Your hotel," she corrected.

His eyebrows furrowed. "My hotel. In the city you love."

"I haven't been here in years and my Spanish isn't even that good anymore. Dr. Montero would be so pissed at me," she said, and he laughed.

"He's probably still pissed at me. Did I ever tell you that I ran into him a few years ago?"

Candace shook her head.

He smiled and Candace swallowed a moan.

"Yeah," Ezra continued, "and he only spoke to me in really basic Spanish, and super slow at that. By the end, he just looked so disappointed in me. Like as a person. He's probably still depressed that he never got through to me."

Candace smiled. "Probably."

Ezra's eyes only darted to her mouth briefly. "I used to wish I'd come on that study abroad trip with you back in college."

She squinted at him. "You couldn't have done that. The Gilder Prize."

"I know," he said quickly, his eyes boring into hers, "but I still used to dream about it."

That Candace didn't shiver when he looked at her that way and said that he'd dreamt about her — about being in Quito with her — was a herculean effort she knew she wouldn't be able to repeat.

"I have to go," she said abruptly and moved past him.

"What's your room number?" he asked again, following her out of housekeeping.

"No, Ezra."

"Okay, what are you doing tonight?" he asked, jogging around her to block her path. He put his arms out to stop her from moving. "I'm here on business and we're having a party in the ballroom tonight. It's on the mezzanine floor."

"No, Ezra," she said again, unsure of what else to say and unable to trust herself with anything more.

"The party starts at eight. I'll put you on the list."

She shook her head.

"And a plus one. You can bring your friend from the airplane. Jorge?"

"Ezra—" she started, but he cut her off.

"No. I know. But..." He blinked at her. His face and neck were red and she could see the tension in the way a vein on his forehead had appeared. She forced herself to ignore that bone-deep desire she always felt to pull him into her arms and soothe him.

"This can't be a coincidence, Candace. You and me in the same place at the same time over New Year's Eve like always. My entire adult life, New Year's Eve has been about you and I've never felt right when we weren't together."

She wrapped her arms around her torso to ground herself. "What are you saying?"

"What I should have said four years ago, and eight years ago, and eighteen years ago at that dumb bonfire. Ever since the day we met, it's always been you. I know I might be way too late but I... if I'm not... I'm asking you to come to the party tonight and talk to me. If we talk and you still think this is the end..." he swallowed thickly, "then I'll respect that. Or if you just want to be friends again, I'd love that. Because I've missed making love to you, but fuck I've missed just being your friend too."

Candace blinked at him, her eyesight blurry with the tears spilling over her cheeks.

"Ezra," someone called.

He turned and Candace saw a short brown-skinned woman in a business suit looking at them. Candace took the opportunity to wipe her face and take a quick breath. Her heart was pounding.

"I'm coming, Martina. Sorry. I'll be there in just a minute."

The woman nodded and walked away.

He turned back to her. His pupils were dilated and his face was red. He really did look like his old self again and it made her heart clench. "I have to go," he said in a soft voice.

She nodded.

"Eight o'clock. Please, just consider it."

He looked at her with a kind of intensity she'd never seen from him; at least not when he was fully clothed. She knew she should say no. She'd just this morning convinced herself of the rightness of moving on. But she wanted to say yes. She always wanted to say yes when it came to Ezra.

"I'll consider it," she said in a choked voice.

His face lit up and he started walking backwards; as if he was running away just in case she changed her mind. And knowing Ezra, that was exactly what he was thinking.

"I hope I see you tonight," he said before he pulled the boardroom door open and disappeared inside.

When the door closed, Candace blinked rapidly, trying to understand what had just happened as the hotel lobby seemed to come back to life around her. All of a sudden, the lights seemed too bright, the lobby seemed unnaturally loud; everything was too much. She pressed the button to call the elevator to go back to her room.

She needed to talk to Mei.

*E*zra was looking at her again. She could feel it. She was Mei's maid of honor and lots of people were looking at her. Mei's cousin Karen was currently glaring in her direction, still angry that Candace had apparently taken her place. Miles's creepy childhood best friend was also looking at her — staring, more likely — as if he wanted to maybe kidnap her and tie her up. But it was Ezra's gaze she could feel on her skin like a cashmere blanket; soft, warm and arousing. It always had been. His deep blue eyes always felt as if the pads of his fingers were coasting over her skin. It made the hair on her arms stand up and her nipples hard and after three years apart, it made her wet.

Ever since they'd all arrived in Napa for Miles and Mei's wedding, Candace felt as if Ezra had been just on the edge of her peripheral vision as they stood by their best friends at the rehearsal dinner and for all the pre-wedding activities. Their hotel rooms were in different wings of the hotel, but Candace could have sworn that every time she stood waiting in the lobby at the East elevator bank and she looked to her right, there was Ezra, waiting at the West elevator bank.

She'd turn and there he'd be, not looking at her. But her skin would still be tingling as if he had been. Or maybe that was just her heart and imagination playing tricks on her.

Still, everywhere she turned, Ezra was right there. He hadn't spoken more than a few words to her since she'd first arrived. To be fair, there really hadn't been much time for a casual catch-up about their lives for the past three years because Mei had scheduled her wedding weekend down to the second and she was a ruthless taskmaster. No one was going to ruin her schedule. And while Miles didn't care nearly as much about the itinerary besides the ceremony and reception, he adored Mei and so stood next to his future wife and glared at everyone, making it clear that anyone who threatened her plans would have to answer to him.

But now the ceremony was seconds from starting and there was Ezra. And while he wouldn't have to talk to her, they would have to touch. And this time there was no confusion; Ezra was watching her. The other bridesmaids and groomsmen were pairing up. Miles's mother was putting them in the correct order and checking the men's ties and suits, making sure they looked their best.

"Come on Candace, Ezra. You're next," Mrs. Jefferson called to them.

Candace smiled, trying to ignore the fact that her stomach was doing flips. She stepped into line behind Karen and Miles's favorite cousin, Devonte. Karen turned to glare over her shoulder at Candace one last time. Candace smiled smugly at her in return. But then the sleeve of Ezra's tuxedo grazed her forearm and Candace shivered. She turned to him. He wasn't looking at her now, but his left cheek and ear were bright red. He was blushing. About her, probably. *That* was the Ezra she knew. She smiled at his profile and he turned to her — almost as if he'd been watching her in *his* peripheral vision — and they locked eyes.

"Alright," Mrs. Jefferson said, "it's time!"

Candace and Ezra turned to watch her cup Miles's face in her hands, beaming up at him. Candace smiled at the sweet tableau. Miles bent down to let his mother kiss both of his cheeks and then smile up at him one more time, before walking into the hall to her seat. Once she was out of earshot, Miles turned to them, the glare back on his face.

"Alright people, you heard my mama. It's show-time. All y'all gotta do is walk semi-on beat down the aisle and stand still while me and Mei do all the hard work. If you mess this up, you're dead to me. But I love you all. Let's go!"

They all watched him with opened mouths until the music started and the first couple began to walk down the aisle.

"How was that?" Miles whispered to her and Ezra. Candace grimaced at him.

"Terrible," Ezra said.

"You said we'd be dead to you," Candace added.

"*If* you can't walk kinda on beat," Miles shrugged. "That's a low bar."

"I really hope you and Mei go back to normal after this," Candace said.

Miles smiled at them and clapped Ezra on the shoulder. "So do we. This bridezilla thing is weird. And apparently contagious. Anyway, make me proud," Miles said, shooing them forward.

She and Ezra shook their heads and turned around. They inched forward slowly, waiting for their turn to walk down the aisle. Together. When Karen and Devonte were off, Ezra turned to her and held out his arm. Candace tentatively moved her hand to his forearm. She held her breath as they touched and she ran her hand from the inside of his elbow up to his bicep. Her touch was light, tentative, but she heard him hiss at the contact. She did the same.

"Go," Miles whispered behind them.

They stepped forward and began to walk mostly on beat down the aisle. Everyone was watching them but for Candace, it was all a blur. The entirety of her focus was on the solid presence of Ezra to her right, his hard bicep — much harder than she might have expected — under her hand and the spicy scent of his cologne. It was near overwhelming.

They hadn't seen each other in three years. And

over the past few months her happiness at watching their friends get married had warred with her apprehension about what it would be like to be face-to-face with him again. She worried that he might be cold; that he might not blush when he saw her anymore. She wondered if her response to him would change as well. If she would feel the same flutter in her chest when she saw him. The good news was that he still blushed adorably and the bad news was that she still loved it.

"You look beautiful," Ezra whispered to her at the head of the aisle, just before they separated.

Candace gasped. Her hand dragged down his arm and she stepped left as he stepped right. She walked to her place at the head of the line of bridesmaids and then turned, her mouth still open, to look at him and found him aiming that small grimace at her; that level one smile that she loved.

Three years and it was as if nothing in her heart had changed at all.

$\sim$

*E*zra's knee was bouncing. He was sitting at the head table, listening to Miles's creepy childhood friend, Bobby, talk about his collection of sword replicas, but watching Candace across the room. She was standing in line with Miles and Mei's moms for more dessert, chatting excitedly at them. It was adorable. She was adorable. She was beautiful. He'd missed her.

All he'd been thinking about for months was seeing her. Sure, he'd been ecstatic to see their friends get married, and true to form it was a beautiful production, but nothing was more beautiful than Candace. Especially not Candace in her bridesmaid's dress. He'd been a tense wreck all day watching her, her sparkling dark brown eyes glassy with tears as Miles and Mei said their vows; the sheen of her gorgeous skin in the sunlight as the wedding party took pictures, and the sound of her laughter.

He hadn't been sure what he would do when he saw her again after all this time. Probably nothing. Ezra might have been older. He might have let Miles force him into the gym so he didn't have to lift weights alone and had accidentally developed a few more muscles than he'd had in college. He might even have been on the verge of securing his first funder. But with Candace in front of him, he had to face the uncomfortable truth that he was still the same eighteen-year-old kid who could hardly think in her presence.

But it had been three years since they'd seen one another and his excitement was doused with fear. What if they left the wedding and it was another three years before they saw each other again? What if it was longer than that? What if they *never* saw each other again? He realized that that kind of doomsday thinking didn't make any sense and yet there had always been something about Candace that reminded him of the passage of time. Unfortunately, it never spurred him into action. He never asked her out like he wanted to and when he'd finally almost mustered up the courage, it was too late. That was the lesson about time that Candace taught him again and again; that there was never enough of it.

"You know what I mean?" Bobby asked.

Ezra turned to him and frowned. He shook his head. "Nope. Excuse me," he said hastily and stood from his chair.

"Where you going?" Miles called out to him.

"Dessert," Ezra said, when the right answer was Candace.

"Ooh, can you bring us some cupcakes?" Mei asked, leaning over Miles to smile at him.

Ezra sighed. "Yeah, sure," he said and then slipped off the raised dais.

He walked through the crowd toward her. His path was direct. Normally, he might have skirted along the edges of the ballroom but he was worried that if he took his time, someone might intercept him or whisk her onto the dancefloor or maybe she'd simply disappear. He couldn't take that chance. Not this time.

He let out a relieved huff of a breath when he made it to her.

"Ezra," Mrs. Jefferson exclaimed.

Candace turned to him.

"There you are," Mrs. Barnes said. "We were just talking about you."

He frowned. "You were?" His eyes darted to Candace. She looked quickly away.

"Yes," Mrs. Jefferson said. "We were saying how sad it was that your parents couldn't make it."

He hid his disappointment well. "Yeah, they sent a gift but they're on a cruise to celebrate mom's official remission news."

Mrs. Barnes reached up to Ezra. He stooped down to let her pat his cheek softly. "So lucky," she whispered at him.

He smiled at her and then stood up straight to smile at Mrs. Jefferson who rubbed his other cheek lovingly.

"How's your mom doing?" Candace asked.

Her voice made his stomach clench. He turned to her, nodding. "She's good. Really good. She misses you," he said. It was maybe underhanded. He didn't want to guilt-trip her, but his mother had missed her. And he'd missed her too. But he couldn't quite say that to her face, even if he was forcing himself to be bolder than he'd ever been. To tell her that he'd missed her, that he'd thought about her nearly every day, and maybe even ask her if she remembered their last night together? That was too much for the dessert table at their best friends' wedding in front of the mothers of the bride and groom.

But as he was internally spinning, Candace just smiled at him, "Yeah, I've missed her too."

"Are your parents here?" he asked.

Her smile widened and she turned to the dance-floor. Ezra followed the shift of her body but his eyes lingered on her profile a few seconds longer than was probably appropriate. When he did turn to look, he laughed. He wasn't sure how he'd missed Candace's parents slow dancing to a fast song in the middle of the dancefloor, but she was so beautiful there could have been a fistfight next to him and he might never have known.

"They're cute, huh?" she asked, turning to him and lifting her eyebrows.

He smiled and nodded.

"Are you single, Ezra?" Mrs. Jefferson asked.

He and Candace turned away from one another quickly. His ears warmed. "Um, Mei and Miles said they wanted cupcakes."

It was a cheap fake, but it was the exact thing he needed to get the older women's attention away from him and his pathetic love life.

"Did they say what kind?" Mrs. Barnes asked.

Ezra shrugged.

"We'll just grab one of each," Mrs. Jefferson said.

"Good idea."

Candace and Ezra stepped back and watched as they filled two plates with every dessert on the table and ferried them across the room to their newly married children.

"Smart," Candace whispered to him. "Meddling elders need a definitive target for attention."

"They did ask for cupcakes," Ezra said.

"So everyone's happy," she shrugged, turning back to the dessert table.

Not everyone, he wanted to say. Not yet.

"There's gonna be a fireworks show," he said abruptly.

"Yeah, I know. I got the itinerary too. All five single-spaced pages of it," she said around a laugh.

"Are you going to stay for them?" he asked, swallowing thickly.

"Yeah, of course. Where else would I go?"

"My hotel room," he blurted out.

She turned to him with a frown and then shifted her weight to her right leg, putting her left hand on her hip. "Excuse me?"

Ezra's entire body felt as if it was overheating. Had he really just said what he'd said?

"Are you propositioning me, Ezra Posner?" she asked with a soft, unsure smile.

He shook his head. His throat felt as if it had closed. He didn't think he could say anything else. He wasn't even sure if he was breathing.

"No?" She raised her eyebrows at him.

He started nodding his head.

"So you are propositioning me? I wouldn't have thought you had it in you."

And maybe it was that he, too, hadn't thought he'd had it in him. Or that now that he'd said the words, there was no taking them back and he didn't want to. Or maybe it was the way she said his full name. He'd always loved that. The way it sounded on her lips. The way her voice crawled under his skin and made him feel strong and weak all at the same time. The shock he felt — even after all this time — that Candace Garret knew who he was.

He swallowed thickly and clenched his fists. "We can watch the fireworks from my room."

Her lips quirked. "The show doesn't start for another hour. What do you think we should do until then?"

He swallowed again and decided to be as bold as ever because, even though his entire brain felt as if it had shut down, he was older, slightly more built and on the verge of bringing his Gilder Prize project to reality. So he wasn't entirely the same person he'd been three years ago.

"We can do whatever you want," he said in a slow, hesitant voice. And then he stepped forward, closing the distance between them. "But I was thinking we could finish what we started last time we were together."

"You remember that, huh?" she asked, and her eyes were bright, her pupils dilated.

"Of course I remember that," he said, his eyebrows bunching. And then he smiled. "I hope we didn't traumatize Teddy."

Candace's peal of laughter was deep and husky and it made his balls ache. Then she licked her lips and lifted her hand. Her index finger grazed the top of his bow tie, her nail just barely pricking the underside of his chin.

"Lead the way," she whispered in that dark honey

voice she'd used when she was teaching him how to eat her out.

It took a few seconds for him to process her words, but when he did, he smiled at her in relief. He grabbed her hand and led her from the ballroom.

They'd done all their maid of honor and best man duties. Miles and Mei probably wouldn't even miss them for the rest of the evening. And knowing those two, they'd probably slip out of here soon anyway. Whatever guilt Ezra felt about leaving early disappeared in front of the West elevator bank. He pressed the call button and Candace pressed her body to his side. Every part of him became rock hard and hot. He hadn't felt like this in years. Three years to be exact.

The elevator doors opened. He led her inside and pressed the button to the twelfth floor as he squeezed her hand in his.

~

For the past three years, Candace had travelled from Ecuador to Nicaragua, Jamaica, Mexico (to get to Cuba without having her passport stamped), Puerto Rico, New York, Toronto, Vancouver and then home. She hadn't planned any leg of that travel except the last part. Mei had asked her to be her maid of honor over Skype. She'd emailed Candace's official invitation. Candace had sent her measurements by email to Mei and Candace's cousin Lisa — who was a similar height and weight — had stood in at her fittings. Mei didn't care as long as Candace made it to the wedding. That was her only request. And she'd only had to ask once, because there was no way Candace would miss Miles and Mei's wedding. There was no way she could bear to miss seeing Ezra one more time.

But she'd thought all she'd do was look, because that's all she'd really been accustomed to doing in college. Except for those three nights when there had been hugs and a little light making out, and that one time when they'd defiled Teddy. But now Ezra was holding her hand, leading her down the hall to his hotel room, turning every now and then to smile at her as if to reassure himself that she was still there. She squeezed his hand and their warm palms pressed together, because she needed to be reminded that this was real too.

When Ezra's hotel room door closed behind them, the quiet was deafening. She blinked into the darkness and gasped when she felt his soft breath on her skin. His lips tentatively touched her back just at the top of her spine. She moaned as his wet tongue traced the skin over her right shoulder before his forehead pressed against her skin and his big hands settled on her waist.

She'd had dreams like this, but she'd never believed they'd come true.

His breath was ragged against her skin. This wasn't the Ezra she knew. The boy who'd been blushing at her longer than she could remember right up until a few hours ago. This new Ezra was more like the Ezra of her dreams. The Ezra she'd been carrying around with her all over the Americas. The Ezra she sometimes conjured to mind when she touched herself or even when she fucked her ex-boyfriend. The Ezra she'd wanted so desperately she could taste him on her tongue, imagining what he would feel like in her hand and mouth and pussy since she'd never gotten the chance.

But she didn't have to settle for dream Ezra, she realized. For the first time in so long, he was right behind her. Holding her.

She turned in his arms and he stepped back just enough to let her move. But he never let her go. She swallowed a groan as his hands rubbed along her waist and over her stomach, his hard body still so close. His eyes were focused on her mouth and she sucked her bottom lip between her teeth.

Ezra groaned.

Candace smiled. God, she'd missed him. She raised her hands to his chest and lifted her right eyebrow. "You been lifting weights, Ezra?"

His chest hitched before he spoke. "Miles made me start going to the gym with him."

She smiled. "Just like he used to make you come to our dorm room freshman year?"

His fingers flexed and dug into her hips. "He never had to make me come to your room," he whispered.

It was her turn for her chest to hitch. She leaned into his body, the smell of his cologne engulfing her as she pressed herself to him. The hard points of her silk-covered nipples touched him first. Her mouth fell open on a soft sigh. Her hands moved up his chest to glide around his neck, and then her fingers sunk into the hair at his nape. "God, Ezra," she whispered just as he captured her mouth with his own.

Candace wouldn't have said that Ezra had been her best kiss ever, especially not that first kiss. But what she could say was that every kiss with him was always better than the last. And this kiss was by far the best. Not because it was perfect, but because they poured themselves wholeheartedly into it. Candace loved Ezra's awkwardness, his blushing, all that nervous energy and banked intensity, and this kiss was that times infinity. He plied Candace's lips open with his own and slipped his tongue into her mouth, groaning when her tongue eagerly met his. She smiled and he kissed her deeper, gripped her hips tighter and pulled her close. Candace sighed and wrapped her arms around his neck, meeting every thrust of his tongue and press of his lips with equal fervor, reveling in a kiss she'd been too scared to hope for. As Ezra kissed her, she let her bruised heart imagine that he'd missed her almost as much as she'd missed him.

*But he never contacted you,* some poor bitter part of her mind reminded her. She pulled back from him sharply and Ezra immediately stepped back, letting go of her waist.

"Did I do something wrong?" he asked quickly.

She shook her head. "No, I just..."

The light blinked on and Ezra turned from the

switch on the wall to peer at her with worry in his eyes. She blinked at him. She wanted to ask him why he'd never emailed her during that final semester or in the past three years. She wanted to ask him if, errant New Year's Eve behavior aside, she'd completely made up their friendship, because that was the only thing that made his complete radio silence make any kind of sense. She wanted to ask him why she only ever heard about what he was up to through Facebook or second-hand from Miles via Mei. She wanted to ask him how it was possible that he could look at her right now, dilated pupils, flushed cheeks and a prominent mound in his pants, as if he'd been waiting for this as desperately as she had, but not once even put a message on her Facebook wall.

But if she asked him that, she knew he could throw those questions back at her and she felt too fragile to even consider the answers. Because if he asked her, she was certain she'd spill all of her hurt and sadness out to him and not just about the last three years, but all those mixed signals when they were in college. And if she did that, then he'd know how much she'd loved him from the very minute she'd first seen him. And if he knew, she was terrified that her greatest fear would come true; that Ezra would frown at her and tell her that he didn't feel the same. That she'd made meanings from all that blushing, and those kisses, and The Teddy Incident based on her own deceptive heart instead of reality. And she couldn't handle that.

She couldn't bear to be rejected by Ezra. Not

again. She'd just barely survived the last time. So she swallowed all that emotion, shook her head and forced herself to smile at him. And then she turned to look over her shoulder at the bed. When she turned back to him, his eyes were still worried, but his jaw was set and there were beads of sweat at his hairline. Candace moved her hands to the back of her dress. She walked slowly backward toward the bed as she unzipped her dress, her gaze locked on Ezra's warm blue eyes.

The metallic rasp of the zipper bounced off the walls. Ezra gulped at the sound, following her as if it was a beacon. At the foot of the bed, she held her bridesmaid's dress loose against her body.

"Do you have condoms, Ezra?"

His eyes widened. He gulped again and nodded.

"Did you come here prepared to pick up someone from the singles table?" she asked, pretending it was a joke even as her heart shriveled at the thought.

He grimaced and shook his head. He turned to the desk against the far wall — trying and failing to subtly adjust his hard cock as he walked — and moved to a basket on the table.

She smiled when she saw it. She'd recognize Mei's handiwork anywhere and there were near-identical baskets in all the bridesmaids' rooms as well.

Ezra rifled through the basket and then turned to her, a box of condoms in his hand.

Candace frowned. "We didn't get condoms in our basket."

"I feel like this was Miles's contribution," Ezra offered.

Candace pursed her lips and rolled her eyes. "I can't believe he took all those Women's Studies classes with Mei and learned nothing."

Ezra shrugged. "I don't know about nothing. He made me go see the new *Stepford Wives* like twice when it came out. It was not good," he said with an awkward laugh.

Candace smiled at him and then dropped her dress. Ezra's laughter cut off on a strangled groan. She pushed it over her hips and let it pool at her feet, never taking her eyes from him.

"Ezra," she whispered.

He nodded.

She smiled. "Come here."

He nodded again.

She laughed. "You have to walk, Ezra."

His eyes lifted to hers and he grimaced, still nodding, and finally moved.

Candace's heart felt as if it might beat straight out of her chest as she waited. When he stopped in front of her, he had a death grip on the box of condoms. She plucked it from his hands and he sighed in relief. She threw the box on the bed and then put her palms flat on his chest.

His breath hitched again and she loved the feeling of it under her palms. She moved her hands under his lapels to his shoulders and then pushed his jacket from his body. It fell to the floor and was soon followed by his bowtie, shirt and belt. Ezra toed off his shoes and socks and then waited for Candace's direction. She smiled at him and trailed her fingertips through his chest hair, down his stomach — his abs flinching under her fingertips — to the top of his pants.

Candace licked her lips and marveled at how much she loved touching Ezra. She was happy she'd never gotten to experience this while in college because she knew she'd never have been able to stop herself. The way his body heated and flinched and melted under her hands made her feel powerful and so horny her skin felt like it was covered in electricity. If she'd known Ezra would be like this, she was certain she'd have flunked out in a semester. Happily.

She wedged her finger into his belt buckle and began to pull it loose. She locked eyes with him as she pulled it slowly from his pants loops. A part of her wanted to yank it free quickly and push his pants just barely down his hips, just enough to get his dick free. But she hadn't waited three years to rush through this. Who knew if it would happen again?

She slowly unbuttoned and unzipped his pants, leaning forward to push them over his hips. He dipped his head to brush his mouth against hers, but she pulled back before he could pull her into a kiss, smiling wickedly at him as her gaze dipped.

And then there he was, just the thin cotton of his underwear between her and her greatest regret. There was nothing worse than spending years of your life having a singular, but incomplete, masturbatory focus.

Of knowing the intimate feeling of Ezra's mouth and tongue, but no clear image of his dick. She knew what it felt like to desperately ride the hard mound of his erection but she had no idea of the weight of him in her hand, his girth, or the way that silky steel tasted. More than once she'd gotten herself off on her own fingers or her ex-boyfriend's tongue trying to imagine all of that.

She slipped her fingers into the waistband of his underwear and his own hands followed. They took off his underwear together. He straightened, his hands at his sides as he waited. For her.

"Get on the bed," she whispered, her voice hoarse with need.

There was no hesitation this time. He scurried onto the bed so fast Candace couldn't help but laugh as she followed. He turned onto his back, his legs spread and she crawled between them. He groaned and his head fell back to the pillow, but only for a second. He lifted his head, unwilling to look away. That realization made her feel powerful in a way she'd always longed for with Ezra, as if the life she wanted with him was just at her fingertips.

She thought about reaching into her underwear, knowing that she'd find herself wet and warm. But she wanted to wait. She wanted his fingers to be the first to touch her in so long. So, she sat on her knees between his legs, her hands on his thighs.

"Candace," he moaned.

She smiled and leaned over him, pressing a firm, closed mouth kiss to the center of his chest. She felt the deep rumble of his groan against her mouth and her sex clenched. She kept her eyes on his as she kissed her way down his chest and stomach as all of his muscles twitched and tensed. She smiled up at him as she settled onto her stomach, making sure she was comfortable and her cleavage looked amazing from this angle.

He huffed out a laugh that sounded like a moan and his hands gripped the sheets at his side.

And then she indulged herself. Finally.

His abs jumped when she wrapped her hand around his half-hard cock. She bit her bottom lip as she stroked him gently, just testing his weight and girth with her right hand.

"Candace," he hissed, when her left hand moved to massage his balls.

She smiled up his body and then lowered to lick the head of his dick with the flat of her tongue.

"Shit," he said, and so she licked him again.

She dragged her tongue up the underside of his growing erection and then let the tip of her tongue flit through the slit at the head. It was her turn to moan as she tasted him after so many years of dreaming about this.

"Oh my god," he groaned, and let his head fall back onto the pillow.

She smiled and stroked him just a bit faster with a tighter grip, enjoying the way he hardened and grew in her palm. She suckled on the head, stroking him up and down as he squirmed underneath her. She pressed her thighs together just as she swallowed as much of his dick as she could. She was rewarded with a loud, incoherent cry at least an octave higher than Ezra's regular voice.

It was amazing. Maybe even more amazing than she'd ever imagined. So good that she lost track of her own desire and began to suck him with deep strokes and pressure, licking and pumping his shaft, massaging his testicles, living for every moan that fell from his lips. His hips lifted from the bed momentarily and he bunched more of the sheets in his fists. She clenched her sex as the room filled with his cries.

Her eyes closed in ecstasy. Giving Ezra a blowjob was everything she'd ever hoped it would be and more.

"Fuck, wait," he hissed suddenly. His thigh muscles went rigid and his strong hands grazed her shoulders.

She lifted her head, the head of his dick popping from her mouth obscenely. He groaned and shivered, gently pushing her away.

"Did I do something wrong?" she asked, even though she was certain the answer was no.

He shook his head quickly and rolled to his side. "Don't want to come in your mouth."

"What if that's what I want?" she asked with an arched eyebrow.

He moaned and grabbed his erection, burying his face in the pillow beneath him.

She laughed and waited for him to get himself together.

When he turned on his back, his hand still gripping his shaft tightly, she almost worried that it might hurt.

"Next time," he ground out.

Her smile faltered for just a second. She wanted to ask him if he meant that they would be having sex multiple times tonight — which she was very much into — or if he meant tomorrow or the day after or the day after that — which was what she really wanted, but was too afraid to tell him. So she sat back on her heels, put her hands on her hips and smiled down at him.

"So what do you wanna do now?" she asked, sounding cocky even though she felt just as off-kilter as he looked.

When Ezra looked at her, Candace felt as if the world had shifted. Sometimes when he looked at her, she could have sworn that his eyes were filled with awe and something like love. His gaze made her feel beautiful and desired, but it was so fleeting. It never came with declarations of love or action. And over the past three years, she'd convinced herself that what she thought she'd seen in his eyes wasn't real; just a reflection of her own desire for him. But even she couldn't explain this look away. When he lifted his eyes to hers, Candace shivered as his eyes traveled from her face and then up and down her body as he licked his lips.

"My turn," he whispered absentmindedly.

It was Candace's turn to groan.

*E*zra was the king of nervous energy and it usually presented itself in the obvious flush of his neck and face. But the reddening of his skin when he was around Candace hid a deep clenching in his gut, a rapidly beating pulse, an almost painful pounding of his heart, a constriction of nearly every muscle in his body as he fought a marrow-deep longing to be closer to her, touch her, taste her or just hear her say his name. He was always shy and maybe a little socially awkward, but around Candace, Ezra hardly knew up from down or left from right.

He'd been thinking over the past three years that the next time he saw her in person he would be more in control of himself, and on some level he was. There was a time when looking into Candace's eyes was impossible to imagine and there wasn't a fantasy world that he could have conjured where Candace's hands and mouth stroked his aching dick and he didn't come prematurely. He'd held out as long as he could, but he had to stop her before he came so hard he passed out. That wasn't the image he wanted Candace to have of him after so long.

Besides, she was in the sexiest black lace underwear he'd ever seen and all he wanted to do was rip them off.

He struggled to his knees and faced her. She watched him and licked her bottom lip, making his dick throb. He flexed his hands and she laughed.

"You stretching before you touch me?"

He raised his eyes to hers and not for the first time today, she took his breath away. He'd missed her so much. He smiled shyly. "Don't wanna get a cramp before you come."

Her mouth fell open in shock. "Ezra Posner!"

"I love the way you say my name," he finally admitted to her, six years too late, as he reached out and slipped his hand behind her neck and pulled her face forward. He could taste himself on her tongue and he groaned into her mouth. She shivered against him.

His other hand moved slowly to her collarbone. He reluctantly let go of her lips because he wanted to see her face as his fingertips tickled the fragile bone there, moving down her chest to the edge of her strapless lace bustier and over the soft cleavage that spilled over the top of her bra in a way that had been distracting him all day. He hadn't been ogling her — of course he never would — but the amount of effort it took not to stare at her face or drool at her cleavage had actually made him miss his cue to give Miles Mei's ring during the cere-mony. He'd been embarrassed, but feeling that soft skin under his fingertips soothed the awkwardness of that memory. And when he looked at Candace, her eyes closed and eyelashes fluttering as he dipped a finger into one of her bra cups and grazed her hard nipple, he knew that he wouldn't remember that gaffe, not after tonight.

She moaned.

His body tensed and he accidentally gripped her neck harder. She didn't open her eyes but she did smile, that knowing haughty smile that he'd always loved.

"I want to tear all this lace off you," he whispered.

Her eyes opened quickly and she stared at him as if she was seeing him for the first time.

"You've changed," she whispered to him.

He didn't know what she meant by that or if it was a good or bad thing, but she was right. He wasn't the inexperienced boy who'd happily — if nervously — knelt at her feet and had his first taste of her. He wasn't the same Ezra who'd let himself hope they were on the precipice of something real. And thankfully, he also wasn't the guy who'd spent the entire summer after she didn't come back sad and moody. The man who'd lost his virginity to a girl he met at his cousin's wedding but whose name he couldn't even remember. Who'd hated himself after it was done because he didn't feel more mature, he just felt regret, because he'd always wanted Candace to be his first. His only. He was older and a touch more confident. And even though Candace still made his throat dry, he wasn't as inexperienced as he used to be and he wanted her to know that.

"In some ways," he said and pressed his lips to hers. "But not totally."

He kept his eyes locked on her as he wrapped his arms around her and pulled apart each small clasp of her lingerie.

She exhaled heavily when she was free of her bustier. "I don't know what that means," she whispered.

He cupped her breasts, a bit of flesh spilling from his hands. And then he lowered his mouth to lick across each mound and up her neck. He placed a chaste kiss on the corner of her mouth as he rolled her nipples between his fingers. She moaned.

"I'll show you," he whispered against her skin. And then he lowered his mouth to her breasts to kiss, lick and suck at the soft flesh.

"Oh god," she moaned when he sucked her left nipple into his mouth on a hard tug.

Her hands plunged into his hair, her fingernails scraping along his scalp. He wanted to grab his dick again and squeeze, but he also didn't want to stop touching her, not even for a moment.

He lifted his head from her breasts. She whimpered and frowned at him. He smiled. She moved one hand to cup his face, running her thumb over his lips. He tried to decipher what that look on her face meant. Maybe on another person it might have reminded Ezra of reverence. Maybe on any other woman whose breasts he was currently holding, thumbs gently stroking her nipples, he might have read this look as something like love. But not with Candace. Simply because he wanted to see love in her eyes, made him certain that it must be something else.

So he blinked and looked away, pressing his lips to the pad of her thumb as he helped her lie back onto the bed. He swallowed the loudest groan of the night at the image of her lying beneath him, her soft hair fanned out around her head like a halo — just like that first

New Year's — naked but for a pair of lacy underwear, her breasts drooping slightly to her sides and the gentle rounded slope of her stomach. He felt the prick of tears at the back of his eyes and he had to swallow hard to hold them back, his hands shaking as he reached for the waistband of her underwear.

It wasn't enough. It wouldn't be enough. He could fuck her tonight, all night, and he planned to. He could wake up tomorrow and fuck her again and again and he would if she would let him. But the problem with him and Candace was that she'd leave. The wedding was over. There was a brunch tomorrow, but after that she'd go back to wherever she lived now and he'd hop on a flight back to New York. And no matter how good the sex was sure to be — no matter that he'd been waiting for this moment for years — a world where he couldn't keep Candace with him for longer than a few hours would never be enough.

She lifted her hips from the bed and he pulled her underwear over the curve of her ass, down her legs and off. He leaned over her to press his mouth against her soft stomach, letting his mouth sink into her flesh, the smell of her surrounding him. It wouldn't be enough, but he'd remember every second of this night for the rest of his life. And that would have to do. For now.

Candace's hands moved back to his hair. She stroked his strands slowly and let him stay like that, pressing his face into her stomach. If she felt the wetness of the few tears he couldn't stop, she was kind enough not to mention them. Or maybe she thought it was his tongue, because eventually it was. He licked his salty tears from her skin and then circled her belly button. She giggled. He moved his mouth to the apex of her legs and she opened for him automatically.

He crawled between her legs and ran his hands under her thighs, spreading them more.

She moved one hand from his hair to her sex, reminding him of three years ago. He unconsciously thrust his hips into the bed as her fingers moved through her slit, becoming slick with her own arousal. He looked up her body, over the peaks of her stomach and breasts to find her staring back at him with hooded eyes.

"Did you miss me, Ezra?" she asked in a hoarse voice.

"Every day," he admitted honestly. "Did you miss me?" He held his breath as he waited for her answer.

She laughed. It sounded soft, maybe even sad. "Every minute," she said.

He couldn't have hoped for a better answer. It might have been a lie, or not in the same way he'd meant it — like love, not friendship — but he'd been waiting so long for this that he decided to let himself be seduced by the perfection of her laugh, her body, those words, her scent as he lowered his mouth to her sex.

She moaned loudly and scratched his scalp with one hand while the other spread her lips open for his tongue. She tasted better than he remembered and he lost himself in the sweet salty taste of her. He sucked her from clit to opening and pushed her legs higher and further apart.

"Oh god yes," she whispered.

He could feel her orgasm nearing. Her thighs shook in his hands, her moans becoming a beautiful melodic song even as the words that flew from her mouth grew filthier. He wanted her to come on his tongue again. But there was something he wanted more.

She growled when he took his mouth away and sat up on his knees. She pushed up onto her elbows only to return to her back when he pressed her left knee to the bed with one hand and then slipped two fingers of his other hand inside her.

"Oh fuck," she said, shivering beneath him.

His eyes focused on her face, watching the minute details of her facial expressions as she came fully undone on his hand. He pumped his fingers into her forcefully, the wet tip of his dick resting against her thigh.

She grabbed her breasts and he moved his thumb to her clit. He fucked her like that, watching her moan and gasp and shiver underneath him, bringing her slowly to the brink. Candace's back arched when he added a third finger and increased the pressure of his thrusts as she fell over the edge. Ezra's palm filled with her release and he shifted next to her on the bed. He covered her sex with his wet hand, cupping her as he fucked her with his fingers. She spasmed again and her back arched from the bed as her sex clenched with an obscene squelch around his fingers.

Ezra gritted his teeth to keep from coming with her.

He slowed his hand, stroking her through the aftershocks of her orgasm. He ignored the fact that his dick ached, or at least he'd planned to.

Candace wasn't interested in that. She pushed his hand from between her legs and practically ripped the box of condoms open with her teeth.

He laughed and then slipped one of his wet fingers into his mouth.

"Ezra," she squealed at him with a smile.

He smiled back and sucked her essence from another finger as she tore open a condom wrapper.

He jerked when her hand covered his dick again. He held his breath as she rolled the condom on and threw a leg over his body to straddle him.

"You might want to breathe," she said, that beautiful smile spreading across her face.

He let out the breath he was holding and moved his hands to grab her hips again. They locked eyes and the room filled with their mingled moans as she lined his erection up with her opening and then sank down onto his length.

She threw her head back and laughed as if everything was right with the world and for him, it was. As Candace started to move on top of him, rotating her hips in slow circular motions, he dug his fingers into her waist and thrust his hips up to meet her. They rocked slowly into his every fantasy. She was as warm and wet and tight and shuddering as he'd always hoped she'd be. And when she started to move faster, her palms planted firmly on his chest, their eyes still locked, she smiled down at him. It was even better than his fantasies, he thought, as he smiled up at her. The distant sounds of fireworks spurred them on. It was all so familiar and new at the same time that it caught him off guard. In that moment of vulnerability, he let himself imagine that this wasn't the culmination of his college dreams but the start of something new.

They changed position.

She turned on her side and he moved behind her and re-entered her slowly. She contorted herself so that their mouths and tongues could meet and he fucked her slowly, as if there was no rush, as if they had all night and the next and the next. He let himself imagine that this felt as good and right to her as it did to him; that each stroke only strengthened her resolve to never let this feeling go. He let his imagination conjure an infinity of days for them, where they could have this and their old friendship and so much more. He let himself hope.

And maybe that's why it hurt so much when he woke up the next morning in his hotel bed alone, an empty box of condoms and Candace's smell still clinging to the sheets and his skin. That and the debris from the now empty box the only signs that last night hadn't been another dream. Maybe that's why when he rushed downstairs to the brunch reception only to find the seat next to Mei — Candace's seat — filled by Karen, he felt a kind of foreboding he had no idea what to do with.

Finally, Candace's dad put him out of his misery. "She had to leave. She starts a new job today. Mei didn't tell you?" Mr. Garret asked.

Ezra swallowed a lump in his throat that was certainly full of tears and confusion and regret. "No. She didn't tell me anything. She never does," he said. But he meant Candace, not Mei, because not telling him that she was leaving felt a whole hell of a lot like telling him that she was coming home for graduation, and then not.

So he guessed Candace had been wrong, he thought to himself. He hadn't changed at all. And neither had she.

# CHAPTER 9

"*M*ei, I need you to WhatsApp me as soon as you get this message," Candace said into her phone. She didn't want to worry her best friend but this was an emergency. She needed to talk to someone who knew her. Who knew Ezra. And soon. "Call me as soon as you get this, Mei. Not once you've had a cup of coffee. Not when you get to work. Not when your boss pisses you off and you need to vent. You hear this message and then you WhatsApp me. Love you, bye."

Candace sent the voice note to her best friend and stared at the chat screen as if Mei might feel her concentration through the phone and wake up from a dead sleep. She wished — not for the first Ezra-related time — that she and Mei were telepathic. But they weren't, and she was going to have to wait for her best friend to wake up and call her back. Unfortunately, knowing Mei she wouldn't call Candace immediately, not even with the express request that she do so. Mei was a great friend, but easily distracted. She might have the best intentions of calling Candace back and then find an article on the probability of mermaids really existing or realize that she didn't have any coffee creamer and just forget. She didn't mean to be MIA and she so rarely was, especially where Candace was concerned, but life happens.

It used to be that when Mei was unreachable, Candace could call Miles and have him walk across their house, tap her on the shoulder, and just hand her his phone. For year, Miles had been like a trap door to her best friend, but that door had been closed for over three years and it had become harder and harder to catch Mei at the exact moments she needed her.

It didn't help that Mei was pretending as if the divorce hadn't devastated her and avoiding everyone who might be able to see the truth, which meant she and Candace saw each other less than either of them liked. Miles and Mei's separation had rent the fabric of all their relationships and none of them quite knew how to move forward in this new world where Mei and Miles lived in different cities and she and Ezra couldn't count on their best friends to pull them back together. Candace didn't know how to help Mei besides just waiting and avoiding all Miles-related topics, which included Ezra.

But Candace needed Mei now, even if it was going to hurt.

Her phone chirped and she unlocked it in the

desperate hope that the telepathy had worked. It hadn't. Jorge's message was brief as ever.

Lobby.

"Oh, thank god," she breathed. She grabbed her purse and headed out of her hotel room. As soon as she stepped into the lobby, her eyes darted to the board-room Ezra had disappeared into.

"Girl, how much did this hotel cost?" Jorge asked none too quietly as soon as he saw her.

Candace rolled her eyes and grabbed his arm. "Let's go." She dragged him onto the street. It was warmer than when she'd walked here this morning. The sky was clear and it felt as if the sun was beaming right down on them.

"Does this mean you got that raise?" Jorge asked.

Candace frowned. "No. Stop asking," she mumbled. That was a sore topic and it had been for a few years.

Candace had been with AeroPlan for her entire career and she'd risen relatively quickly up the ranks to purser, but no further. She'd applied to become an instructor in the flight attendant training program three times in the past four years and been rejected each time. She'd applied for raises based on her always near-perfect performance reviews every other quarter — company policy — and been either lowballed or denied. She was beginning to think that her time with AeroPlan was coming to an end and she had no idea what to do with the next phase of her life.

"You okay?" Jorge asked.

Candace bit her bottom lip and shook her head.

"Is it the billionaire?" he asked, turning her toward him. "Did you see him again?"

She nodded her head.

"Where? When? How? Tell me everything," he demanded excitedly.

"Not...not here."

"Why? Oh, holy shit, is he staying here too?"

She grabbed his hand and pulled him toward a taxi stand on the corner.

"Candace, come on, give me the gossip."

She didn't answer him until they were in the back of a cab heading to one of her favorite parks in all of Quito and away from Ezra. "He owns it," she whispered.

Jorge started and turned to her with big eyes. "Are? You? Kidding me?" he yelled. "Why are we leaving? Why are you wearing this?" he asked, moving his hands in the air to indicate her blue jean shorts and loose gold and white baseball tee.

"Hey," she whined.

His face softened and he put a warm hand on her shoulder. "No offense, girl. You're gorgeous and I love you. But if we're trying to snag this man and his *hotel*, you're gonna need a better look than 1970s tomboy chic. We need to go shopping." He turned to the driver and Candace stopped him.

"Can we back up like ten steps? I'm not trying to snag him. I just want to go sit in the park and talk to my friend."

Jorge sighed and smiled at her. "Okay. That's fine." He sat back in his seat and sighed, "We can go shopping later."

Candace pushed Jorge's shoulder and they both laughed. They rode the rest of the way in silence, enjoying the scenes of the city as it passed. Locals going about their day to work and church, school children playing soccer in a grassy field, the driver's radio providing an easy soundtrack of drums and horns as his hands tapped out the beat on his steering wheel. It was a moment of calm that Candace needed desperately.

~

Stepping onto the grass of Parque La Carolina was more like coming home than landing in Quito. When she'd been a broke study abroad student, she and her friends had quickly figured out how to enjoy the city while spending as little money as possible. They ate breakfast and dinner in the university dorms for free. They ate cheap lunches from the food carts around the city. And when they needed to get out of the university bubble to experience the city they were studying, they brought their schoolbooks to the city's parks, staked out a stretch of grass and shared cheap bottles of wine in the equatorial sunshine. This way, they reserved the bulk of their money for traveling around the Andean region on weekends by bus and sporadic nights out at the city's dance clubs with locals where they practiced their Spanish and everyone, including Candace by the end of the trip, flirted with locals.

But of all the city's parks, Parque La Carolina was Candace's favorite. She'd always found the lake at its center peaceful and used to come here on her own to sit and read, write, draw and sometimes cry. She'd planned to do that on this trip and had packed her worn copy of *Plum Bun* to reread on the grass nearby and try to find herself again.

Jorge had other plans.

"Oooh, paddle boats," he screeched.

"No, I just wanted—" Candace started, but Jorge was already pulling her toward the boathouse. And before she knew it, she was sitting in a paddle boat with a life jacket on and a smiling Jorge pumping his legs happily.

"Help anytime you want," he snarked at her.

She rolled her eyes and began to move her pedals begrudgingly.

There weren't a lot of other boats on the water and after a few minutes it was almost as if they were completely alone. They could see people in the park, riding along the bike path, playing soccer and flying kites in the grass, but the water dampened the sounds of the park and it was peaceful.

"Alright, let's get this therapy session started," he said.

"You're good."

He smiled and shrugged. "I try. Look, you can tell me as much or as little as you want. I won't tell a soul. Not even your billionaire."

"His name's Ezra," she said irritably.

"I know."

"And he's not mine."

He ignored that. "So, of all the hotels in all of Quito, you end up at the one owned by your ex-man? Sounds super romantic to me."

"It's not romantic. It's a coincidence."

"It's fate. If my mother was here, she would probably have already taken out her rosary and started praying for your babies. Like seriously."

Candace looked away and tried to blink away the tears in her eyes.

"What happened?"

She laughed as she turned back to him. "We ran into each other in housekeeping. He told me he'd wanted to come here with me when we were in college. And he invited me to a party tonight."

Jorge's eyebrows furrowed and he looked at her intently before leaning forward and putting his hand on her knee. "I don't understand what any of that meant or why it's making you sad, but I'm here for you. Did he give you a plus one?"

Candace burst into laughter and he squeezed her knee.

"God, I love you," she breathed.

"The feeling's mutual, sweetheart. Now come on. Spill. The whole story, this time."

Candace wiped at her eyes. "When we were in college, Ezra had a four-year plan. He was the most organized person I'd ever met. Focused. And studying abroad wasn't in his schedule. So for him to say that he even thought about studying abroad just to be with me…"

"Romance," Jorge added with a sage nod of his head. He ignored her rolling eyes.

"He told me he missed me and he looked at me like…"

"Like he loved you?"

She nodded, too afraid to actually say the words. She'd been so accustomed to never saying aloud how often Ezra looked at her as if he loved her, because she'd convinced herself years ago that those looks were deceiving. She couldn't bear to say it, just in case she was wrong and inadvertently revealed how desperately she wanted it to be true.

"You ever look at your life and wonder how the fuck you got here?" she whispered to Jorge.

He huffed out an ironic laugh. "Is that a joke? Of course I have. I wear the worst uniform to a job where I serve small single-use plastic cups of soda and packets of peanuts to people who take their shoes and *socks* off in a small metal tube full of recirculated air. I hardly know what city I'm in day-to-day. I can't save more than a few hundred dollars before life fucks me up. My roommate keeps trying to pay his portion of the rent in

Bitcoin. And my last relationship ended three years ago. Every day I wonder what my karma was like that this is my life. Go on."

Candace covered his hand on her knee and squeezed.

"The first time I came to Quito, I thought that I'd be leaving here with a paid internship at an art gallery and a new boyfriend. Ezra. Instead, Ezra didn't bother to contact me until it was almost time for me to come home and every job I applied to said I didn't have enough experience for an entry-level job. Meanwhile, Ezra got this super prestigious award. My best friend graduated summa cum laude and Ezra's best friend walked out of college with a junior executive position at the architecture firm of his dreams. Our best friends were also completely in love."

"Geez," Jorge breathed.

Candace nodded sadly. "I was the broke failure of the bunch and I couldn't..." She swallowed and shook her head, "I couldn't go back to that."

"But you've seen him since then," he prompted.

She nodded. "When I saw him in his best man's tux at our friends' wedding, he looked fine as fuck."

"I believe every word of that," Jorge said with a hand to his chest.

Candace laughed. "We hooked up for the first time at the wedding."

"I would honestly disown you if you hadn't. So, what happened after?"

She smiled. "I'd just gotten this job actually. And he got a three-million-dollar investor for his company."

"Three million!"

"Three. Million," she nodded. "A few months later he got another multi-million-dollar investor and then write-ups in all the tech magazines. My mom sent me clippings," she laughed. "*Actual* magazine clippings of articles from *Time* and the *Chronicle*. Whatever she could find. My parents were so proud of him."

"That's amazing. Isn't it?"

"No, it was. It is. He's the smartest person I've ever met and the best person. It was everything I ever wanted for him. But he was a rising star in the world of innovative transportation and I was putting on that ugly uniform to serve tiny drinks and peanuts."

"Oh," Jorge said, and sat back in his seat.

"He lived in New York and he didn't come home much. He dated models or women with PhDs in like, biomedical engineering. If that's a thing. For years, we almost never saw each other."

"But he came home for New Year's Eve?"

Candace nodded sadly. "We hooked up every year for a few years. But it was like I didn't exist for him for the rest of the year. When I left Quito after college, I promised myself that I wouldn't wait for Ezra to run after me anymore. But then I did."

"Did you ever call him?" Jorge asked carefully.

"I should have," she admitted just as carefully. "I know that. I should have called him when I flew into New York or when I knew he was home. But you don't know what it was like when we were in college. Every time we were around each other, he just... clammed up. And no matter what I did, no matter how much I brought up his favorite musicians or engineering shit I didn't understand, no matter how close I thought we were, he never got any better. For three years I felt like I was sticking my neck out over and over again but never getting that same effort in return. And I just..."

"Couldn't do it anymore."

She nodded, fighting back tears.

"So, you never called him while you were in Quito or all those years because you were still waiting."

She nodded again.

Jorge's eyes shifted to the domestic scene in the park. He seemed to be contemplating her words. She took advantage of the silence to wipe away the tears she refused to let fall.

After a while, Jorge cleared his throat. "Okay, this is some heavy shit," he said. "And I don't know him or what you two were like in college but it sounds like he was shy and socially awkward, especially when around you."

"Very," she laughed. "He basically spent three years beet red, he blushed so much."

"And you thought a guy like that would suddenly change his entire personality and reach out to you?"

"Ouch."

"I'm sorry, babe. I don't want to be mean, but it seems to me like the problem with you two is that you've spent years beating around the bush. It's cute.

A bit like a telenovela, which I'm actually super into, but not if you're crying in a paddle boat in a foreign country. That's sad. You're too fabulous to be pathetic."

"I'm gonna hold onto you calling me fabulous, while you apparently drag me for filth."

Jorge smiled, "That's my girl." He sat up, rocking the boat gently, and looked at her with serious eyes. "I totally get you wanting him to show you how he felt. You deserve that, but why not tell him that?"

"I tried," she said.

He squinted at her. "Did you though?"

"I did," she said. "Before I hopped on the plane, I called him at my apartment."

"Like his landline? Jesus, how old are you?"

Candace ignored him. "I told his best friend to tell him to email me and he never did."

"Okay, and you never emailed him, not even to tell him he was trash for not emailing you? Like that's the part that I don't get. You're smart. You're more than smart, but he's not the only person who clearly can't think straight in this relationship."

"Meaning?"

"*Meaning*, would you ever let any other man you've messed with go this long without being one hundred percent clear about his feelings?"

"Never."

"Exactly. You'd drag them to hell and back and then invite me over to laugh at their groveling text messages, because you deserve better than that and you know it. But somehow you've been doing this dance with Ezra for twenty years."

"Eighteen," she corrected pathetically.

"Yeah, that's much better. You've been running around in a circle with this man for *eighteen years* and there are only two reasons I can imagine why."

Candace's back straightened. "I'm listening."

"Either you're a masochist or you already know deep down how he feels but you're just such a helpless romantic that you're still waiting for his grand gesture."

Candace turned away from Jorge quickly.

"How'd I do?" he asked after a few seconds of silence.

"Nail on the head," she admitted.

"Yeah, I thought so. And I get it, maybe if he hadn't become a billionaire and you weren't so unhappy with your life... maybe this wouldn't have dragged on so long. Maybe if you were both struggling or you were some fancy art dealer, you'd feel worthy of him."

Candace cringed to hear those words even though it was exactly how she'd felt for too long.

Jorge reached out again to squeeze her knee. "But you are worthy of him. Your job might pay for shit and management might be sexist and probably racist as fuck, but you're the best flight attendant I've ever worked with. You're also kind and funny and can make even the worst passenger love you. And if Ezra is the kind of guy who thinks the work you do is beneath him, then he's abso-fucking-lutely not the guy you should be wasting any more time on. Although he seems like he *is* the kind of guy you should waste just a little bit more time on at least."

"How do you know?" she whispered.

"I already told you. I saw the way he looked at you. Whenever you weren't looking, his eyes were on you. I might have called security on him but he didn't seem as if he was planning to kidnap you. He just looked like he loved you. Like loving you was the same as breathing. And you might not want to hear this, but you look at him the same way."

She laughed and then let her face fall to her upturned hands. "I sound so pathetic."

"Girl, my younger sister is pretending to be in an open marriage right now to keep a man who won't keep a job. You're good," he said and they laughed.

"So, what should I do?" she asked.

"Ooooh, sorry, I have no idea. But I mean, I guess you can start by having a conversation with the man. Sounds like you two are way overdue."

Candace sucked in a deep breath, straightened her back and nodded. "Yeah, okay, you're right."

"Always."

She rolled her eyes and then smiled at him. "He did give me a plus one tonight."

"Bitch, and you're *just* now telling me?" Jorge screamed. "Get to paddling. We need to find a mall. Rich people hang out with rich people. I still need to find a man for tomorrow night. Let's go."

Candace laughed as she and Jorge began to paddle back to the dock. She focused on his enthusiasm to distract herself from his hard truths for her and the thought of seeing Ezra again. But for the first time in longer than she could remember, she didn't feel fear. She didn't know what would happen with Ezra or her job, but she'd lived her life by fear and shame and if she didn't want to have to run to Quito in another fifteen years, still lost and alone, she couldn't let that fear paralyze her anymore.

~

Candace's suitcase was open on the floor of the large closet in her hotel room. She was standing in a matching set of black lace underwear trying to decide between the best two dresses she'd brought. There was the slinky, shiny champagne spaghetti strap dress she'd bought with Ezra in mind. It fell demurely to her knees, but left so much of her shoulders, chest and back exposed. The thought of him seeing her in it made her shiver, even now. And then there was the slightly less flashy deep plum wrap dress that hugged all her curves and showed a lot of leg.

The rational decision was to wear the wrap dress and save the shiny number for tomorrow night, but she was hesitating. There was a chance — however small Jorge thought — that after she spoke with Ezra, their relationship would be over. And if this was the last night that he looked at her with flushed cheeks and wide eyes, she wanted him to remember her literally sparkling. But she also thought there was a case to be made that if they ended things, she should save the glittery dress for tomorrow. For someone else.

Her phone rang.

She rushed back into her bedroom and snatched it up. It was Mei. Hours late.

"Fuck, I'm sorry," Mei breathed as soon as Candace answered.

"I smashed my phone yesterday and had to leave it at the store. And then I didn't have time to go pick it up this morning. And I got a ticket." She sighed. "This has been the worst day. But I'm here now. Very late. What's up with you and Ezra? Are you pregnant?"

Candace's mouth fell open. "Okay, hold the fuck up. Breathe." She and Mei took deep breaths together over the phone.

"Sorry. I'm good now," Mei said in a calmer voice.

"Great. I'm not pregnant," Candace said. "And I don't know why that's even a thing you'd ask."

Mei scoffed. "Because it's Ezra, duh."

"What does that mean?"

She could see Mei rolling her eyes in her head.

"It means that I've been waiting half my life for you to stop fucking around in my spare bedroom and finally lock that down. Also he texted me yesterday to ask if I thought he had a chance with you."

"He what?"

"Yeah. Thankfully, I had my tablet on me."

"Wait a minute, he asked you if *he* had a chance with *me*?"

"Yeah, why are you talking like that?"

"Ezra's a billionaire," Candace screeched.

"His company's worth billions. He's only worth a few million. Few hundred million. Something like that," she said nonchalantly, as if a few hundred million was akin to the few hundred dollars in Candace's meager savings. "And shut up. He could be worth trillions and he'd still blush whenever someone even mentions you. He's been head over heels in love with you since at least homecoming freshman year. He was staring at you the entire time."

"How are you just now telling me this?"

"How could you have missed this? Ezra is lots of things, but subtle has never been one of them. Not with you. Jesus, Can, did you really not know?"

"No!" she yelled into her phone. "I didn't know. He wasn't..." She stopped herself just in time and pressed her lips together.

Mei's voice was soft, hurt. "He wasn't Miles," she said. "I know."

"It was just... Miles never stopped talking about you or talking *to* you. He was basically our third roommate sophomore year. He bought you flowers and candy and you dorks always had matching Halloween costumes. It was sickening. But it was also clear that he was head over heels in love with you."

There were a few seconds of silence before Mei replied. "You're right. Miles was the best boyfriend. For me. You would have hated all that. We're two totally different people who like different kinds of men. You never would have dated a man like Miles so I can't understand why you ever compared Ezra to him. They're as different as we are."

Candace fell to her bed in shock. Today was apparently the day of very hard truths about how foolish she'd been.

"You and Ezra are basically the same person. I mean you know, not on the outside, but definitely in all the ways that count. Only you two geniuses could somehow be obsessed with each other and never realize it. It's kinda cute if you don't think about it too hard."

"Okay, Mei, I get it. We're pathetic."

"Very. But like, adorably so. Are you in Quito?"

"Yeah. Ezra was on my flight."

"Oh wow. This is some fated shit. I'm gonna tell my ma when we get off the phone. She'll light some incense for you two. Again."

"Again? Your mom knew?"

"Yeah. She's been rooting for you guys for a while. Maybe this'll take her mind off trying to set me up with every eligible Chinese man in the East Bay."

"Doubt it," Candace said.

Mei sighed. "Worth a try though. Anyway, so you and Ezra are both in Ecuador. I guess that means Miles isn't having his New Year's party again?" she tentatively suggested.

"I don't know. I can ask Ezra if you want."

"No, no. That's okay. Don't...I mean if it comes up organically, I guess that would be okay. But don't ask. Don't make me seem..." Mei trailed off and even though Candace knew the perfect word to finish the sentence, she could tell Mei wasn't ready to hear it.

"Okay. If it comes up organically. I'll let you know."

"Cool. Um...cool. So when are you going to see him again?" she asked, her voice brightening with the topic change.

"Tonight. He's having a work party or something and he invited me."

"Wear something short or tight or both," Mei offered.

"So we've moved quickly from impregnation to seduction, eh?"

"Yes, because we're working our way to impregnation. I need nieces and nephews asap."

"You sound like your mother."

"When the lady's right, she's right."

Candace smiled and rolled her eyes. "I have two dresses I'm deciding between. If I send you pictures...?"

"Yeah, duh. Send them now. Hurry."

"Alright," she laughed.

"I'll text back quickly. I promise. I'm here for you, Can. I love you."

"I love you too, Mei."

They hung up the phone and Candace smiled down at it for a few seconds in a soft, warm daze. Between Mei and Jorge she felt... well, maybe not optimistic about tonight, but certain she could survive it, nonetheless. She moved back to the closet, slipped both dresses on, one at a time, and took pictures to send to Mei.

She knew which one Mei would choose even as she sent the images. But when she got back two full rows of exclamation points under the shiny, sparkly dress, she felt the rightness of the decision she'd been too nervous to make. And Mei knew her and Ezra — apparently better than they knew each other and themselves — so she decided to trust in her friend.

But as Candace slipped on her shiny, slinky dress and sat down to do her makeup, there was an edge of sadness to her mood. Preparing to see Ezra so close to the new year inevitably reminded her that Miles and Mei weren't together, and that sometimes love just wasn't enough.

# CHAPTER 10

*E*zra wanted to pace the entire perimeter of the room to expel some of the energy currently coursing through his body. Actually, what he really wanted to do was knock on every door in the hotel until he found Candace's. It had taken every inch of restraint he had not to just go to the front desk and get the information he needed earlier in the day. But he felt that control wearing thin. The only thing that stopped him was the fear that he would go looking for her and find that she had gone. He knew he wouldn't be able to handle that.

Also, as much as he wanted to find Candace, he really did need to be in this room tonight. Even though the paperwork was signed and notarized, he knew how important it was for him to be here to announce that his company was now majority employee-owned. If he left, he knew there'd be gossip that it had been a hostile takeover, which might tank them in the future. They'd been planning for this night for almost two years and he wouldn't do anything to jeopardize that since this was really a party for the members of his Board to have face time with investors. In the future they'd slowly take over his role as the face of the company — a job he was more than ready to relinquish — and he wanted to give them all of his support.

So he paced instead, choosing to believe that Candace was coming. That this time she'd come back to him.

"Ready?" Tommy asked.

"Um..." Ezra's eyes darted to the ballroom doors. "Can we wait for a few minutes?"

Tommy shook his head. "No can do. We're already half an hour behind schedule. What are you waiting for? Jesus, you're not backing out, are you?" he asked, panicked.

Ezra brought his hand to his beard and scratched, shaking his head slowly. His eyes darted to the door again. "I'm not backing out. Calm down."

"Then what? We don't want to wait much longer for your speech."

Ezra sighed. Tommy was right. There was a science to these kinds of parties. Anything important he wanted his investors to know, he needed to tell them in that delicate period of time after they'd had at least one glass of champagne but before the waiters brought out the expensive bourbon he'd had shipped in specifically for this purpose. He needed to give his speech and hit them up for money in just the right way to get the funding they needed.

"Nothing," he said to Tommy. "You're right. Let's go."

He followed Tommy to the front of the room, but his attention — and his heart — stayed focused on the doors.

~

"You sure I look okay?" Candace asked Jorge. Her heart was pounding in her chest and the humidity, even in the air-conditioned hotel, was slowly turning the soft curls on her head into a crown and the skin exposed by her dress was covered in a slight sheen. She had no idea if she looked radiant and alluring or just like a humidity-drowned rat.

Jorge rolled his eyes and barely even glanced at her in the mirrored wall. Instead, he straightened his tie as he spoke.

"You look like a sexy disco ball," he said with a lifted eyebrow. "That was the look you were going for, right?"

"I hate you," she hissed.

"Okay, and I'm hungry. And there's certainly good food and free booze in there," he said, pointing toward the doors to the hotel's ballroom. "Can we go in now?" he whined.

"I'm nervous," Candace said in a small voice.

"You should be."

She gasped.

He rolled his eyes again and turned toward her. "Not because he's gonna reject you, but because all change is hard. If you walk in there in *that* dress and the two of you talk about your feelings, your entire relationship could change. Girl, your entire life could change. That man got *money*," he whispered. He grabbed her shoulders and shook her gently. "It's fine to be nervous or scared or unsure right now. But don't you want to know for sure how he feels? Don't you want to stop breaking your own heart?"

Candace swallowed. "Have you thought about becoming a life coach?"

Jorge put his hands to his chest and smiled. "I actually have. You don't grow up with four sisters with terrible taste in men and not learn a thing or two about all the bad decisions people make every day. But let's be real, I'm great at giving advice that I never take for myself. So let's get in there and find me a rich man to bring in the New Year."

Candace crossed her arms over her chest.

"*And* get your cute white boy," he chuckled. "Of course."

Candace rolled her eyes and walked away from him without a word. She pulled the ballroom doors open just as Ezra walked onto the stage with a smile. He looked sexy as hell in a dark tuxedo with velvet lapels, his dark brown hair parted on the left and styled.

"Oooh girl, he looks good," Jorge whispered to her.

"Shush," Candace said, never taking her eyes from Ezra.

She watched as he shook hands with another man on stage and then settled at the clear dais there. He placed his phone down and looked at it for a few seconds before smiling and looking up.

And then he saw her. She knew it by the way his smile widened and that slightly wonky tooth he'd never gotten fixed peeked through his lips, but also by the way her bare skin began to tingle.

Ezra's face flushed, and for a second he was flustered, laughing nervously and stumbling over his words. He was her Ezra in that moment. The same Ezra who used to avert his eyes when they accidentally ran into one another in the dining hall freshman year. He wiped his hands on his pants legs and tried to get his bearings.

She watched him and smiled. Because Ezra saw her. And Candace saw him.

Maybe for the first time in nearly two decades, Candace thought she saw Ezra Posner clear as day.

~

*E*zra knew his speech by heart but he kept looking at his phone, stuttering on the words he'd written and rewritten dozens of time. Every word he'd planned to say had flown completely out of his head the minute he'd seen Candace. In that dress.

She'd shown up.

"Sorry, just..." he said and laughed. "Just give me a second to—" He laughed again even though he had no idea what was funny about this situation. He could just imagine the horrified terror on his Board members' faces. He probably looked deranged.

He thought to look at them reassuringly, but as soon as he lifted his head his eyes skipped completely over the crowd to find Candace again. She was standing in shadow and he couldn't see her face, but her dress caught every errant ray of light and sparkled as she inched forward just a bit. He smiled and decided to forget the speech completely since he apparently couldn't read and could hardly speak. Because Candace had shown up.

"I'm going to go off script for this. I promise not to talk your ears off." Ezra took a deep breath and began. "I had the idea for this company when I was in high school," he said, clearing his throat and never taking his eyes from Candace's frame. "My parents were obsessed with trains. My nursery had trains everywhere. When I was a kid, my mom bought me every stitch of clothing she saw with trains on it, especially the matching sets. I was a train conductor for Halloween at least six years in a row," he said, and the crowd laughed. "I had this massive train set that took up the entire living room. We went on train rides around California in the summer. They even loved the trains that go around like amusement parks and the zoo. They *loved* trains. I didn't." The room erupted into amused laughter. "I didn't love all those train rides. They were long and boring and I just wanted to play basketball with my friends like everyone else. But as much as I hated trains, I loved my parents so I pretended to love all the train paraphernalia they bought me and the long train rides and that massive train set that wasn't even electric, because it made them happy.

But my entire life, they told me the story about this massive cross-country train trip they'd always wanted to take. On my parents' first date, my mom told my dad that she wanted to see the country by train for her ideal honeymoon. And my dad, being the huge train geek he was... is," he laughed and the crowd laughed with him, "basically decided to marry her on the spot. Apparently, that was like the sexiest thing he'd ever heard.

But my dad's also like me. He was shy and nervous and it took him a year and a half to finally get up the nerve to propose. And apparently they were so excited to be engaged that they immediately conceived me." The room laughed again and Ezra smiled, shaking his head. "By the time they were married, they were too nervous to take the trip with a newborn. And then they couldn't get time off work. And then it was too expensive, and on and on and on. Life. So I grew up thinking about this unfulfilled dream my parents had, to take a cross-country train trip.

But I could never understand why they'd want to.

Like I said, the trip would take forever. It was expensive and not particularly comfortable. And it felt like every year someone was writing an article about the sad state of the American rail system. A network of hundreds of thousands of train tracks that at the turn of the twentieth century connected the country for the first time. It put American citizens, including newly freed slaves, immigrants and itinerant workers from dozens of races to work as never before. All of that innovative track from the Second Industrial Revolution had been left to decay for decades. Why in the world would they want to make that trip?

Also, I was a kind of scared kid, so the idea of my parents traveling from California to Maine terrified me. I used to wake up in cold sweats from nightmares of them on a derailed train. I was terrified.

So, you probably see where this is going. When I first had the idea for this company, I had a super tech bro name: Innovative Transportation Industries. Boring, right?" He smiled as the crowd chuckled and Candace's dress shimmered under the lights.

"All I wanted to do was make a transportation system that was safe enough for my parents." Ezra took a deep breath and looked at about where he thought Candace's eyes would be. "But then in college I met a girl." The room tittered and he smiled, blushing. "She was the girl of my dreams. She was tall — taller than me in heels — with the biggest brown eyes, big curly hair and the best smile ever. The first time I saw her, I thought she was the most beautiful girl I'd ever seen. So beautiful it hurt to look at her but I could never look away. But best of all, she was so smart. I swear, every time she opened her mouth, she'd say something that would make me rethink everything I thought I knew. I was in awe of her." He paused for a second to swallow and take a deep breath. "I'm still in awe of her.

It took me our entire freshman year, but I worked up the nerve to give her the early draft of my proposal to read over the summer. And she ripped it to shreds." Ezra laughed along with the crowd this time. "I got it back and it was just bleeding on the page. But I read every comment. And then I got up the nerve to talk to her about them. Thankfully, I had the foresight to record our conversation, because what I remember most about that day was feeling complete shock that she was talking to me," he said, pointing at his chest.

"But when I went back to listen to the conversation, once again she blew my mind. She asked me questions about access over and over again and some of those questions have stuck with me ever since. 'What's the point of rebuilding and repairing the trains if it's still too expensive for poor people to access? What's the point of using fuel that pollutes the air and waters and affects poor communities first? Who will this benefit in the end?' And she was right.

She's the reason Innovative Transportation Industries eventually became the Community Railway Project. She's the reason I changed my proposal from refreshing train travel in the US to rethinking ground transportation of all sorts to make high-speed, efficient, safe, accessible, and affordable travel a possibility for people first and businesses second.

Because of her, I've dedicated the past fifteen years of my life to advocating for renewable energy sources, lobbying to dig up old track and lay new tracks in areas that haven't seen industry since the 1970s. We've advocated for clean fuel, created workarounds for diesel engines to run on these new fuel sources and lobbied local and state governments to make infrastructure a priority in all neighborhoods, not just the pretty white suburbs. And we've done all this while also working on our new efficient engine that runs on several fuel sources while also converting solar energy, which we are right now, as I speak, manufacturing for our first fleet of trains that we'll pilot on an exploratory trip from San Diego to Seattle."

The crowd erupted in applause and he smiled at them and then sighed. "I haven't always been successful. I won't pretend as if every local government has been receptive to building local rail systems or retrofitting woefully outdated ones. But I'm young," he said with a smile.

"And it's not just me. And that's really why we're here tonight. For two years, I've been working with my Board of Directors who represent my employees rather than our generous investors, to make this company commercially successful *and* socially conscious. And while I get all the attention — whether I want it or not — it's never been just me. My employees have been with me at every part of the process. My friends and family have supported me every step of the way, especially my parents, who are still obsessed with trains, by the way." He smiled. "So we're here tonight, not for me to give you some inspiring lecture about where we're going, but to remind you of how far we've come. Everyone in this room has helped make the Community Railway Project what it is today. I'm here to ask you to invest, not in me, but in the people in this room and our offices in San Francisco, and the single mother who can't afford a car, and the kids on their gap year who want to see the country, not take out student loans.

I'm here to tell you that wherever we go in the future, it won't be because of my dreams in isolation. It'll be all of us together. And now, finally, that's reflected in company shares. I've enjoyed being the primary owner of CRP, but it's cost me a lot of sleep, a lot of forgotten meals, and a lot of time away from the people I love. That's a price that I wasn't prepared to pay." He swallowed and took a few beats to breathe, to settle his nerves.

"Some of you are probably wondering why we're here in Ecuador for this meeting. Couldn't we have done this in the States? And the answer is absolutely yes. We could have. But that really smart, tall girl with the great smile once traveled to Quito without me. She was supposed to only be gone a few months and I threw myself into my work while I waited for her. I got my first investor from all that hard work, but she didn't come back for three years. I was too shy and nervous and caught up in my work that I let her leave without telling her how important she was to me. I let her leave and nothing between us was ever the same.

I'll never regret building CRP, but I've thrown

myself into my work to avoid acknowledging how much I missed her. We're here for me to hand over some of the responsibility of running the company to the Board so I can maybe, hopefully, retrace my steps and get back some of what I've lost. I have faith in our future as a company, but I look forward to finding a balance between the good work we do and the good people who've always been there for me. Thank you all for coming. Especially you, Candace Garret," he said. "Now please eat all the food and drink all the alcohol I'm paying a fortune for. Happy New Year."

Ezra smiled as the room erupted into applause. The spotlight on the stage lifted and the rest of the room was finally illuminated to his eyes. He looked up in just enough time to see Candace pushing the ballroom doors open and leaving the room.

He blinked back tears as her sparkly dress disappeared behind the closing doors.

# CHAPTER 11

*E*very hair on Candace's body was standing on end. Her arms were covered in goosebumps and her stomach felt the way it sometimes did when a plane hit unexpected turbulence and dipped suddenly. Her mouth was dry and she could feel beads of sweat at her hairline and down her back. Even though Jorge was the only person in that room who knew Ezra was speaking to her, she'd felt exposed, as if everyone was looking at her. But maybe what she was feeling wasn't about anything else but finally knowing how Ezra felt about her. How long he'd loved her.

She'd been waiting nearly two decades for this information and she felt exhilarated, but also over-whelmed. She felt powerful and vulnerable at the same time.

She'd felt something like this before; many times before, actually. Every New Year's Eve when Ezra and Candace slipped away to be together, she'd felt a faint echo of this feeling, her heart pounding with expectation and fear, but those feelings were like whispers compared to the way she felt right now. Because underneath the adrenaline spiking through her veins was regret.

Candace's eyes filled with tears as she realized just how much time they'd wasted being young, dumb and scared.

The ballroom doors opened behind her and she whirled around.

"You're crying? Did I say something wrong?" Ezra asked in a panicked rush.

She couldn't see his face clearly through her tears. "You came after me?" she cried.

"Of course, I came after you."

"Did you mean everything you said?"

"Of course, I did," he said, taking tentative steps toward her.

"You really wanted to ask me out?"

"Yes. I told you that."

"I was the girl of your dreams?"

"No," he said quickly.

"What?" she screeched, wiping at her eyes as her stomach dropped.

"I mean yes, you were the girl of my dreams, but you still are. You always will be."

Candace's mouth fell open as her vision blurred again.

"Miles told me that I put you on a pedestal. That I never let you be a real person, and he was right. And maybe that stopped me from telling you how I feel. I was so certain that you wouldn't feel the same way that I never gave you the chance. I was so worried about losing you that maybe I pushed you away." He shook his head and stepped closer. "I won't do that again. I want to be completely honest with you. So, yes, you were the girl of my dreams from the moment I saw you walk into freshman orientation in that gray Oakland A's t-shirt and those really tight jeans with your afro out."

Candace wiped her eyes, wanting to see him smile as he seemed to be remembering that first moment they met.

"But you *are* the woman of my dreams right now in this dress," he continued, his eyes dipping quickly to take her in, "and your makeup smeared by tears. I want you to know that I *can* be completely honest with you, Candace. But I don't think I'll ever take you off that pedestal."

Candace's mouth fell open in shock and she blinked up at him. "I saw you first," she blurted out.

Ezra frowned. "Huh?"

"Mei always tells that story of how she and Miles met. She says she spotted you and Miles in the housing registration line and she practically turned me around to show me Miles. And she did. She told me he was the guy she was going to marry. But that wasn't the first time I'd seen Miles, because I saw you first. You'd just stepped into the line in that ugly green sweater and khakis. You looked terrified. And then Miles stepped into line behind you and whatever he said made you laugh." Her eyes started to fill with tears again. "And I thought to myself that you were supposed to be mine; just like this overwhelming desire to be with you. But I didn't know what that meant, so I looked away. And then Mei saw Miles. I never told you that. I've never told anyone that before, but *I* saw *you* first."

Ezra's eyes were filled with tears as well, but he stepped forward, tentatively lifting his hands to cup her face. He used his thumbs to brush over her wet eyelashes and cheeks. Candace waited expectantly for him to say something, but he just kept gently stroking her face and looking at her with wide, warm eyes.

And then the ballroom door opened again.

"Candace, are you o—" Jorge said, concern replaced by surprise and then a smug smile as he took them in.

"Ezra, right?" Jorge asked.

"Yeah, hi again."

Jorge's eyes bounced from her to Ezra and back. He winked at Candace. "Thanks for the plus one. You two kids be safe," he said as he pulled the doors closed again.

Ezra turned back to her. "Do you have to go back inside?" she asked quietly.

He shook his head. "I don't care. I was telling the truth about that too. The company isn't the most important thing in my life anymore." His eyes focused on her mouth. "If it ever even was," he whispered.

"Then do you wanna get out of here?"

He smiled and lifted his gaze to her eyes. "Of course. What do you want to do? We can go sight-seeing? Or to dinner? Anything."

She shook her head. "I want to fuck you, Ezra," she admitted. "I want you."

Candace smiled as Ezra's eyes lit up.

They walked hand-in-hand to the elevator, staring at one another shyly as they waited for it to arrive. He inserted a key into the elevator, turned it, and pressed the button to the penthouse.

"Fancy," she whispered.

His eyes raked over her body from head to toe. "Not nearly as fancy as you deserve," he whispered back.

Candace smiled at Ezra and leaned into his side, relaxing when he leaned into her as well. Finally, after all this time.

~

*E*zra Posner could remember every detail about every kiss he'd ever shared with Candace Garret. The first time she'd kissed him, he'd been too terrified to move anything but his lips, thinking if he reached out to grab her waist the way he wanted, she'd realize who he was and what she was doing and stop. The second time had been much the same, although when she'd put his hands on her ass, he'd felt relief at knowing that he was actually the person she wanted to be kissing, at least in that moment.

In hindsight, he could see a pattern he hadn't noticed over the years. He'd spent every year waiting for her to make the first move and set the pace, too afraid to ask for more than he thought she was willing to give. He could see now all the cues he'd missed along the way as he held himself rigid, still too afraid to move too fast or take too much, just in case Candace took her entire self away. And now that he saw it, he knew he could change, but as the elevator ascended, he realized that he needed to convince Candace of that; he needed to make her see that their future could be so much different than their past.

When the doors slid open directly into the living area, Candace gasped at the sight. But it wasn't the lavish furniture that caught her attention. She practically ran across the room to the windows, pulling him along after her by their joined hands.

"Oh my God. The view. It's beautiful." She threw her purse onto the coffee table as they passed and then pressed her free hand against the warm glass.

He knew the view was beautiful. It was part of the reason he'd bought this hotel. He'd stood in this room looking out over the city, the mountains in the distance, and Ezra the businessman had known that anyone would pay top dollar for this view. But Ezra the man had been in control of that acquisition, because he'd looked out at the silhouette of the Andes and thought only of Candace. Ezra Posner, the not-quite billionaire, had bought a fancy — but not the fanciest — hotel in Quito, Ecuador on the slim hope that one day Candace

Garret would be here with him and her eyes would light up when she looked out at her favorite city. Even when he hadn't wanted to, his heart couldn't help but dream that one day she'd be here with him in this room and she would love it. That she would love him.

And she did.

"It is beautiful," he whispered, his eyes focused on her face.

Ezra reluctantly let go of Candace's hand to shrug out of his suit coat and let it fall to the floor. She turned to him and smiled, almost shyly. He wasn't sure that he'd ever seen Candace be shy around him. Or maybe it was just that he'd never let himself notice it. But he noticed now.

Ezra moved slowly behind Candace, trapping her between the window and his body. He leaned forward to press a single kiss to her bare left shoulder. She gasped again.

He could feel himself hardening in his pants, but he wanted to take this slow. It wasn't their first time; not by a long shot. But this one was special, he thought, as he gently circled her wrists and lifted her hands to the glass. As soon as the thought formed in his mind, he realized that it was a lie.

Every time he'd made love to Candace had been special.

He felt her shiver against him and he had to close his eyes and just breathe her in as he fought to center himself.

"You're an interesting guy, Ezra Posner," Candace whispered in a deep voice, full of arousal.

He smiled as his mind hurtled nearly eighteen years into the past. Back then he'd gulped back his reaction, all the startled glee as she looked him directly in the eyes and said his name, when he felt her lips touch his. He'd held himself stock still, waist averted, so that she wouldn't know how he'd been pining for her like so many other guys around campus. But he didn't have to hide that. Not anymore.

He moved his hands down her arms. He felt and heard her inhale and hold her breath. He placed another of those soft kisses against her neck and then smoothed his hands over her breasts, massaging them in his hands. She moaned and shivered more violently as he stepped even closer, letting the bulge in his pants settle against her backside.

She moaned and he smiled against her skin.

Reluctantly, his hands left her breasts to travel over her stomach in gentle circles and out to her hips where he squeezed.

"Ezra," she moaned and laughed at the same time. He kissed her shoulder again.

He moved his hands to the hem of her dress and began to pull it slowly up her legs.

She groaned in lust and frustration. He smiled and she leaned forward, her forehead resting against the window.

"You know I came here to get over you, right?" she

asked, her breath momentarily fogging the patch of window by her mouth.

Ezra didn't know why but for whatever reason, that puff of condensation by her lips turned him on. But then he realized it was just because it was Candace. He'd yet to encounter a thing she could do that he didn't love.

"So did I," he said, resting his chin on her shoulder. His hands continued to pull her dress up her thighs.

"I've been terrified of admitting that I'm a failure. Everything I've touched since college has failed. And I thought—" Her voice broke on a small, swallowed sob. He kissed her shoulder again and waited for her to continue. "I thought that I'd failed with you and I just couldn't bear it."

His hands froze on her thighs, filled with the shimmering fabric of her dress. He shifted slightly to see her face more clearly as she spoke.

"I was the scholarship kid who had to pull all-nighters just to survive. Part of the reason I came to Quito senior year was just to escape the pressure. And then I couldn't find a job after graduation. I didn't know what I wanted to do with myself and I was terrified that my parents would think less of me."

"And I didn't email you."

She nodded but didn't turn to look at him. "It was the icing on the worst cake. All the plans I'd been making, and dreams I had, amounted to nothing."

"Miles never told me you called," he said.

She turned sharply toward him.

"He was hungover and forgot until I asked him about it today. But I should have emailed you. I was always just so nervous to push you. To get too close. I thought if I did, you'd run away." He leaned forward and rested his temple on the glass next to hers. They made eye contact finally. "I'm sorry, Candace. I should have told you how I felt so many years ago."

She smiled at him. "I'm sorry, too. I should have told you that you were my dream boy, at least after I let you eat me out on top of my favorite stuffed animal."

The laughter that burst from them sounded to Ezra like old times again. Before they'd built so many walls between them.

He pulled her tight against his body, his short fingernails grazing the sensitive skin of her thighs. She choked on her laughter and moaned. And then his hands started to move up her thighs again until his fingers were at the edge of her underwear, playing with the delicate lace he couldn't wait to see.

"You never really failed though," he said.

"You sure about that?" she asked, and then swallowed loudly as his fingers moved along the crease of skin where her leg met her torso.

She spread her legs without him having to ask. Before he answered her, he let his fingertips move under her underwear and just barely graze the soft, curly hair at her mound for a second. Her breathing was labored, her body shivering against him. His heart was pounding in his chest. And then he slipped his fingers over her mound, between her legs and across her lips. She was soaked.

"Do you remember that first-year breakout session we had at orientation?"

"No, of course not. It was forever ago," she gasped and panted as he just stroked her sex, up and down without any pressure.

He smiled. "I remember. I remember you, every minute we ever spent together," he admitted, kissing her shoulder one more time. "One of the questions we had to answer was about what we wanted to do with our lives."

"Okay, I vaguely remember that." She groaned as he slipped his middle finger into her cleft.

He could hardly believe how normal his voice sounded considering the aching erection in his pants. "Mei said she wanted to change the world. Miles said he wanted to build the tallest building in San Francisco."

"Fuck," Candace gasped. "And you said you just wanted to make your parents proud."

He gently pushed his finger inside her. This time they both moaned as her wet pussy contracted around his digit. He didn't sound nearly as normal when he spoke this time. "And you said you wanted to see the world, which is exactly what you've been doing all these years."

Candace's head fell back to his shoulder. She looked at him with wide eyes and her mouth parted. Small moans and pants fell from her lips as he slowly dragged his finger out of her only to push it back in. His movements were slow, deliberate, agonizing.

He never let up because she felt so good and he didn't want her to speak just yet. Ezra knew Candace. He was certain that whatever quick thing she would say to him now would be a brutal refutation of what he'd said. She'd find some way to deny what he knew was true. And before tonight, he would have let her.

But what Ezra knew now that he couldn't have fathomed before was how differently she saw herself versus how everyone else viewed her. Especially him.

"You were never going to travel anyone else's path, Candace. That's why everyone loved you. That's why I love you."

He could see the tears in her eyes. He didn't know if it was emotion or arousal but he hoped that what he said was sinking into her head, just as he was sinking another finger into her sex.

She cried out and he covered her mouth with his own, needing to taste her excitement.

He wasn't certain how he'd gone this long without feeling her this way, but he didn't plan to ever experience that kind of absence again. He stroked her in sure strokes, his palm grazing her clit. And he held her close as she shuddered against him, silently promising that he planned to stay with her for as long as she'd let him; the same promise he'd have made her at eighteen, twenty-three, thirty, and every other year they'd known each other.

As he watched Candace come completely undone

on his fingers, he let himself make real plans for their future. Places they could travel together, places he would make love to her that weren't their best friends' spare bedrooms. And he made himself promise that he would tell her all the things he hadn't; he'd remind her of all the things about herself she couldn't see.

"I love you," he said again, whispering the words against her lips.

Her hips were moving in tight circles. She rode his hand and ground her ass into his dick. The room was filled with her moans and his ragged breath and the pounding of his pulse in his ears.

"I love you, too," she moaned just as her pussy clenched around his fingers like a vice and her orgasm wracked through her body in shuddering waves. "Fuck, I love you, Ezra," she panted and then moaned again as she gushed into his palm.

Ezra's cheeks hurt from smiling and his dick was aching to be inside her, but they had so much time. They didn't have to ever rush again. So he kissed her. It wasn't the best kiss of their lives as she panted and moaned into his mouth because he'd never stopped moving his fingers inside her. The kiss was kind of sloppy with a lot of tongue and maybe too much teeth as they murmured how much they loved each other over and over again, but it was perfect.

When Candace put her hand on his wrist to stop his ministrations, she giggled.

"What's so funny?"

She turned in his arms, her lush body brushing

against his chest, his hip, his dick. "I was just thinking about how awkward our first kiss was."

"So bad," he said and gripped her hips, pulling her to him. And then he frowned.

"What's wrong?" she asked.

"I just realized that I don't have any condoms. I didn't come here to get over you with someone else," he admitted.

"God, you're great," she whispered and pressed her lips to his. And then she nodded toward her purse.

"Jorge very generously donated a few condoms to get us through the night. He was optimistic that we would work things out."

Ezra laughed and lifted his eyebrows. "I appreciate everyone else's faith in us."

She smiled and lifted her hands to his beard, running the pads of her fingers over the soft hair. A groan slipped past his lips.

"You going to take me to bed now?"

He shook his head and she frowned.

It was his turn to kiss her and he'd planned for a small peck like she'd given him. But Candace had other plans.

"Bed, Ezra," she mumbled against his mouth even as her hands circled his neck and she pulled him closer.

"Next time," he said as he reluctantly pulled away. He walked to the coffee table and pointed at her purse. "May I?"

She nodded quickly. He picked up her small clutch and plucked one of the condoms from inside, counting three as he did. He knew that wouldn't be enough but after three years, it wasn't a bad start.

He walked back to the window, the condom between his teeth and his hands already opening his belt. Candace laughed and reached under her dress. He groaned when her underwear fell to her ankles and she stepped demurely out of them. He couldn't push his pants and underwear down his legs fast enough. His hands were shaky with need so Candace had to open the foil packet excitedly. He groaned again when her warm hand circled his dick, squeezing him before she rolled the condom down his length.

He was afraid that he might come prematurely, so he closed his eyes and breathed deeply to center himself. Candace laughed at his distress.

When he opened his eyes, her hand was still wrapped around his dick and she was still smiling mischievously at him.

"God, Candace," he breathed as he pushed her back against the window.

"I love it when you say my name like that," she whispered, her arms circling his shoulders.

Their mouths crashed together as he lifted her leg and wrapped it around his waist. "I love this dress," he whispered against her mouth.

Her right hand moved between their bodies and she angled his dick at her opening. He pushed forward and they both moaned, their eyes locked.

"I bought it for you," she gasped.

"Fuck," he said, his hips jutting forward.

They groaned in unison as he moved his hips, fucking her in long, deep thrusts. Their gazes never wandered, as if they wanted to see every detail of the other person's ecstasy.

Candace wrapped her other leg around Ezra's waist and he stooped the tiniest bit to sink deeper inside of her. Needing to be as close to her as possible in this moment. Forever.

When she came, he smiled as his name mixed with curses and proclamations of love. And when he followed her after a series of fast thrusts into her, his fingers digging into her hips and his tongue in her mouth, "I love you," was the only thing he could say. Over and over and over again. As many times as she needed to hear it, for as long as she would have him.

"Do you have plans tomorrow?" he asked when they finally fell into bed so many hours later. Their bodies were covered in sweat and they'd never felt happier.

"You asking me on a date, Ezra Posner?" she panted, curling against his side.

"I am. Will you have breakfast, lunch and dinner with me tomorrow... today, Candace Garret?"

Her answer was a feathery breath that ruffled his chest hair. "Yes," she said and then placed a soft kiss against his skin.

They fell asleep in each other's arms.

*T*hey could still hear the party downstairs, but Ezra's room was dark, quiet. They'd opened the window above the bed and a soft breeze gently rustled the curtains and moved over their still hot, sweaty bodies tangled together. Candace lay on her side, and Ezra had practically molded himself around her from the back, one of his strong arms under her head and the other locked around her soft middle.

"I'm not going to sleep," Candace whispered.

"I am," Ezra said, nuzzling his face into her neck as he pressed a firm kiss there.

"Okay." The word was a breathy moan and she scraped her nails over his forearm, enjoying the way the hair on his arms felt underneath her fingers.

They lay in silence for a few moments. Candace could hear the faint pops of fireworks outside. She wondered if Mei had noticed that she'd disappeared, or if Miles was looking for Ezra so they could tell the story about the time they'd gotten matching trashy tattoos on a boys' trip to Vegas. She was worried that Mei would send Miles to look for them and knew she should probably get up and tiptoe across the hall to the other spare bedroom, just in case. She knew that, but she snuggled deeper into the bed, inside the warm cocoon of Ezra's body.

She'd leave in a little while, she reasoned to herself.

"Why aren't you going to sleep?" Ezra asked after a while, his voice deep and thick with sleep.

Candace shivered in his arms. "Me and Mei are going to the Oscar Grant protest," she said.

It shouldn't have been possible for him to hold her tighter, closer, but he did and it made her entire heart clench with emotion.

Ezra kissed the column of her neck again. "You don't want to get a few hours of sleep before that?" he asked carefully.

She shook her head. "I'm afraid I'll oversleep."

It was true. She and Mei had agreed to help a friend who'd volunteered to take her students to the protest and needed extra chaperones. They couldn't be late. She didn't want to be late. And she knew that if she closed her eyes now, she wouldn't wake up on time, not even with the alarm she'd set. And if she didn't wake up, Mei would come looking for her. She'd wake Miles up, no matter when he'd fallen asleep, and the two of them would look all over the house. Eventually someone would open Ezra's door and find her in his bed.

She couldn't let that happen. She wasn't ready for anyone to know about their annual arrangement. At least not until she understood it herself.

But that wasn't the only reason she didn't want to fall asleep.

She and Ezra had been hooking up every New Year's Eve for four years. For the past four years, she'd spent three hundred and sixty-four days waiting to see him again, relishing his rare likes on Facebook or when he popped up in the group chat they shared with Mei and Miles unexpectedly. Each time, she felt overwhelmed by just the digital imprint of him and the force of her own longing. Their time apart was an extended lesson in patience as she fought against the bone-deep urge to write him the long email confessing her feelings; the email she'd had written in her head and heart for seven years.

But all that perseverance paid off, at least for a single night each year; just a few hours really. For the past four New Year's Eves Candace allowed herself to revel in her time with Ezra; cataloguing him the way she used to in college, noting all the small changes in him as he became some version of the boy she'd loved.

Her favorite point of observation was his voice. She drank in every word he said and marveled that every year, the timbre seemed to dip, taking on a raspy edge that had never been there before and made her shiver with arousal. It made him seem more confident, sexier; not quite like the Ezra she'd known, but just as fascinating. She also liked to note the way his accent was changing year-to-year. It wasn't a New York accent really, but it wasn't that weird Bay Area accent, the fast-paced slow drawl she loved, anymore either. She'd mourned it once and then over the course of the night, it had re-emerged as he spoke to their friends and drank with Miles; becoming — at least aurally — the Ezra she'd always known.

During their night together, Candace tried to memorize every detail of him. The sound of his laughter. The tickle of their arm hair when they almost touched. All his different facial expressions — frowning at Miles, playfully rolling his eyes at Mei, smiling at Candace, biting his bottom lip at Candace, staring hungrily across a room at Candace — she mentally catalogued them all, saving them up to get her through their year apart.

And when it was just them alone, she tried to memorize the feeling of his strong hands slipping under her dress and up her legs, his tongue on her breasts, the taste of his skin, the feel of his dick in her hands and mouth and sex. The way he groaned her name in her ear in that new voice but that old accent. There was so much to see and feel and know and relearn in their dark, quiet room and she didn't want to miss a thing, because this night was all they had.

But she couldn't tell him that. He wouldn't understand. He might stop holding her so close and she couldn't bear that loss. Not right now.

Candace had been up for a promotion at AeroPlan. She'd received the rejection letter three days ago right after she'd returned from a hellish cross-country trip with an inexperienced and unprofessional crew. She'd had to stay at Oakland airport three hours after landing to fill out incident reports and write up crew members; performing the responsibilities of a purser, even though she wasn't one and according to her rejection letter, she wouldn't be any time soon.

Being denied for yet another promotion she wanted — and more importantly, deserved — was a blow she wasn't yet ready to deal with. And looking forward to seeing Ezra had been the post-rejection distraction she needed. So, she didn't want to miss anything; not even the sound of his even breathing as he slept.

Ezra shifted and his dick prodded her hip.

"I thought you were going to sleep?" she whispered with a laugh.

He smiled against her skin. "If you're not, I'm not. I'll keep you company. I have a meeting in the city and can't go to the protest, but I can make sure you don't miss it," he said.

She turned her face to the pillow to hide her smile. She thought about telling him her other reason for wanting to stay awake in that moment. She wondered if maybe he felt the same way. If maybe he could. If maybe this didn't have to be their only night.

Ezra's leg slipped between hers and he pressed his thigh against her wet, aching core. He raised his mouth to her ear and sucked her lobe into his mouth.

She groaned.

"I'll stay up with you. But only if you want," he whispered.

"I want," she said quickly, turning toward him. "I want you."

His face was shadowed, hiding his reaction from her. She didn't know if he frowned at her words or if his eyes lit up and he blushed again from his ears down his neck the way he used to in college. But with the recent sting of rejection she decided to be happy about the mystery of his emotions. She only wanted to memorize the best things about their time together. Only the things she could hold close for the rest of the year to get her through the worst days and loneliest nights. She had enough mediocre or bad things in her life; she didn't need more, especially not with Ezra.

So she allowed herself to imagine that he did blush and smile.

But she didn't have to imagine when he lowered his head and kissed her deep and slow for what felt like blissful hours that she couldn't track. And there was no mistaking how real it felt to fumble around with Ezra's penis to roll on another condom in the dark without breaking their kiss, or the pleasure of how good it felt when he moved on top of her and entered her so tenderly that it brought tears to her eyes. These were the moments she wanted to remember and carry with her. And she did.

here used to be days — sometimes full week stretches — where Ezra would wake up before the sun had risen, covered in sweat, hard as a rock, his heart pounding and his mouth so dry he could hardly speak. It wasn't nightmares. It was Candace. More times than not, he'd come to full consciousness with unfortunately vivid memories of wet dreams where she'd been the star. Those mornings made him want to buy a physical calendar, tack it to the wall by his bed and every morning cross off another day; counting down until New Year's Eve when he could see her again.

But the worst mornings were when he woke up with his alarm, rested, calm, relaxed even — well, except for his dick — but his brain still clogged with vivid memories of dreaming about Candace all night. During those nights, his dreams weren't filthy but mundane. He remembered their best times together and subconsciously pined for her for hours. His favorite memory-dream was of that time sophomore year when they'd shared a plate of nachos while Miles and Mei had their first real fight.

Their friends had been going back and forth about whether the A's stood a chance of making it to the World Series that year. The fight had been loud, but maybe kind of adorable. The nachos had lasted longer than the fight, and he and Candace had finished eating and talked about Ezra's Gilder Prize submission while their friends made out on the other side of the booth. It was such a normal moment but it was one of Ezra's most cherished memories of Candace, because of the way she'd lifted her eyebrow and rolled her eyes at him as Mei and Miles gesticulated wildly about the team's current roster and RBI, things he and Candace didn't understand or care about. It felt as if they had a secret to share. As if the two of them were a team.

That was what had made those dreams somehow worse than the erotic ones. It reminded him of all the other times he'd imagined that the future held so much more for them than a single night once a year and lonely desperation for the rest. On those mornings, he often turned over in bed to the extra pillow next to him and felt a deep ache to hop on a plane and fly to wherever she was. So many days in the past four years, he'd been obsessed with wondering what if. What if he'd given into that urge?

But this morning, for the first time in a long time, he didn't have to wonder or regret. He might have gotten it wrong with Candace more times than he'd gotten it right, but this morning he woke up with Candace in bed next to him and reminded himself that none of the past had to matter more than this moment and their future.

Candace pressed her face into the crook of his neck and wrapped her leg around his, her naked body molding to his. He slung both arms around her and kissed her temple.

"Again?" she mumbled against his skin, her knee nudging his hardening dick under the sheet atop them.

He could feel his entire body flush. "Not yet. Not if you're not ready."

She chuckled and rubbed her leg up and down his, making the hair on his body stand on end. "I've been ready for eighteen years."

Ezra held her tighter against him and kissed her temple again.

"Are you going to cry?" she asked.

He nodded. "But I'm okay with crying during sex, if you are."

There was a second of silence before the room filled with Candace's laughter, her body shuddering with glee in his arms.

Ezra loosened his grip only so she could push up on her forearms and he could watch her laugh. He'd always loved watching her laugh.

"Let's save the emotional sex for an anniversary or something," she said with soft eyes and a smile.

He lifted his hand to her face and stroked her cheek, blinking back tears. "Too late."

"It was 'anniversary' that did it, huh?" she asked, covering his hand with hers and pressing it harder into her skin.

Ezra nodded.

"Figured," she whispered, as she moved to straddle his waist.

Ezra's hands moved down her sides and he gripped her hips and thighs, letting his fingers sink into her flesh. When she leaned to the side to grab another condom from the bedside table, he lifted his head to suck her nipple into his mouth. She moaned and pressed her sex against his stomach.

"Do you remember that time you damn near twisted my nipple off?" she whispered to him.

Candace's nipple popped from his mouth. His head fell back on the pillow and he laughed.

She leaned down and kissed his chin, nuzzling into his soft beard. "See," she whispered. "No more tears."

Ezra could hardly believe that this was real and it didn't have to be temporary. He held onto her as she rolled the condom down his shaft and then sank onto his dick carefully. He kept his eyes trained on hers as she rode him slowly, because there was no rush. For once, there would be more and more and more after this. They gasped and moaned as the room brightened along with the sky outside and the speed of their movements increased. They clasped their hands together as their hips moved in slow tandem, reveling in their easy, early morning orgasms.

When they settled back under the sheet, Ezra held Candace tight to him. Their right hands were clasped together palm-to-palm and their fingers threaded as they fell back to sleep. It was only then that Ezra let himself finally accept the reality of the situation. That, corny as it sounded in his drowsy brain, all of his dreams had finally come true.

~

They woke up mid-day and had to rush.

"I really want to take you out on a date," Ezra had said as he'd jumped out of bed and ran to the bathroom. Candace sat up in bed, still groggy from sleep and confused. She heard the shower turn on and then he'd rushed back into the bedroom naked and pulled her into the shower with him, further delaying the start of their day. Not that either of them complained.

He said it again when they went to her hotel room many floors below his so she could get dressed. Ezra helped Candace undress and they'd lost a bit more time having quick, near desperate sex in her closet; the joy of being able to touch each other whenever they wanted once again overwhelming all other emotions and plans.

But they had finally made it out of the hotel. It was late afternoon and they were both so hungry their stomachs were growling fiercely. Just outside the hotel, they'd spotted a cluster of food carts, rushed across the street to them and proceeded to buy themselves enough empanadas, fresh fruit, mote con chicharron and juice to feed themselves three times over. And then they'd sat on a nearby bench to scarf it all down.

"Is this the date you had planned?" Candace asked him with a smile, a half-eaten empanada in her hands.

He shook his head and blushed. "Considering the fact that I first wanted to ask you out on a date when I was nineteen with thirty-five dollars in my bank account, this actually isn't that far off though."

She took a sip of guayaba juice and then offered him the cup. He accepted it and drank; unsure he'd ever be able to get over the possibilities for this kind of easy intimacy with her.

"I would have said yes, you know?" she whispered, examining the empanada in her hand as if she were shy. "Just to be clear."

Ezra smiled, or maybe the same smile he'd been wearing since last night only widened and deepened. He wasn't sure. He didn't care. Around them, the streets of Quito were packed with people, locals and tourists alike, cars whizzing down the streets, the smell of roasting meat and vegetables making the air seem warmer and calm, but as far as Ezra was concerned, nothing existed beyond this bench. No one mattered in this moment more than Candace.

"The next date will be better," he said seriously; a solemn promise.

She looked around them with a smile on her face. "I don't know, this is the best empanada I've ever had, in my favorite city in the world," she turned back to him, "with the shy nerd of my dreams and my best friend. I'm not sure you can top this, babe."

His smile faltered as every muscle in his body tightened with need. "Say it again," he rasped.

"Say what again?"

"Call me 'babe.'" Candace Garret had the most beautiful smile, he thought in that moment, not for the first time. Not for the millionth time.

"Babe," she whispered at him, her eyes full of mischief.

Ezra put his food down.

"Babe," she said again around a chuckle.

He stood from the bench and then leaned over her, their faces close.

"Babe," she whispered again, this time against his lips.

They laughed and kissed as the city teemed, no one paying them any mind as everyone prepared to celebrate the end of yet another year, while Ezra and Candace celebrated the beginning of something new and more precious than they could define.

~

"ou sure you don't want to go back to the hotel?" Ezra asked for the third time.

"Very sure," Candace said, leaning into

his side as they waited for his driver to pull the car around to the front of the hotel.

"Because it looks like it might rain."

"It's Quito. It'll rain or it won't and then it will. We'll survive. Besides, I want to show you something," she said.

He was about to protest when the car appeared. His driver stood from the driver's side, walked around the car, and opened the back door for them. After they'd all climbed inside, Candace leaned forward. "La Mitad del Mundo, por favor," she directed.

The driver nodded at her and pulled off.

"My Spanish is rusty," Ezra said. "Where are we going?"

"It's a surprise."

He pulled his phone from his pocket. "I can just Google it."

She covered his phone with her hand and pulled his face to hers, distracting him with a kiss.

When the car stopped, the driver had to cough more than once and loudly before they understood what was happening.

"Aqui," he said, maybe not for the first time.

"Lo siento," Ezra said, his face and neck probably bright crimson.

Candace laughed, "Dr. Montero really failed you, huh?"

"My accent isn't that bad," he said as they crawled out of the car.

The driver choked back a laugh, which only made Candace laugh harder.

Ezra blushed but he couldn't feel bad about her teasing him. Not when she smiled and laughed like that. Not when she seemed so happy to be with him. As happy as he felt to be with her.

He shook his head and turned to his driver, letting him go for the night. He didn't know what Candace's surprise would be, but he felt certain they could find their way back to the hotel together. He turned to her and found her waiting for him in the setting sunlight, smiling expectantly, lovingly. He knew in that moment that they could do literally anything together. But he'd always known that.

When Candace extended her hand to him, he grabbed it quickly and let her lead him up a hill to a busy square with plots of grass, stone benches and walkways leading to a stone building in the distance. The open space was filled with small groups of people, the edges of each group blending into the next. He saw families and young people and even a few older people on benches, everyone milling around, drinking, setting off fireworks, clearly planning to welcome the new year in the open air. The square was filled with music from speakers and even a small live band in a distant corner playing for tips. The sky was clear above them. The clouds he'd seen just a few minutes ago had moved on. It wasn't fully dark yet, but Ezra could see the moon and the faint twinkle of stars in the darkening sky.

Or maybe it was just that with Candace's hand in his and everything felt sharp, crisp.

"Here we are," she said and turned to him.

A soft, warm breeze disturbed the ruffles of her dress. He bit his lip as his eyes drank in the dark purple fabric and the hidden curves underneath. He squeezed her soft hand in his and lifted his eyebrows. "Where are we?" he asked in a hoarse voice, not that he really cared as long as they were together.

"La Mitad del Mundo," she said.

He sighed. "I told you my Spanish is rusty."

"Half of the world," she translated and rolled her eyes.

"What does that mean?"

"It means that we're at the equator." She pointed to the ground; a faint line on the concrete between them. "We're standing where the two halves of the world meet."

"On New Year's Eve," he added, stepping forward, the toes of his shoes meeting hers over the painted line. He wrapped his arms around her waist and smiled at her, the pressure of tears forming at the back of his eyes again.

"I thought this might be the perfect way for us to start fresh; where our past and present can meet and we can move on. Together." She sucked her bottom lip into her mouth and her eyebrows furrowed. "I mean, if that's what you want."

Ezra nodded quickly so that there was no confusion. Not this time. Not ever again. "I've wanted exactly this since we were eighteen," he said, and leaned forward to kiss her again.

"Better late than never," she mumbled and then kissed him back.

The sparkly sound of fireworks — too early for midnight — sounded and neither of them startled. This wasn't the first time they'd kissed with a celebratory soundtrack and Ezra smiled against Candace's lips because it certainly wouldn't be the last.

*M*ei had spent nearly her entire life in Oakland. She was born and raised here. She'd gone through the Caldecott Tunnel for college but made the trip home at least twice a month to reassure her parents that she was alive, eat as much of her mom's cooking as humanly possible and sit on the couch to watch a sports game — whatever Bay Area team was playing — with her dad in near silence. To soak up the sounds and smell of home. Their small two-bedroom apartment above an import market in Chinatown was the safest place in the entire world as far as Mei was concerned. So the decision to move home after she left Miles had been a no-brainer.

She'd thrown a couple of suitcases in her trunk, driven the twenty minutes across town, and folded herself into maybe the only place in the city that didn't feel soaked in memories of the life she'd built with him.

She'd wanted — needed — to feel safe in the

cocoon of her parents' home in the heart of the city she loved. She wanted the familiar sounds of her city within a city. She wanted to sit at her mother's feet and let her comb, oil and braid her hair. She wanted to cry silently while her mother's sure but gentle hands reassured her that nothing was as bad as it seemed. She wanted to walk into the kitchen early in the morning, before the sun was fully out, and see her dad at the kitchen table reading the morning paper in his work uniform, a cigarette burning out in the ashtray on the windowsill and her mother fussing at him in Cantonese about the smell while she cooked. For weeks she'd needed to putter around the apartment in nothing but old pajamas stained with tears and the fading scent of him. She'd wanted to hide.

Eventually though, she had to venture back out in the world, mostly just to appease her mother. At first she only left the house for a few hours at a time, rediscovering familiar streets she knew like the back of her hand even as they had seemingly changed in big and small ways. Her small forays reminded her that Miles wasn't the center of the world; he'd just been the center of her world. But now it was time to restructure and build something new.

Outside had its own perils. Every now and then she'd look up from a book she was pretending to read in the park to find an old woman staring at her in a way she found as familiar as disconcerting. Those looks wondered, "Are you Ahn's granddaughter? Are you married? You should meet my grandson." She had to

fight the urge to run from those inquiries and invitations. She wasn't Ahn's granddaughter. She wasn't
married anymore. She wasn't ready to meet anyone's
grandson; she maybe never would be again. But she
didn't run. Instead, she bore those inquiries with a stiff
back and pained smile that she hoped seemed polite,
before grabbing her unread book and purse and then
walking briskly — not running — home.

In that small apartment she loved, Mei got to
pretend to be a version of herself before Miles was
even a thought in her head. She was her parents' only
and favorite child; her dad's most persistent and
corniest joke. In Chinatown, she was "you, girl," to the
woman with broken English who didn't bother to speak
Chinese to her because she assumed Mei wouldn't
understand, but needed help getting her grocery cart
across the street, nonetheless. She was "Mei. Yin and
Jimmy's daughter, Homecoming queen," at Mr.
Wang's shop when she stopped in to pick up bones for
her mother's soup. He always introduced her that way
to other customers before unfurling a near perfect
recitation of her life-long achievements. She used to
find it grating as a teenager, hating that she couldn't
just pick up her mom's order and leave. But now that
she was older, wiser, and more bruised by life, she
appreciated the butcher's obvious pride in her and
sometimes stayed for a few minutes to chat if the shop
wasn't too busy.

Coming home was a kind of relief if only because
no one introduced her as Miles's wife. She wasn't Mrs.

Jefferson here. No one even made a tv show-related joke about her married name. Because she wasn't married anymore. And at home she could pretend for a few minutes — sometimes even hours — that she never had been. It gave her as much relief as agony. But what didn't, these days?

The only people she ran into on a day-to-day basis who knew that she'd once been Miles Jefferson's college sweetheart and wife were her parents, because she still wasn't ready to see any of the people she'd invited to their wedding on a regular basis. Even after more than three years. She didn't want to see pity or judgment in their eyes. She didn't want to feel like more of a failure than she already did. She could only just handle the way her parents sometimes looked at her, as if she were bruised fruit; still cherished, but tender in some places and maybe skinned raw in others; someone they had to handle with just a bit more care than before.

But sometimes the weight of their soft voices — much softer than normal — made her want to shrivel up and die, because they knew what she had lost and they didn't know how to help her fix it. Because Mei, only child of Yin and Jimmy, was in her thirties, childless, divorced and sleeping on the twin bed she'd had most of her life. And she'd never felt like more of a failure.

All of her cousins and friends were having babies, moving to the East Coast for new jobs, or going on treks around the world to "find themselves." But she was in her childhood bedroom, sometimes too afraid to venture further than the living room just in case she started crying unexpectedly in the middle of a very public place and couldn't stop. Again.

At first, her parents had been understanding. Her mom put her hair in detailed fishtail braids so she felt pretty. Her parents plucked food from their own bowls at each meal, depositing them on her own dish or at times directly into her mouth, so she would know how much they loved her. Her dad even volunteered to watch reruns of *The OC* with her, even though he hated it.

But after four years, they were done handling Mei with kid gloves.

She couldn't count the number of times her mom had suggested she move in with Candace or even get her own place. Her dad had sounded almost excited to tell her that his boss's daughter was getting a divorce too. "Maybe you two can move in together," he'd suggested kindheartedly.

At another point in her life, Mei would have jumped at the opportunity to get out from under her parents' protective wing. Or she would have been offended at them trying to pawn her off. But now, she pretended as if she couldn't hear their suggestions, fear paralyzing her heart at the prospect of starting over again.

She'd never been alone before.

But apparently even her parents' hospitality was running thin, especially her father's.

He'd made no secret of the fact that they hadn't minded being empty nesters and were eager to go back to that. Mei had shuddered at the implication and fiercely ignored him when he brought that up, running back to her room with her ears plugged. As pathetic as it sounded, she was perfectly prepared to spend another four years hiding away at home, only leaving for work and to run errands around the neighborhood for her mom, avoiding their overt suggestions that she move out.

But then, just after Christmas, she'd accidentally pushed her dad over the edge.

She'd just gone down to the kitchen for a late-night snack. She'd been halfway through a plastic container of her mom's glass noodles when her dad had turned on the kitchen light. Mei's chopsticks froze halfway between the container and her open mouth. She'd met her father's hard gaze with wide eyes and then cringed. He'd clearly been planning to have this dish for his late-night snack too.

"Sixty days," he'd ground out, shaking his finger at her. "I want you married or in your own apartment in two months."

"Dad—"

"No. I've worked too hard not to be able to eat my own leftovers in the middle of the night. We raised you. You're an adult. Get your own leftovers," he'd said, before turning the lights off and walking back to bed. "I love you," he'd called from the hallway, his voice annoyed, but still kind.

And just like that, the holding pattern of Mei's life post-divorce came to an end.

She'd hoped that in the clear light of day her dad would change his mind. The next morning, she'd set a basket of his favorite pork buns in front of him. She'd woken up early to make them with more than a little help from her mom. She folded her hands in front of her and smiled awkwardly at him as he plucked a single bun from the bamboo basket and ate it. Just the one. Then he got up from his chair, kissed Mei and her mother on their cheeks and walked from the kitchen.

"Sixty days!" he'd called from the front door.

That was a month ago.

Her impending homelessness should have lit a fire under her ass, but it only made her anxiousness spiral. It was hard to imagine her life getting any worse than being a mid-30s divorcée about to be kicked out of her parents' house like a freeloader. She'd entertained the idea of asking Candace to let her crash on her couch just until her dad changed his mind. But she couldn't bring herself to do it.

And then Candace and Ezra had hooked up in Ecuador over New Year's Eve and the idea of telling Candace about her life, knowing that she'd tell Ezra, who'd tell Miles... No. She couldn't bear that. There had to be another way, she'd thought. But in a month she hadn't managed to find a way through her predicament and as her eviction loomed, her life only seemed to get worse.

She hadn't told anyone, but ever since the divorce

she'd hardly slept. It wasn't the small bed or the fact that one of their neighbors liked to watch reruns of *Law & Order* between the hours of midnight and four, loud enough for Mei to hear every word. It was because, for over a decade, she'd gone to bed nearly every night practically cocooned inside Miles's too long arms and legs. Apparently four years wasn't enough time for her body and mind to stop needing him to fall naturally asleep.

It was a chilly late winter morning and she'd been up for most of the night. She could see the sky lightening through her bedroom window as she waited for her alarm to go off. She contemplated the day ahead of her knowing that it would hold nothing more fascinating than the possibility of picking up sushi for lunch.

When her phone beeped that she had a new text message, she yawned as she typed in her pass code, pressed the text message app and then froze.

She hadn't seen that particular group message labeled "United Friends of Benetton" at the top of her app in years. It ate up so much of her phone's memory that when she'd taken it in to get fixed last month, the guy at Sprint had suggested she delete it. He'd also pointed out that another message thread was eating up even more of her available memory and her phone would work so much better if she cleaned them out.

"It's with someone called 'Dead to Me,'" he'd told her.

She'd upgraded her memory instead.

Because it was one thing to divorce Miles. It was another thing to get rid of a decade and a half of their text messages. And an entirely different thing to get rid of their group chat with Candace and Ezra. She could chart so many of her most significant moments by messages in those threads. And the group chat in particular was as precious to her as the file folders full of images on her laptop of the four of them together over the years. But seeing it at the top of her app made her heart stop for what felt like minutes.

Her finger hovered over the bold text for a few heartbeats. She held her breath and then exhaled, pressing the message open at the same time.

The block of gray text was so long Mei sucked in a hard breath, thinking it was from Miles. He always used to send such long messages that Ezra was perpetually annoyed, and Candace once admitted to catching up on his messages only when she was bored on a plane with literally nowhere else to go. But Mei had loved every one of those essays.

Miles's enthusiasm for literally everything had always been one of the things she'd admired about him. When they'd just started dating, she used to read and re-read all of his text messages, marveling not just at how excited he was to tell her about failing his chemistry midterm, but also that he'd pressed the buttons on his flip phone so many times to do it. That felt like dedication. Like love, her young heart had decided.

But this message wasn't from Miles. It was from Candace.

Hey nerds. Wanted to let you both know that we're alive. We haven't eloped (Miles tell your mom, my cousin Shar is lying for clout). And I'm not pregnant. But I did quit my job. Also Ezra gave away a bunch of money and I saw his tax return, so he's just a regular multi-millionaire these days. Someone tell People mag.

Now let's get down to business.

Pack a bag bitches, we're going to Paris for Valentine's Day! (Not to get married. Ezra's cousin Yosef is also lying for clout.) And we want our bffs there with us. All expenses paid by Ezra of course. (No one should have this much money.) Oh, Ezra wants me to tell you that he would never type bffs.

Mei, you can wear that ugly beret you bought against my sound advice! And Miles, you can practice that French you're always lying about studying!

*I*t was such a Candace message that it pulled an unexpectedly hoarse puff of laughter from Mei's dry throat. She missed her. She and Ezra had been traveling around South America since New Year's, only popping up online sporadically to post pictures — without captions — on their social media, completely oblivious to all their family and friends going nuts in the comments because they were together. Finally.

Mei didn't comment, but she did sometimes lie in bed in the middle of the night, alternating between tossing and turning and swiping through the pictures of her friends, smiling at how happy they looked together. Hating the small sliver of bitterness ruining that joy.

Another message appeared before she could even fully process the first.

We know things are weird right now, but please don't say no. We were all friends before we were anything else. Think about it?

*T*here was so much in these messages to take in that it made Mei's stomach roil. She was happy for Candace and Ezra. Watching them tiptoe around one another and break their own hearts for so long was sad and frustrating. But it was impossible to think of them without thinking of Miles.

They used to lie awake some nights and talk about the latest in their own personal long-running television drama starring their two best friends. *How often had Ezra indirectly asked about Candace in an hour span? At what point in the night did Candace give up the pretense of not being interested in the latest Ezra news? What new romantic relationship had they tanked on the off chance that the other person was finally ready?* She and Miles had secretly — and shamefully — taken small solace in the fact that their own love story had been much more straightforward.

But now the entire world was turned on its axis.

Miles had a bachelor pad in El Cerrito — according to her cousin Karen's boyfriend, Rick — and she was sleeping on a twin bed older than wi-fi. Meanwhile, Candace and Ezra were their friend group's #couplegoals.

Her phone beeped again. This message was just a picture.

It took a while to load with her parents' slow wi-fi, but the picture made Mei tear up. It was a picture of Candace and Ezra in an open-air square, the Andes mountains behind them, the sky a fiery orange and people milling in the background. But she only passively took in those details because her eyes zeroed in on Candace. Her best friend was wearing the deep plum wrap dress that made her look beautiful and delicate. Ezra was standing next to her, his arms wrapped around her waist as he pressed a kiss to her left cheek; but even the angle couldn't hide the smile on his face. And Candace's smile was clearly a laugh that Mei could practically hear ringing in her ears.

She'd known them for more than half her life and had never seen either of them look so happy.

Count me in.

She typed the message quickly and hit send before fear and sadness could overtake her. Because this request wasn't about her and Miles. For once, it was about Candace and Ezra. And no one knew how much this picture meant — how much they'd had to go through to get there — better than Mei.

And Miles.

How could I say no?

Somehow Mei felt the vibrating notification of his message deep in her chest. It boomed like a four-ton weight. It made her gasp and sit up in bed. She pressed the phone down into the tangle of covers and sheets around her, as if she could push it straight through the mattress, the floor, the apartments below, the concrete, and straight into the earth's core. But she couldn't do that. She didn't even really want to.

Instead, she lifted her hand and began to scroll up through the latest months and years of their collective friendship. She scrolled past the tense message she'd sent, telling Candace and Ezra that they all needed to talk. It was one of the last things she and Miles had done together: breaking the news of their divorce to the two people they loved liked family.

She kept scrolling up and up and up, until she found the thing she was looking for.

It was an old picture Mei had found during their move into what was supposed to be their forever home. The house they'd planned to raise kids in. This was the house where they'd planned to have their multicultural barbecues each summer and Miles had joked that the neighbors would probably have the police on speed dial. That had been the house where they'd planned to grow old.

"Not too many stairs," Mei remembered saying with approval, "so when your back and my hip give out, we can just move to the first floor and give the kids and grandkids the second floor when they visit."

"The kids and grandkids chipping in on this mortgage?" Miles had joked, and then swept her into a one-armed embrace against his side and pressed a kiss into her hair.

But this picture was older than that memory.

She didn't know exactly who had taken it, but she knew for sure that it was from their sophomore year. It was during that short but awful period of time when they were all experimenting with their hair. Miles had a head full of stubby dreadlocks, Mei had neon pink highlights, Candace was wearing her thick curly hair in two buns on her head, "like a Black Princess Leia," Miles had noted, and Ezra's hair was in long, shaggy strands that fell limply around his shoulders. They looked terrible.

"Like a mashup of every c-list cartoon gang," she'd said to Miles, just before taking a picture of the image with her phone and sending it to their group chat.

If she could go back in time and tell her twenty-year-old self that those streaks would haunt her and Miles would only be hers for about a decade more, she wouldn't have believed it. Because that Mei had been certain that Miles was her soulmate. That Mei couldn't have ever imagined the slow, painful dissolution of their relationship. That Mei didn't yet know what it felt like to watch someone you love grow and change and succeed as they became someone you still liked but didn't love anymore. And that Mei didn't know what it felt like to watch someone else come to the same realization about her.

That Mei couldn't have imagined what it would be like to slowly grow apart from the only man she'd ever been in love with and be unable to figure out how to stop it.

But this Mei knew the painful realities of that all too well. She'd lived through it and just barely survived it. Or maybe she hadn't. That was still unclear.

She put her phone face down on the bedside table and lay back onto her pillows, covering her head with the blanket. She'd have to get up soon. And apparently, she had a trip to Paris to pack for. And she needed to put in a request for time off from work. These new things would be distractions from apartment hunting, she supposed, trying desperately to see the silver lining around her shattered heart. It had been so long since she'd had something to look forward to.

But first, she needed to cry.

HAPPY NEW YEAR!

If you made it this far, I hope you enjoyed Candace and Ezra's long ride to love! It was more emotional than I normally write, but it felt right to me in the end. Or the beginning really, since I like to imagine them heading off into the future, making up for all the time they lost. But we'll see...! This story was also randomly personal for me. I set it around the cities in the Bay Area where I grew up, had my heart broken a few times and enjoyed laughing with my friends many more times than that. I also based their unnamed college on my alma mater, where I lost and found myself more times than I can count. Go Gaels! And unexpectedly, it's been helping me deal with some unexpected grief after losing my favorite cousin, who was always optimistic and kind with the biggest smile on his face. His memory is a lovely reminder for me that life rarely turns out the way we expect, but there's still so much to be thankful for. I hope that gives each of you a bit of comfort.

If you're inclined to leave a review wherever you feel comfortable, I'd appreciate it. Or if you have a friend who you think might enjoy this story, please share! But more than anything, I hope that 2020 is good to you all. If 2019 was hard for you, I can more than relate and I hope this new year treats you kindly. If 2019 was the best year yet, I hope 2020 is even better. Be kind to yourselves in the new year, even when it's hard.

And lastly, look out next year for the rest of the Love At Last trilogy: One More Valentine (Mei and Miles aren't over just yet!) and Just Another Pride (Jorge's blast from the past might not be a billionaire, but he's always had his heart).

## ACKNOWLEDGMENTS

There were a few times I thought about scrapping this story, even though I loved it. Thank you so much Kai, Chencia and Agata for reading early versions and offering feedback and encouragement along the way. Thank you also for letting me whine and cry in your dms and emails every now and then. haha This story didn't take the path I expected in some ways, but it did in so many others and I love you all for being in my corner and offering support and corrections when necessary. That friendship seems more than fitting for a story like this! <3

Beautiful & Dirty

The Hitman

Standalones

Encore

Layover

Office Hours

The Tenant